All Of My Sundays

SARAH DELANY

Paperback ISBN: 978-0-6488144-5-0

Cover Design by: Amanda Walker

www.amandawalker.pa.com

Editing and Proofreading by: Rebecca Andrews

To a Warrior named Chelsea,

In this vast universe you may feel like a speck of dust who goes unseen but, in my world, you are one of the brightest stars in my sky.

Don't hide your authentic self when you are destined to shine.

I'm lucky because out of the billions of people in the world I get to call you, my friend.

Until the day we meet,
Your friend in Jurassic World.

Table Of Contents

Chapter One

SOPHIA

"Have you seen the new guy?" my friend Kelsey whispers beside me, as I slam my grey locker shut. The weight of my history textbook in my hands is heavy so I tuck it into my side to ease the load. My black perfectly shined shoes tap along the linoleum floor as we walk side by side down the hall.

"No, I just arrived," I tell her. My fingers pull my slick ponytail over my shoulder so I can smooth the hair down. My mother ingrained in me from a young age how we were never to be seen in public with even one hair out of place. In my father's words, we had a reputation to uphold and had to always look the part.

"He's totally gorgeous, even you won't be able to resist him," she gushes. Her dramatic statement pulls an eye roll out of me.

"You know I have no interest or time for guys. My focus is on finishing school with the best scores then hightailing it out of here to a great college as far away as humanly possible from my parents," I remind her. To say my parents are controlling is the understatement of the century. I can't have friends or associate with someone without them passing an unwritten test by my parents. Kelsey's parents are friends with mine, so we got lumped together from a young age. We get along well, and we share similar views about our parents which is a bonus. Why do all the rich parents around here have their noses stuck up in the air or other people's arses?

"I wish we were in our last year of school. I don't know how I'm going to survive two more years of this torment," I whine, as we continue down the hallway to our class.

"Trust me Soph, this guy is delicious. Just the look of him will have you begging him for a chance?" she whispers.

"I don't beg. Plus, how many times have I told you, I have no time for boys," I grunt, as my feet stop in their tracks and turn to face her.

Her smile pulls up, reaching her eyes as she says, "Well he's gonna have everyone else begging. Just you wait and see. They will be lining up around the block for a piece of him," she says. I roll my eyes directly at her this time as I clutch her forearm and pull her towards our class. The moment we begin our trek down the hall, I stumble over nothing. Oh, not nothing, it's the sight of the beautiful boy walking towards me. His fingers run through his raven-coloured hair pushing it back off his forehead. It's longer on the top with the sides shorter and looks sexy as hell but I won't admit it to anyone. The hallway quietens as he walks through it. A new student is always a big deal, but I feel this guy is a bigger deal than usual. This school is filled with the pretentious and rich offspring of the town's elite and something about this boy feels like it doesn't fit in. Maybe it is the black leather jacket he's wearing combined with the confident strides he makes as if he owns the school. With his head held high, he pays no one any notice Everyone has halted, Kelsey and I included. We all have stopped to stare at the new kid.

I shake myself out of the fog and pull on Kelsey's arm. The student body can be relentless, and they'll cast you as an outsider for any little menial thing. His leather jacket alone will have everyone giving him a wide berth, if not, the vibe he gives off like he couldn't

4

care less about anyone here will do the job. Kelsey resists my pull, her wide ogling eyes stuck on him. Rolling my eyes for the third time today, I walk down the hall alone as everyone else is rooted to their spot.

The new boy ignores them all. He must notice it though, no one could be that oblivious, it's as if time has frozen everyone except for him. My shoes sound louder as they click against the floor. The distance closes between us, his head faces forward, unfazed. I internally tell myself not to look at him when every fibre of my being is telling me to get a closer look to see if he's as beautiful up close. I follow his lead and keep my eyes facing forward, fighting the urge to look at him.

As we pass each other, I see him glancing my way in my peripheral vision. My heart beats quicker as I walk past him, knowing he broke his trance to look at me. His own steps fade behind me and the chatter begins.

"Soph. Wait up," Kelsey yells out from where I left her. With a squeal, my shiny shoes pivot back her way. I wait until she reaches me then turn back around as she falls into step beside me. "Didn't I tell you? He looks like a fallen angel from the heavens," she sighs, between catching her breath.

"You're exaggerating a bit, don't you think?" I state, as we enter the classroom.

"You saw him. You can't tell me he's not drop dead gorgeous?" She slides into her chair, and I take the seat at the desk beside her.

"I admit he's cute, but could you reign in the drooling?" I tease, which makes her roll her eyes at me this time.

"I'll try but I make no promises," she whispers, as the room fills with the other students. "What do you think his name is?" she asks, as she leans towards me.

"Don't worry I'm sure with him being the talk of the school, you will know by next period," I whisper in return, before I shuffle in

5

my seat and straighten my spine as the teacher takes his place at the front of the class. For the next hour, the new boy is forgotten, and I focus on Ancient Rome.

The rush to exit the class when the bell rings is chaotic. Everyone is in a hurry to find out the gossip on the new kid. Kelsey and I have different classes, so we split off and head in opposite directions.

"Don't gossip too hard," I call out to her, as I walk away. Her laughter floats to me as we drift apart. She has Camilla in her next class who is the go-to person in situations like this. She's up in everyone's business and knows everything about everyone. You want dirt on someone? Camilla is your girl. There's no doubt in my mind Kelsey is headed straight to her to get the dirt on the new boy.

I make it to the changing rooms for Physical Education with enough time to change into my sports uniform. My crisp white blouse is carefully removed so as not to crease it. The yellow t-shirt glides over my head and then I replace my black skirt with navy blue shorts. The black shoes are swapped out for my white sneakers, and I tie the laces before checking if my hair is still in place before walking out the door.

The changing rooms are right beside the gym, so I follow my other classmates into the gymnasium and see there are two volleyball nets set up across the room. As we enter, Mrs. Valen points to us and gives us a number which assigns us to a team. I'm given number three, so I walk to the far side of one of the courts where my new teammates are. Physical Education isn't my favourite subject as I'm not coordinated when it comes to ball sports. A gut feeling tells me this isn't going to go well at all.

"Hey Sophia," my friend Delilah greets me, as I walk towards her.

"Hey, how's your morning been?" I ask, as we stand side by side and wait for the teams to be ready.

"Great. Did you see the new guy?" she squeaks.

"Yeah, Kelsey is as excited as you are."

"Come on Sophia. He's hot. Oh my gosh did you see his jacket? He looked so cool," she continues.

"Alright kids, get to it," Mrs. Valen calls across the open space, and we all move into position. Delilah pushes me to the front of the net which makes the back of my neck sweat. I know my team is going to get annoyed when I start missing the ball.

Before we begin, someone walks through the doors late and draws everyone's attention. I look up to see the new boy standing there.

"Come on kids, snap to it," Mrs. Valen hollers out, so the others slowly move into position. Ricki grabs a ball and sets up to serve it while everyone tries to discreetly glance towards where Mrs. Valen talks with the hot topic of the school. I force myself to focus on the game and not look at him. He's got enough eyes on him as it is, and he can probably feel them. As I'm staring straight ahead, I catch a glimpse of him walking towards the bleachers to take a seat. He's new so I assume he doesn't have his sports uniform yet and the P.E teachers have strict instructions. No sports gear, no play time means he'll have to spend the period watching us.

Ricki's hit sounds in the room then it travels over the net a second later and I follow it as the other team sets it before spiking it over. It comes straight at me, and I manage to do a forearm pass

7

without looking too gangly. We fall into a rhythm and move around in a circle as points are scored and everyone takes turns at serving.

We are evenly matched and I'm up next to serve.

The only warning I get is an "Aaah," that Delilah screams before the ball whacks me in the back of the head making me stumble forward. My eyes screw shut as I clutch the back of my head with two hands as it pounds from the pain. The beginning of a headache is already forming.

"Sophia, are you okay? I'm so sorry," she says, as her and my teammates surround me.

"Do you need to sit down?" Ricki asks, and I peel my eyes open. A few tears have sprung to the surface from the pain.

"Yeah, I think I'll sit down for a bit," I tell them, walking the best I can around the side of the court.

"Sophia, do you need to go to the nurse's office?" Mrs. Valen asks, as she moves around the court to come and check on me.

"No, I think I'll be good once I sit down for a bit."

"It was a hard hit so if your head is still hurting when the bell rings, go and see her even if it's to get some paracetamol for the headache you are sure to get."

"Okay Miss," I reply. She pats me on the shoulder as I step past her and head to the bleachers to take a seat. The closer I get, the more I notice the new kid. His knees are bent with his elbows resting on them as he leans forward, enticed by the games of volleyball like he wishes he was out there. My butt drops onto one of the wooden beams a few rows down from him. Resting my own elbows on my knees, my head drops into my hands and my eyes close. My palm runs over the back of my skull in search of any bump the hit might have caused to erupt. Delilah is as uncoordinated as I am but jeez how did she hit it so damn hard?

Shuffling behind me draws my attention before a deep voice speaks. His voice is quiet, so it doesn't carry far but it has me lifting my head to look at him and his brown almost black eyes stare straight back at me.

"Hey, is your head, okay?"

"It's pounding now," I admit, which makes him wince.

"Do you need an ice pack or anything?" he asks, which makes me smile at his kindness.

"No, I'll be okay for now. Thank you."

"Lorenzo," he adds. Lorenzo. I mull the name over in my painful head. It suits him.

"Sophia," I tell him, which makes the faintest hint of a smile light up his face. His top lip pulls up in a miniscule movement, but I notice it and that tiny movement makes a huge difference to his face.

"Nice to meet you," he adds.

"You too," I tell him, before my brain slams around in my head with the pressure. I physically wince, scrunch my eyes and place my head back in my hands, hoping if I don't move the pain will lessen. Lorenzo lets me be, not talking anymore but not moving back to his original seat. The whistle blows some time later and Mrs. Valen tells us to head to the sheds to change.

"You should go to the nurse like she said," Lorenzo's smooth voice says, as he stands and picks up his bag beside him.

"Yeah, I think I will. Thanks." He nods before strutting down the steps towards the bathrooms. I pass Mrs. Valen on my way to get changed.

"Change then go straight to the nurse. How is it now?"

"Not as bad as it was but I do have a headache."

"I'll write you a note for next period if you need it," she tells me.

"Thanks Miss." She writes me a note and hands it to me. On my way to the changing room, I meet Delilah coming out.

"I'm so sorry Sophia."

9

"It's fine, it was an accident. Luckily it got me out of serving," I joke, making us both laugh which makes my head hurt more.

"Do you want me to wait for you?"

"Nah. I'm gonna change and then go see the nurse."

"I can come if you want?"

"No. I'll be fine. I'll catch you and Kelsey in the cafeteria for lunch."

"Sure. I'll see you then," she says, as she waves goodbye. I strip out of my clothes and pull my uniform back on. Lucky for me I hardly worked up a sweat. I make my way across to the other side of the school where the nurse's office is and knock on the open door.

"Hey, how can I help you?" Miss Torres the nurse greets me.

"I got hit in the head hard with a volleyball. I was hoping you could give me some paracetamol for my headache."

"Sure thing. I'll be two ticks," she says, turning and opening cabinets to find what she's after. She pops two pills out, hands them to me, and fills a plastic cup with water from the cooler in the corner of the room. I tip the pills into my mouth and wash them down with the water before handing the cup back to her, which she chucks in the bin.

"Do you want to lie down and rest? I can write you a slip for the missed period if you like?" she offers.

"Yeah, that would be great, my head is killing me," I confess.

"If it's as bad as you say, do you want to go home?" she asks.

"No. Hopefully after a rest I'll be good to go," I tell her. Dread fills my body at the thought of going home. I couldn't think of anything worse than having to call my parents to pick me up for getting hit in the head with a volleyball. It's not my fault but they would find some way to turn it around on me. Nothing is ever good enough in their eyes.

She pats the bed for me to hop up on. My bag drops to the floor, and I lie down on the hard surface and try to get comfortable.

These beds are not designed with comfort in mind. She kindly shuts the lights off as I close my eyes, leaving the door open as her footsteps fade and she leaves me to rest.

My head thumps but I try to ignore it, hoping it will fade soon. Instead, I focus on the nearly black eyes of the new boy named Lorenzo and his hint of a smile.

Chapter Two

Lorenzo

"Hey old man," I call, as I open the squeaky front door to my house.

"Who are you calling old, boy?" he replies from the couch, where he sits with a jigsaw puzzle splayed out on the coffee table. "How was your first day at the new school?" he asks. I shrug off my bag and it drops to the carpet as I sit down beside him.

"It was okay. School is school," I tell him, picking up a piece and placing it into the slot next to a border piece where it fits.

"School is not just school. I'm hoping this one will open doors for you. I want better for you Lorenzo," he tells me again for the hundredth time.

"Yeah, I know Gramps."

"You gotta want better for yourself too boy. You can't settle. What have I always told you?"

"You gotta grab life by the horns and go after what you want," I say.

"Damn straight and don't you ever forget it." He twists a piece around trying to make it fit before he drops it and picks up another piece.

"Your advice is ingrained in me, I doubt I could forget it if I tried," I tell him, laughing.

"Good. Now for the important things. Did you see any pretty girls?" he teases.

"Gramps!"

"What? There's nothing wrong with that. You know I met your grandma when I was your age," he starts, and I know I've fallen straight into his trap. He just wants a reason to relive memories he has of his one true love, my nana. She passed away when I was nine years old, and Gramps has stayed true to her. Even in death, his love for her lives on.

"There was one girl that caught my eye," I blurt out, and I don't know why I'm telling him this because it's only going to set him off.

"What's her name?" he asks.

"Sophia," I confess, as her face comes to my mind.

"Ahh that's a beautiful name. You got a class with her?"

"Yeah P.E. She got hit with a volleyball, so I asked if she was okay. She has the prettiest hair I've ever seen. It's this bright orange like fire and her skin is covered in these faint freckles," I tell him, which makes him lean back and look at me. "What?" I ask.

"Don't forget why you are there. You need to focus on your studies and get good grades before you finish school. Girls can come later," he tells me.

"Yeah Gramps, I know the deal. She made me too nervous anyway," I confess.

"Well, you know what that means."

"What?"

"It means she must be worth it. If you get that nervous around a girl, it means she's worth fighting for. But like I said, girls can come later, you have your whole life ahead of you."

"But you didn't wait for Nana," I remind him.

13

"That's because I had to convince your Nana to give me a shot. I knew it in my soul when I met her there was something about her that drew me in, and I never stood a chance. I grabbed life by the horns and held on for dear life. I want you to focus on your grades Lorenzo. I didn't pull you away from that bad crowd you were hanging with at your other school so you could mess up this opportunity," he sighs, as he stands to head to the kitchen.

"Yeah, Gramps I hear you," I reply. He stops in the hall to turn back to me.

"When the right girl comes around, you'll feel it in your bones, boy. Life has a funny way of making things work out, so if this is the girl meant for you, it'll work out. You're sixteen. Focus on yourself for now. The rest will come later." He leaves me to think as he heads into the kitchen. I place pieces into the puzzle where they fit and leave the images of the girl with the fiery red hair behind me. Like Gramps said, if it's meant to be, it'll be. Plus, I don't know this girl. I'm sure I'll forget about her soon enough.

Chapter Three

Sophia

Days turn into weeks and weeks into months and before I know it, the end of the year is closing in on me. It's stressful with exams coming up so the pressure is getting to me. My parents expect nothing less than the best and anything else is a disappointment. My best isn't enough most days.

It's the Tuesday before exams start and I find myself holed up in the library at one of the tables with Kelsey and Delilah during our free period. Everyone is cramming for the exams next week. It's not a new thing. All the rich parents who send their kids here have high expectations of them, mine are just as bad if not worse.

The tables are full as the sound of scratching pens on paper surrounds us. The sound of the library door closing perks my ears up, but my eyes stay on the page I'm writing on, needing to focus.

"Did you hear the latest gossip about Lorenzo?" Kelsey starts, and I roll my eyes inside my head at her. She hasn't stopped gossiping about the boy since the day he arrived.

"Aren't you tired of talking about him yet?" I whisper.

"With all the stuff I hear about him, how could I ever be tired of it?" she asks, and this time I roll my eyes so she can see.

"What did you hear?" Delilah asks, and I try my best to ignore them, as my eyes drop back down to the paper in front of me.

"I heard he had a threesome with Gaia and Trisha on the football field on Saturday night," she says with glee, which has Delilah choking in shock. I lift my head at her news and my own eyes widen as Kelsey waggles her brows at me with a huge smile on my face. It isn't her I'm focussed on though. It's the main character of her story that happens to be standing right behind her, and his eyes are on me. Now I realise why Delilah was choking.

With his eyes still set on mine he says, "Ladies, do you mind if I sit with you?" which has Kelsey's own eyes about to pop out of her skull.

I swallow with the hope it will ease the dryness, but it doesn't, so I nod instead of speaking, worried my voice would come out squeaky if I tried.

"Thanks," he says, as he pulls out the remaining seat next to Kelsey and sits down. He pulls out his books and flips to the page he needs. "Oh, don't let me interrupt your conversation. Carry on," he encourages Kelsey, as he settles into his own studying and focuses on his textbook. I avert my gaze and follow his lead, focusing on my books and from the lack of noise coming from Delilah and Kelsey, I'm guessing they are doing the same.

The rest of the period we work silently surrounded by our awkward bubble until the bell goes and everyone rushes off to their next class.

"By the way there was no threesome. The girls asked if they could spread the rumour to mess with their exes who they caught cheating on them. It was no skin off my nose, so I let them. If you wouldn't mind keeping that information to yourselves, I'd appreciate it. Those guys deserve what was coming to them," Lorenzo whispers, which has us all nodding before he packs up and leaves us to it.

"I knew gossiping would get you in trouble one day," I direct at Kelsey.

"You guys could have warned me he was behind me," she chastises, as we leave the library behind and walk to our next class.

Chapter Four

Lorenzo

I spent the summer working with my gramps at his auto shop. He gives me smaller tasks to keep me occupied. We fixed up my motorbike too. We worked on it every day during the summer. It was a piece of garbage Gramps bought off someone cheap knowing he could fix it up. He's allowing me to ride it to school now instead of taking the bus which took nearly an hour. I passed all my exams at the end of the year, so Gramps was happy. Only one more year to go and then I'll be out of school for good. Gramps wants me to go to university, but I already know I want to work in the shop with him.

Pulling up to school, the hum of the engine causes the other students to stop and stare. It's nothing new. All last year they gawked and spread rumours about me. I know I don't help the situation. I couldn't relate to most of these kids. They were worrying about their daddies not buying them a new boat for their birthdays where I was worrying about making sure I pass each test so as not to let my gramps down.

I hop off my bike and hang my helmet on the handle. It's not like these kids are gonna steal it. They could have their parents buy them a brand-new bike by tomorrow if they wanted. My fingers rake through my hair, pushing it off my face as I walk towards the front doors of the school. Once inside, conversations cease as they notice me, but I pay them no mind as I head straight to my home room which isn't too far. Taking a seat, my teacher Mr. Carr slides my timetable in front of me.

"Thanks sir," I say to his retreating figure, as he moves on to the other students. My schedule doesn't look too bad as I glance over it. The bell rings and I head to my first period which happens to be English. A seat in the back calls to me in the hope no one will sit close to me. At least the rumours cause most of the students to keep their distance. Still, it doesn't deter everyone and I have the odd girl throwing themselves at me or starting rumours about hooking up with me which isn't true at all. I haven't hooked up with anyone at this school. The only one who ever caught my interest was the red-haired siren but like everyone else, she gives me a wide berth. I wouldn't mind if she came closer. With thoughts of her in my mind, she magically appears. Her bright red hair captures my attention as she steps into the room. The bored expression on my face remains in place but I watch out of the corner of my eye as she glances around the students to find a desk. She's with her friend Kelsey and they take seats on the opposite side of the room together. Her hair is straight down her back today, not one hair out of place. I'd love to run my fingers through it to see if it is as soft as it looks.

Class begins and thoughts about the red head are pushed aside as I focus on why I'm here, determined to get good grades before I leave this place.

The rest of the day is uneventful. Everyone is talking about all the places they visited for their summer holidays and their summer homes. I avoid it all and as the bell rings, I pack up my stuff and head out to my bike. Sliding onto the back, I pull my helmet on and slide the visor down to cover my eyes. It gives me the perfect chance to watch as Sophia walks out of the school doors. Turning the ignition, I watch

19

as the roar of the engine draws her eyes to me as it does everyone else. Her steps slow, the only indication she's checking out my bike like everyone else is.

What I wouldn't give to have her eyes on me. One thing I've noticed is everyone stares at me, they don't care. They do it openly and whisper lies to their friends except one. Sophia. Her eyes are never on me as if I'm invisible to her. And that is the last thing I want. I'd trade everyone else's eyes on me for hers if I could. I'm not sure why she does it. I don't think she's stuck up but I'm too chicken to ask her. Out of everyone I've ever come across, she's the only person who makes me nervous. My gramps can make me nervous for a different reason, it's usually because I don't want to disappoint him, but not Sophia. She makes my heart race. I worry if I talk to her, I'd stutter over my words.

I've waited long enough so I kick up the stand and slowly back out before I peel out of the school leaving them all behind as my bike takes me to my gramps' auto shop to help him out.

"Hey boy, how was your first day back?" he asks, as I walk into the shop where I find him in his office.

"Same old. Nothing new." He lets out a chuckle before he stands but then staggers and grips the edge of the desk.

"Gramps? You okay?" I ask, my brows furrowed as I watch him. He clutches his chest before falling back into his chair.

"Think I'm having a heart attack," he rasps, squeezing his words out. I react and grab the phone off his desk and dial emergency services. It isn't long before they arrive and wheel him into the back of the ambulance where I jump in beside him. I leave his main mechanic Lewis in charge. At the hospital they confirm it was a mild heart attack and he needs to stay overnight for observation. I settle in for the night, too worried about him to leave his side.

Chapter Five

Lorenzo

I peel my eyes open as I feel a shake on my forearm.

"Hey boy, time for you to head to school," Gramps tells me. My head rested on his hospital bed while I sat in the chair beside him all night waiting for any update.

"I don't want to go to school. Can't I miss one day?"

"No, come on. They probably won't have much to tell us anyway and you aren't gonna do anything but sit here all day. You'll be more useful at school," he urges.

"Fine then," I relent.

"Good. Ring Lewis to come get you and take you to the shop to grab your bike," he tells me.

"I'll be back straight after school. Let me know if there are any updates," I instruct him.

"Yeah yeah. Now get going before you're late," he says.

I pull out my phone from my pocket and dial Lewis. Luckily, he was already on the way to come check on us. With reluctance, I say my goodbyes to Gramps and head out the front to meet Lewis.

After grabbing my bike from the shop, home is my next stop to shower, grab a muesli bar to eat and then I'm back on my bike headed to school. I'm cutting it close so I drive faster than I usually would. The last thing I need is to get detention for being late.

Pulling up into the school car park, I park in the same spot I did yesterday.

"You should take your piece of crap straight to the dump, Moretti," Devon says, as he walks past with his followers behind him. He's Gaia's ex so is sour towards me after the threesome rumours spread like wildfire.

I'm hungry and tired and usually I'd let it slide but today it gets the better of me and I fire back.

"Come on now Devon, don't be jealous cos I gave it to your girl better than you ever could," I tease. Removing my helmet, eyes on Devon, I hook it on the handle.

"What did you say?" He stops, his nostrils flaring as his fists clench at his sides. His friend Peter grabs his forearm to pull him away, but Devon shakes him off.

"You heard me. And the whole school knows what Gaia, Trisha and I got up to when your shit team didn't make the play-offs, so how about you run along and go cry about that. It'll teach you not to cheat on girls and treat them like shit," I cuss at him. A small crowd has gathered now to watch us. A glimpse of bright red hair alerts me to Sophia's presence, without seeing her face.

"You better watch your mouth," he threatens.

"Why? What are you gonna do about it?" I ask, as I hop off my bike. I usually avoid conflict and let their whispers slide off my back but today I'm too wound up to let it go. He lunges at me, and his fist connects with my cheekbone. My fist balls before I throw a punch back, connecting myself. Then his friends jump in and it's three against one. I've got punches coming from all sides and I can't fend them all off. They wrangle me to the ground and one of them kicks me in the stomach knocking the wind out of me.

22

"Lorenzo!" I hear someone scream my name, which registers before another foot kicks my leg. "Get off him," the female voice screams again, and then the guys are pulled away from me. I glance up to see Sophia standing there with her friend Kelsey, Kelsey's brother, and his friend.

"All of you, detention after school," Mrs. Lancaster the principal calls out, as she walks up to the scene.

"Who?" Kelsey asks.

"Devon. Chad. Peter and Lorenzo. The four of you have detention this afternoon. I could see you fighting from my office which is not acceptable behaviour at this school. If you don't show up to detention, I will be ringing your parents," she threatens.

"That's not fair. It wasn't Lorenzo's fault," Sophia comes to my defence.

"Do you want to see yourself in detention too Sophia? I think you should get yourself to class before you do."

"He was only defending himself. Why should he be punished?" she continues.

"Fine, I'll see you in detention after school too Miss Philips," she says. "Now everyone, get to class."

The crowd disperses, not wanting to get caught in her wrath, and they hurry their steps to get to class in time. I pull myself to stand, my body protesting from the pain. The back of my hand glides across my mouth as the metallic taste hits my tongue. Blood shows on my hand but I ignore it. Picking up my bag I'd dropped, I follow suit and hurry to class not stopping to check how my face looks in the bathroom. Maybe I shouldn't have sped to school after all as I could have saved myself the trouble of detention. This day was already going to be unbearable while worrying about Gramps but now it's worse. I can't wait for it to be over, and I can finally get out of here.

Sophia

As soon as I saw them punching Lorenzo, I raced over to stop them. His cheek has a bad bruise on it but I'm not sure if it's gotten worse as the day has gone on as I haven't seen him.

Here I sit inside detention waiting for someone else to show up. I know Devon won't. His parents don't care if he gets detention so it's not like he's going to care if his parents get called. Mine wouldn't let me hear the end of it though so there's no way I want mine called.

Footsteps sound behind me but I focus on the paper in front of me. There are lines on the board I've been instructed to copy. I shall not get into fights at school. How ridiculous when I wasn't the one fighting. A figure drops into the seat at the desk beside me and my head can't help but turn to glance to see who it is.

"Mr. Moretti, write the line on the board three hundred times, then if the hour is still not up you are to complete any work you have or else get a head start on some reading material," Mrs. Lancaster says to Lorenzo.

My eyes flick back down to continue to write but I hear him moving around in his seat, pulling out a book and pen to get started. A few minutes pass in silence and Mrs. Lancaster begins tapping away at her laptop in front of her.

"Thanks for sticking up for me today. I wish you hadn't though because now you're stuck in here too," Lorenzo's voice carries across the desk to me.

"I wasn't gonna stand there and watch them beat the crap out of you in an unfair fight," I huff.

"I could have taken them. I was just warming up," he jokes.

"Well, the concrete you were lying on would disagree with that statement," I joke back, which has a soft laugh leaving him.

"Do I need to remind you two you're in detention and it's supposed to be done quietly. I can get you back tomorrow and the next day if you would like."

"No Miss, we will be quiet," I rush to say. My focus reverts to the tedious task in front of me instead of on the boy beside me. After a while my hand cramps and I shake it a few times to get some feeling back into it.

"Very well you two, you are free to go. I don't want to see either of you involved in any trouble again or else next time I will be calling your guardians. Do you understand?"

"Yes Mrs. Lancaster," we both reply.

"Well off you go," she says, so we pack up our books, hand in our lines that are likely to get thrown straight in the bin anyway, and high tail it out of there. Lorenzo surprises me by walking beside me down the hall. I guess we are both going to the car park, so it makes sense.

"Thanks again for today," he says, with his hand pushing the front door for the school open for me to exit.

"You don't have to keep thanking me. Any decent person would have stopped it," I tell him.

"That's the thing; I don't think they would have," he states, which makes me look at him properly for the first time in a long time. A dark purple bruise shines against his cheekbone, the only indicator he was in a fight today. "Do you need a ride?" he asks, as I continue to stare at him.

I shake my head and point out my car at the back of the lot. He follows my finger and nods when he sees my shiny red sports car.

"Cool. Well thanks again for today," he says, before he hops on his bike, ready to leave.

"Bye Lorenzo," I say, before my feet carry me to my car. The thrum of his engine grows distant the further it gets from me. He peeled out of the car park before I got to my car. I can't blame him; most of the kids are always in a hurry to leave school and get home for the day. I'm the opposite. Always in a hurry to leave home but never in a hurry to return. I hope one day it will be different. Unfortunately, today is not that day.

Chapter Six

Lorenzo

Gramps stayed in the hospital for a week while they ran tests on him. They couldn't find anything major wrong but prescribed him medication and told him to rest for the next month or two. He isn't supposed to work either but that doesn't stop him from going into the auto shop and doing paperwork.

I help more around home to take some of the load off him and I also go into the auto shop every day after school to help the other mechanics so they can focus on the bigger stuff. The last thing I want is my gramps pushing himself any more than he should.

Valentine's Day is coming up which has never held any interest for me. At my old school it wasn't a thing unless you were in a relationship. These rich kids are something else. People can send roses to people they like with little notes. You can state who it is if you wish, or you can make it anonymous. They have a big red box set up in the front foyer as soon as you enter the school. It has a big slit cut into the top so all you must do is place a zip lock bag in there. In the bag you must include the note you want written and the name of who you want it sent to plus the money. It's five dollars per rose.

The week before Valentine's, everyone has been pushing their bags into the box, everyone excited over the prospect of sending their crushes little notes. I haven't thought much of the tradition as I've never been here for it. I started here at the end of February last year, so I missed it by a few weeks. It's all anyone is talking about now. Especially the girls.

I wasn't planning to send anyone a rose until I catch sight of the red hair, I've consciously started to scan the crowd of students for lately. After the day of the fight, she keeps her distance. I don't blame her. It's not like I've given her any indication I'm crushing on her. Plus, I have Gramps to worry about now so like he said, girls will have to wait. It doesn't mean I can't do something anonymous though.

Sitting in class I scribble down a quick note onto a page in my book before I rip it out as quietly as possible. I ask the teacher for the bathroom pass and then as quick as I can, I rush to the big red box. I push the note into the zip lock bag I grabbed from home earlier and add five dollars. I'd already added Sophia's name to the note, so I seal it and push it into the slit. Not wanting to get caught, I quicken my steps and walk back to class, with everyone none the wiser. Now all I must do is wait until Valentine's Day and hope it brings a smile to that pretty face of hers.

Valentine's Day arrives and as I enter the school, people are already gushing over presents they got from their boyfriends and girlfriends. Girls shove stuffed teddy bears and chocolates into their lockers and there's more than one couple not caring about PDA today. I change my books over in my own locker before heading to home room. I'm not one to usually feel lonely but something about today makes me wish I had a friend to talk to. Someone to confide in about the secret note I wrote for Sophia would be nice. My friends from my other school turned out to not be very good friends at all, just like my gramps said. I've seen them around from time to time, but I have no time for their antics now. The things they get up to like tagging, drinking and smoking is low on my to do list these days. I am grateful my gramps got me away from that environment when he did. If only to show me the true colours of my so-called friends.

The bell chimes and I head to English not knowing when these roses are supposed to arrive. I slide into my usual seat and wait for the teacher to start harping on. About halfway through, there's a knock on the door and in walks a couple of students carrying a box filled with roses for them to hand out. They call out names and hand them to the student when they place their hand in the air. My palms sweat as I wait for Sophia's name to be called.

"Sophia?" the guy says. I watch as she lifts her head, her eyes widening. She raises her hand and as he hands her the single rose, my heart thumps in my chest. I can't help but watch as she pulls the note off, unfolds it and tucks a piece of hair behind her ear. Her skin lights up a pretty pink as her blush coats her freckles. I hope it's the note from me.

"Lorenzo?" my name is called, causing my brows to furrow as I raise my hand. The guy deposits three roses into my palm before walking back to the front of the room to resume his list. There are three notes so they must be from different people. I open one note which reads: 'You're so hot. Your secret admirer.' I didn't know I had a secret admirer. I glance around the room and wonder if they are in here with me now, but no one is watching me. The students are either mesmerised by their own roses or looking at their friends' ones. I open another note that says: 'If you are after a good time, message me.' There's a number attached too but no name. I know the note will be going straight in the bin. I don't have time to be messing around with girls. With Gramps, the shop and my studies, I have no spare time. Girls will just complicate that.

I pull the last note off and read it. My heart beats faster at the fact someone took the time to write something so nice and meaningful to me. I'm lucky I had three people think I was worthy to write notes for but it's this third one which has me wishing it was from a certain someone. The thought would never be a reality though. She may know I exist but I'm still invisible in her eyes.

I close my eyes briefly and let out a sigh. For once I don't want to be invisible to her. With my mind made up, I wait for the bell to ring and then quicken my pace to catch her before she leaves.

"Looks like you have an admirer," I say, as she bends down to pick up her bag. Her smile grows as she looks at me. I wonder if she's thinking about my note.

"Well not as many as you by the looks of it," she says, as her eyes drop to the three roses I hold in my hands. I let out a chuckle, not knowing how to reply.

"That reminds me," I say. I pull the note off one of the roses that holds the phone number on it and toss it in the bin as we walk out the door together.

"Why did you throw that one away?" she asks, her wide eyes looking at me.

"It said if I was after a good time to message the number on it," I tell her, as we carry on down the hall together. I know people are staring at us, but I pay them no mind, my eyes focussed on her.

"You're not after a good time?" she asks, as she tucks her hair behind her ear.

"Nah I've got too much on my plate as it is. Plus, I don't think whoever is on the end of that number would interest me," I say, and I wonder if she's catching on to my hints. Are these hints? Damn it, I suck at flirting.

30

She stops in her tracks and turns to me. "What if it was my number?" she boldly asks, and it makes me gulp, my hands sweating.

"Was it?" I ask, and I fear my voice may have risen an octave.

With a slight tug of her lips, she pats me on the shoulder and says, "I guess you'll never know now since you threw it in the rubbish." She walks away without a backwards glance and leaves me standing there.

"Was it?" I yell out to her, but she raises her hand waving.

"Bye Lorenzo." I shake my head as I laugh and continue to my class. She's messing with me, but it still doesn't stop my body from wanting to run back to the classroom and retrieve the note from the bin. Instead, I head to my next class after I put my three roses in my locker for safe keeping.

During the second period there's a knock on the door as a student enters and they hand a note to the teacher. He reads over it before his head pops up to look at me.

"Lorenzo, you are wanted in the office. Take your things with you," he instructs. Everyone's eyes are on me again as I pack everything up and take the pass from him as I leave and head towards the principal's office. Hiking up the huge stairs I reach the top and I'm greeted by my home room teacher and the principal.

"Hi Lorenzo, could you come into the office with us please?" Mrs. Lancaster asks. I follow behind them and take a seat she indicates for me to sit in. I don't understand why I'm here until she comes and takes the vacant seat beside me. "Lorenzo, we've gotten a call about your grandfather."

"Is he okay?" I ask, as my heart gallops in my chest.

"He had a heart attack not long ago but there was nothing they could do. I'm sorry Lorenzo, but your grandfather passed away." Her voice trails off as she keeps talking but I can't hear her words. It's as if my ears are blocked. Nothing penetrates through as I sit there numb.

"Lorenzo, are you okay?" My home room teacher's voice breaks through the fog, and her hand on my forearm draws my attention to her.

"Where is he?" I ask.

"He's at the hospital. They are going to take care of the body to get it ready for wherever you would like it sent for funeral arrangements. Is there anyone we can call? Have you got any other family?" she asks, and I shake my head. It was only my gramps and I left. It had always been me, my gramps, and my nana until my nana passed.

"Can I leave for the day?" I ask.

"Yes, that's fine. Do you need help with anything?" Mrs. Lancaster asks, and I shake my head again.

"I may be out of school for a few days while I organise the funeral, but I will be back," I tell her.

"Don't worry about that, Lorenzo. Do you need a lift anywhere?" she asks, but I shake my head.

"No, I have my bike. I guess I'll go then," I tell them.

"If you need anything, please come and talk to either of us. We are here to help you," Mrs. Lancaster says.

Both women's faces are etched with sadness. I nod, not able to form words then pick up my bag and head out of the office.

Once on my bike, it's as if I go into autopilot all the way to the hospital. My only thought is to get to my gramps. When I tell the receptionist I'm there because my gramps died, she gives me the same sad look. My body sags into a seat and my foot taps against the linoleum as I wait for someone to take me through to see him.

From the moment I see him, it's as if my body shuts down. It's moving and going through the motions, but my brain and heart are shut off from each other. My brain has shut off access to my heart so no emotions will leak out. I answer all their questions in a robotic tone and when I look at my gramps on the cold table, I feel disconnected. That's not how I remember him.

I'm not sure how long I stay there but then Lewis is by my side and wraps his arm around my shoulder as we stand side by side. He says he will help me with the shop and not to worry about it now. My gramps wanted me to focus on school and that's what I'm meant to do.

Lewis follows me back to my house and we form a plan with funeral arrangements. There isn't a need for a big funeral as there isn't much family and it's mainly the guys from the shop who will be there. It's all a daze and I don't know how I make it through.

The day of the funeral comes and goes and I'm still numb to everything. I took the rest of the week off school. Lewis kept his word and is taking care of the shop. I've placed him in charge until I figure out what I'm going to do. A lawyer came and saw me about Gramps' assets. The shop and the house have been left to me. There's still a little left on the mortgage but with the shop going strong, I can keep on top of that easily enough.

I have no idea about paying bills or mortgages or what not as Gramps always took care of it all. Lewis has been a lifesaver helping me with everything. His wife Helen has been bringing over meals every day for me to freeze and heat up when I need it, so I don't have to worry about food for a while. I'll have to go grocery shopping soon though I have no idea what I'm doing. I guess I'll learn though.

Walking into school the Monday after my gramps' funeral, I've never felt so utterly alone. The clanging of the lockers is background noise as I'm lost in my head which seems to be a recurring theme these last few days. My world has been turned on its head while everyone else's has stayed the same.

Automatically my fingers flick through to the combination of my locker and there sit the three now wilted roses I'd left behind. Grabbing the roses, I switch out my books as I'd left with whatever was in my bag at the time. With a slam of my locker door, I turn and carry the roses to the rubbish bin ready to drop them in but one of the notes is still attached, so I pull it off. It's the one with the poem. Today more than ever, I need a reminder I'm not so alone, so I shove the note in my pants pocket before dropping the roses in the bin.

I turn to walk down the hall towards class and catch sight of her red hair disappearing through a doorway. Just when I thought I could make progress with her, that day turned into the worst day of my life. Now I want to keep to myself.

I walk into the class we share, and my head tells me not to look. I can't help but try to steal a glance. She's looking at me though and I see the smile she offers but I pretend I miss it and continue to my desk on the opposite side of the room. It's better this way. I don't want to bring her down with my mood. My butt drops into my chair and my focus shifts outside the window to daydream. My body may be here physically, but my mind is a million miles away, wondering how I'm supposed to get through this thing called life when I'm all alone.

Chapter Seven

Lorenzo

It's now the third day of the second term. The holidays came and went, and I've learnt something major. How to survive. I may be hanging on by a thread but I'm surviving.

Gramps' business has lost customers since his death. He had loyal customers but since he passed away, they left too, taking their business elsewhere as they don't think I can do a good job as a seventeen-year-old running a business. I'm just shy of eighteen but that is semantics to them and means nothing.

Lewis is still running the shop and has now taken me on as an apprentice. I wanted to be a mechanic anyway, so this is one step closer. He said I still must stick school out though, because it was what my gramps wanted for me. So here I am, hopping off my bike already a quarter of the way through the year. This will all be a distant memory soon and I won't remember these days.

With the loss of business at the auto shop, the bills have started piling up. I found the bar in this town my gramps would frequent as his friend Ted is the owner. He took pity on me and offered me a job so now I'm waiting tables in the evenings a couple times a week. I spent my whole holidays either in the auto shop learning or in the bar working. When I turn eighteen, he said he will be able to let me behind the bar to make drinks, but for now I must wait. Doesn't bother me, money is money no matter how I get it.

I've had to cut down on my groceries so I can make my paycheck last. I keep telling myself it won't always be like this. For now, I must hustle because there is no way I'm losing Gramps' house or his shop. He fought too hard for those things, and I don't want to let him down by losing them.

I walk into class and focus with a new determination in me than I did at the end of last term. I've lit a fire under my own ass as there's no one to do it for me, and I'm set on making my gramps proud. I may be working myself to death seven days a week, but I will get there.

Lunch time rolls around, and I've always sat by myself in the cafeteria. Everyone else chatters away around me. I've spent this time listening to the latest rumours about me or feigning boredom. Now I take the time to complete homework or catch up on my reading. I've had to budget my money so tightly; I skip lunch now or I either have an apple or a muesli bar to get me through to dinner. It won't always be like this; I keep telling myself. And I can only pray it won't be.

The bright orange hair of Sophia I always look for is still there in the background. I catch glimpses of it, but I've noticed I don't seek it out like I used to. We come from different worlds, her and I. If I did want her in some way, there's nothing I have to offer her. I'd never be worthy of a girl like her who has the world at her feet with a rolled out red carpet. So, I've let her go. I've let go of the crush I had. She will be destined for great things, and I'll still be slaving away trying to make ends meet. It is what it is, and I've accepted that fact.

Life deals you a hand and all you can do is make the best out of what you've been dealt. And that's what I plan to do.

Chapter Eight

Sophia

Lorenzo's changed. The rumour mill is still going strong about him. Another girl Mackenzie said she hooked up with him over the weekend and all the other girls are gushing over her about her stories. I've listened a few times to what she has to say though and her story changes, so I don't think it's true. I did find out she was the one who left her number on the rose and that's how they started hooking up, but I saw him throw the number away, so it makes me doubt her more.

It's three weeks into the second term now. I discreetly watch Lorenzo. It's quick glances here and there as if I'm scanning the room but I'm in fact looking for him. We're currently in the cafeteria. It's where I have the best time to observe him. He's always got his head in a book now. He looks like he's lost a bit of weight too and he hardly eats lunch. I'm not sure why but he only ever has a piece of fruit or something small and I'm sure he must be hungry. Kelsey's brother alone eats more than me, her and Delilah do combined.

So, I made myself extra lunch today. It's an extra chicken sandwich and a banana but I packed it with a purpose. The others get their lunches from school, but I never have because of my peanut allergy so it's safer for me to bring my own food from home. Me and my brown paper bag are not out of place this way.

"Guys I gotta go to the library quickly and grab a book I need," I tell the girls. They are busy gossiping with Mackenzie so aren't paying me much attention anyway. So, I grab the extra lunch that sits in my bag and with purposeful strides, I head to the table where Lorenzo sits closest to the doors which lead out of the cafeteria. It's the perfect place to be where you can make a fast getaway.

My pulse speeds up as I close the distance and as I reach him, I place the bag on the table and bend and pretend to tie my shoelace. I stand back up and look at Lorenzo whose eyes are on me now. My gaze glances at the bag and I give him a slight nod. He stares back at me with his dark eyes but where there was once a warmth behind them is now a sadness. He gives me a small smile before I walk away but I can't help but wonder what happened to him to cause him such sadness. I wish I was brave enough to ask.

Every day from then on, I double my lunch and split them into two brown paper bags. As I walk into the cafeteria every lunch time, my feet drag behind my friends so I can drop one bag on the table where Lorenzo sits. No one else ever sits at the table so on the days he runs late the bag sits there waiting for him. We don't acknowledge each other anymore and he hasn't spoken to me since Valentine's Day. I don't think he ever realised I was one of the ones who left him a rose. My note was probably stupid, but I wanted him to know he wasn't alone at this school. He's always by himself and I wonder if he likes it that way or not. I have my friends, but they are surface level. I long for a deeper connection with someone but it is hard to find around here. I have Kelsey and Delilah, but I wonder if there is more to friendship where you can tell each other your darkest secrets and not be judged. I don't feel safe enough voicing how I really feel around them.

I wonder if I'll always be surrounded by a sea of people but still feel lonely. I wonder if that's how Lorenzo feels. Surrounded by people but all alone. Perhaps he likes it that way.

The year passes in the blink of an eye and before I know it, it's my last day at school. We have the graduation ceremony this weekend, but today is our last formal day of school. I've continued to leave lunch for Lorenzo every day since the day I started doing it. We carried on the rest of the year as if it wasn't a thing. It was a small secret we held between the two of us and it would bring a smile to my face when I was alone. I hoped it made him smile too.

Clearing out my locker for the final time I drop all my books into my bag. As I pull out the ones on the top, there sits a white sealed envelope with my name scrawled across the front. The banging of lockers and laughter of everyone excited to finally be finishing school is in the air. I run my finger under the edge to break the seal and pull out the folded piece of paper and read.

Sophia,

I'm not sure where to start but I wanted to thank you for the kindness you have shown me since I started at this school. On the first day of school, you were nice to me when all anyone else did was whisper and talk about me behind my back.

I don't know how to put into words what your kind gesture has meant to me this year. I've been going through a hard time since my gramps died on Valentine's Day and I've tried my best to hold it together. Some days I did and some days I struggled but without realising it, you helped me get through this year.

I'm sorry I never acknowledged what you've done for me or talked to you more. I guess my pride got in the way and it was easier to accept if I pretended it wasn't happening. I hope you can forgive me for that fault.

I didn't want to leave you without saying thank you and for making me feel less alone. Don't let the world harden your heart Sophia because the world needs more of your goodness in it.

If we ever cross paths again, I hope it is in better circumstances. I wish you all the best and hope you find happiness.
Lorenzo

My hands shake when I finish the last line and I scan the hall for Lorenzo. I haven't seen him since lunchtime today when I delivered my last offering to him. He didn't acknowledge me then but that was usual for us, although being the last day of school, I had hoped he may say something, but he didn't. This feels like goodbye, and it makes me sad I never knew his grandad had died. For him to suffer through that with no friends around makes me hurt for him. I hope he's okay. I don't have his number and I know no one else has it. The girls around here have tried their best, but he never gave it to anyone, though some have said they had it. I don't believe they did.

I tuck the letter back into the envelope and place it inside one of my big textbooks to keep it safe. As the final bell rings, the hall clears out and I say goodbye to Delilah and Kelsey telling them I'll see them at graduation. I hope Lorenzo is there so I can talk to him.

Graduation day arrives and Lorenzo doesn't show. So, my hopes of talking to him one last time drift away with the thought of him.

Chapter Nine

4 YEARS LATER

Lorenzo

I haven't had the best start in life and if I could change my parents, I would. Though I would need to know who they were first to be able to change them. I was raised by my grandfather and since he passed away, I've been working my ass off to keep myself above water. It isn't an ideal situation but somehow, I have managed. My gramps wanted nothing more for me than to finish high school so at least I had that going for myself.

He was a proud man and didn't accept help when we needed it and I think I got that trait from him. He lost the love of his life when I was nine years old, and he would tell me stories of their great love. He would always tell me we get one great love in our life and when we find it, we need to hang on to it. He also said my grandma needed convincing Gramps was her great love but there was no way he was going to let her go so convince her he did.

He also told me we don't get many second chances in life but when we do, we need to grab them by the horns and hold on for dear life because we will kick ourselves later if we let the chance pass *through our fingers a second time. So, when the girl I had a crush on for years at high school walked into the bar where I work, I knew I was getting the second chance my gramps always talked about. I was going to gear up and go bull riding.*

The dirty rag in my hand that probably needed changing, slid back and forth over the now rough surface of the wooden table. It was a Thursday night like any other week. The same crowd and the same music ready for line dancing all night long. It was a whole vibe. I had never been one to get up and dance but when my grandparents were both still alive, they'd teach me a few steps in our kitchen when they were having one of their many loved up moments. Those memories of them being happy and in love always gave me hope I'd find the same love in my future.

I had a secret love for country music and the dances, making Thursdays my favourite night to work. Everyone was in a good mood for the upcoming weekend and what's not to love about country music. Friday nights were spent serving rowdier crowds while Saturdays were the nights tempers flared and fights started for some reason. Sundays were mellower, the regulars hung out because they had nowhere else better to be.

So, on a random Thursday in May; my missed opportunity came back into my life dressed in a navy blue off-the-shoulder dress, wearing brown cowboy boots. It was the hair that caught my eye. It has always been the hair. Her bright red hair always had a way of drawing my attention. I'd never come across anyone with hair the same color and I don't think I ever would. The hair drew my eye to her, but it was her lit up smile as she two stepped that had me sucking in a breath. Sophia.

I hadn't seen her since the day we finished high school. I'd crushed on her back then, but I'd been too chicken and too focussed on school and keeping my head above water to do anything about it. She realised I wasn't eating lunch and so started dropping lunch at the table I sat at. Some days it would be sitting there waiting for me and other days she'd place it on the table as she walked past. No words said. No acknowledgment. I kick myself when I think back over those days and wonder if things may have been different if I'd sucked up my pride and talked to her. Thanked her to her face instead of in a letter. It probably wouldn't have changed anything. We are from two different worlds and that's something we can't change.

She had no idea her kindness was the only thing getting me through some days. Especially the last few months after Gramps died when I struggled to make ends meet and keep myself fed. She was the bright star amongst all the dark and gloom in my life. I took her appearance in my life as a sign I was being given a second chance and I wasn't about to blow it.

She held hands with a girl and together they laughed at their missteps as they tried to keep up with everyone else but failed. Most of the people on the dance floor had been dancing here for years continuously but they didn't know that. When the song finished, they made their way giggling to the bar while another song started, and the regular patrons fell into their steps naturally.

Finishing up with the table I'm at, I grab the empty glasses left behind and carry them with one hand while I tuck my rag into my back pocket. I place the dirty glasses on the far side of the bar so I can keep an eye on Sophia without her noticing me. I'd never had the chance to watch her uninterrupted before and I want to savour it. While I wipe down the next few tables, I take my time and keep my eyes on the wild haired beauty who had stolen my heart all those years ago. They make their way to a booth around the other side of the bar, but I can easily still watch her.

Most girls who come in order some fruity cocktail. The owner Ted got sick of telling them we didn't have the fancy stuff so instead he capitalised on it and now has a list of fruity drinks all with matching umbrellas he taught the staff to make. Usually on nights like this when the richer folk come along to try their hand at line dancing, those umbrella drinks make up fifty percent of our drink sales for the night. I notice Sophia's friend has a drink with an umbrella but not Sophia herself. No, she has straight no-frills brown liquor in her glass. I'm guessing whiskey and coke. I wouldn't have taken Sophia for a whiskey drinker but then again there are a lot of things about her I probably don't know.

She always made me nervous. The only girl to ever make me feel nervous. I'm not sure if it was how she held herself or because of her rich family but I always felt like I was never good enough to be in her presence. As if I wasn't worthy. I once told my gramps about her and how I felt, and he told me it wasn't the fact I didn't feel worthy but the fact I knew in my bones this girl was worth everything that made me nervous. He said he felt the same way about my grandma.

I watch Sophia and her friend unnoticed for a good hour. They both order a few drinks, and they start to sway a bit more every time they go up to the bar. It isn't until a couple of regulars who are usually here on Saturday nights starting trouble that I step closer to them. To her.

Billy slides into the booth next to her friend and from the angle where I'm standing, I can't tell what he's saying to her, but I can see Sophia's face and she's not happy. Billy's friend Mick stands at the table and before he can think about sliding onto the black leather seat next to Sophia, I'm by his side, placing my best smile on my face. Sophia is too engrossed keeping an eye on her friend to notice me yet. I quickly glance at the friend and can see why she's concerned. Her friend's eyes are half closed, Billy has his arm wrapped around her shoulder now and she's too drunk to fend him off.

"Billy, Mick, how are things tonight?" I greet them. We've always been friendly as it's my job, but they know I won't put up with any shit they try to start. They both look at me, but my eyes find their way to Sophia's face where she finally turns my way. Her eyes widening in recognition before Billy speaks up.

"Just introducing ourselves to some new customers," Billy tells me, with a smug smile across his face.

"Renzo?" I hear whispered from the table, and the sweet sound of her voice saying a nickname for me has my heartbeat galloping in my chest while I keep a blank stare on my face.

"Hey Soph," I casually reply, as if it's normal to have nicknames for each other. In all honesty, I don't think we uttered each other's names except possibly a few times.

"You know her?" Billy asks, as his eyes flick back and forth between us.

"Sophia and I go way back. So how about you remove your arm from her friend and find someone else to bother. Preferably someone who is conscious."

Mick's body turns towards me as he crosses his arms over his chest, puffing it out. I pay him no attention and keep my gaze on Billy. Raising one eyebrow at his lack of speed, I remain in the same position while I patiently wait. He removes his arm and Sophia's friend's head lies back against the booth, her eyes closing more. Billy pushes up out of the seat getting in my face.

"She's not worth the trouble," he grunts, as he pushes past me. He saunters off to the other side of the bar, Mick trailing behind him.

Sophia slides out of her seat and into the one next to her friend, shaking her arm.

"Ally, come on. Open your eyes," she pleads. I drop down into the seat she vacated and sit opposite her. She lets out a huff at her friend, which flutters her bangs briefly. Her eyes turn to me, and I watch as the bright blue orbs move across my face. As if she's examining every inch of me carefully and unashamedly. I stare back at

47

her, doing my own perusal of her face while I wait for her to speak. Her smatter of freckles still peeks through the layer of foundation she's applied. It always amazed me how one person could have so many freckles. In all my life I'd never come across another person who had as many as Sophia. With her bright hair and beautiful skin, I think she was destined to stand out in my eyes. I can't help but wonder if her freckles coat the rest of her body, the parts that have always been kept covered from view. My eyes trail down her neck to her chest where the faint spots continue to grace her skin.

"So, you work here?" she asks. Her voice brings me out of my ogling before it can go any lower.

"Yeah. I've worked here since I was seventeen," I tell her, as my eyes hold her gaze. Soft snores from her right have us both glancing towards the sound. Ally is fast asleep with her head flopping onto Sophia's shoulder.

"How did you ladies get here?"

"We caught a taxi so we could both drink," she explains, as she looks at Ally. Her nose scrunches like she's regretting them both drinking now.

"Do you want me to call you a taxi?" I offer, trying to be of some help.

"I don't know how I would get her out of the taxi when we get to her place," she tells me. To reinforce it, she lifts Ally's hand then let's go and it instantly drops. Ally sits there snoring away, undisturbed.

"I would offer to drive you, but I have my bike."

"The same motorbike you had from school?" she asks.

"Yep, the same one. I've had her fixed up quite a bit since then. But still the same body."

"Wow."

"She is getting a bit old, but she's still got life left in her," I tell her, with a smile on my face as I think about how Gramps helped me fix her up originally before he passed.

"Lorenzo."

I twist my head in the direction of Ted's gruff voice. I'd forgotten for a minute I was working.

He glances towards Sophia and her friend before yelling, "You can finish for the night. Make sure your friends get home safe."

"Thanks Ted," I nod, in appreciation.

Looking back at Sophia, I realise I don't want our time to end yet and the words slip from my mouth, "I actually live above this bar. I've got a bed and a couch if you guys want to crash for the night and then taxi home in the morning when she's more awake." Biting her lip, she looks at me, mulling it over. Her eyes flick to Ally who is still in the same drunken position she was a minute ago.

"Okay," she sighs, giving in to the only viable option she has. "Can you help me get her up there?"

"Sure," I tell her. Sophia slides out and before she attempts to move Ally across the vinyl seat, I place a hand on her arm, halting her. "I've got her." She steps aside, giving me access to Ally. I lower myself and manoeuvre one hand under her legs, keeping her dress securely in place, while my other arm goes behind her back. Wriggling her out of the booth, I lift her into my arms, her head flinging backwards.

"How much did she drink?" I ask.

Lightly laughing Sophia says, "Ally is a lightweight. Always has been. I think she underestimated how much alcohol was in her cocktails."

I nod in agreement, as I make those when I tend bar and they have a high alcohol content, but you can't tell because of the fruity flavours.

"Stick close to me," I tell her, as I lead her around the back of the bar towards the kitchen.

49

We bypass the main cook Jerry and a couple of servers who are working tonight. Jerry's eyebrows raise as he sees me carrying an unconscious girl with another girl following behind, nearly jogging to keep up with my long strides. I give him a shake of my head as I slip down the hidden hallway which leads to my stairs. Taking the stairs one at a time so as not to fall while carrying Ally, it gives Sophia a chance to catch up with me.

Once we reach the top, I realise my predicament as my keys are stuck in my front pocket, but my hands are full. Glancing down, I see how much shorter Sophia is to me now. I knew I'd grown a lot since school finished but I didn't realise how much until right this minute. Sophia must notice the difference too as her eyes take a lot longer to glide up my body and reach my face.

"My keys are in my front pocket. Are you comfortable grabbing them?" I ask her, as I visibly swallow. She stares at my eyes for a beat before nodding and stepping forward. She angles herself around Ally's feet and slips her hand into my pocket, feeling around for the keys. I'm so distracted by her touch; it isn't until she raises an eyebrow at me, I realise my mistake and throw my head back laughing.

"Sorry Soph, I meant the other pocket."

A deep shade of red spreads quickly across her skin and down her neck. She moves around Ally and this time, steps right into my other side as she pushes her small hand into my pocket. Clutching the keys, she drags them out with her eyes cast down in concentration while I keep my eyes on her face. She dangles them in front of me once she's retrieved them.

"It's the biggest key," I tell her. She searches through the bundle of keys, sliding them through her fingers until she finds the right one. I take a step away from the door to give her room and she pushes the key into the lock, turns it and pushes the door open. I send a prayer to the heavens; grateful I cleaned up this morning. I try to do a thorough clean on a Thursday morning when I have the time.

"You and Ally can take my bed and I'll take the couch for the night," I suggest, as we stand in the foyer of the apartment. From the bar, you wouldn't think an apartment up here would be this nice, but Ted had it renovated a few years back. They ripped out all the walls so it's an open plan living area now. With one bedroom, it's all I need as it's just me. I stay here on the nights I work here because I still have my gramps place. Ted likes having someone here to watch over the place when it's busiest, so it gives him peace of mind and he gives me a discount on rent. She's glancing around, taking in my space but whips her head around at my suggestion of sleeping arrangements.

"Oh, you don't have to give up your bed for us," she says.

"There's only one bed, Sophia, and I can't see you sharing the bed with me while we leave poor Ally on the couch now," I say, my heart racing as more words escape my mouth before I can stop them.

Again, she blushes as she averts her gaze and shakes her head. I let out a laugh because I wouldn't mind sharing a bed with her, even if it was only to sleep and have her in my space, I can tell that's not what she wants.

"Follow me," I say, as I lead her down to my room. I've left the door open, so I manage to gently kick it with my foot and step into my space. Again, I thank my lucky stars I made the bed this morning and changed the sheets. "You wanna pull the sheets back for me?" I ask her, which has her hurrying over to help me.

She pulls one side of the white bedspread back and I gently lower Ally, keeping her dress tucked under her. Sophia sits on the side of the bed and starts removing Ally's cowboy boots. The whole time Ally remains unaware of what's going on. She places Ally's shoes neatly on the carpeted floor at the end of my king size bed.

"How likely is it that she'll puke?" I ask, suddenly aware of my carpet.

"She has an iron stomach. She never pukes," she says, standing and placing the covers back over Ally.

51

I want to spend some time with Sophia to catch up so before she can say she's going to sleep too I blurt, "Do you wanna join me for a drink?"

"Sure," she says, without any hesitation. She follows me out of the room, gently shutting the door behind her. I lead her to my kitchen where she takes a seat at my breakfast bar while I search through my liquor cabinet.

"What do you feel like drinking?" I ask over my shoulder, as I take note of our options.

"Do you have any tequila?"

Chuckling, I reach for the bottle at the back of my collection and pull two shot glasses out of my set as well.

"Are you trying to give us both hangovers?" I ask, with laughter in my voice.

"Don't they say everything is better with tequila?" she asks, as I place the bottle and glasses down in front of her.

I turn my back on her to open the fridge, retrieving a lemon, along with a sharp knife from the block.

"And who are they?" I ask, a smile in my voice.

"I don't know. Someone must," she says, laughing to herself.

I shake my head as I slice the lemon up and place the pieces on a saucer. I flick open another cupboard grabbing my saltshaker. Filling the two shot glasses to the brim I pick up the salt and lick a line across the back of my hand, before shaking the salt on to it. I slide the salt across the marble bench to her which she catches. I watch as her tongue peeks out, swiping a line across her skin before she sprinkles the salt on her own hand.

We each grab a shot as I say, "Here's to everything being better with tequila," which has her throwing her head back in laughter.

"Cheers," she says, clinking her glass with mine after she's collected herself. We both lick the salt, shoot the tequila back and grab a lemon slice in sync. Sucking on the lemons, we both smile at each other showing our lemon skin smiles hiding our teeth which makes our smiles grow.

"So, what brings you to this side of town?" I ask, peeling the lemon from my mouth and dropping it onto another saucer I grab from the cupboard. She follows suit.

"Ally was trying to get me to let loose and have some fun. We'd always wanted to try line dancing and heard this was the best place."

"Let loose from parents or partners?"

"Ugh am I that transparent?" she asks, dropping her face into her hands.

No, she's not transparent at all I want to say, I was only trying to dig up info and see if she had a partner or not.

"Which one is it?"

"Partner…. well ex-partner now. He was cheating on me, and I found out a few days ago." Her voice shakes with the confession, her pain leaking out.

"Well, he's gotta be the dumbest idiot on the planet to cheat on you," I tell her, locking my eyes with hers, hoping she hears the sincerity in my voice.

"I think I get the trophy for dumbest idiot on the planet because I didn't see the signs," she sighs.

"How long were you two together?"

"Just a little under two years. But I found out he'd been cheating on me for a good year," she confesses.

All I can think is what an ass hat. Who would want to cheat on this incredible girl? Don't they realise how amazing and kind she is?

"Let's have another shot," I suggest, as I tip the clear liquor into the glasses. "Here's to being free from loser boyfriends who don't deserve us." I shoot the shot back without the salt and lemon and as I lower my now empty glass, I watch Sophia take a deep breath before tipping her head back and doing the same. She scrunches up her face as she slams the glass down then we both crack up laughing.

"I wouldn't exactly call myself free though," she tells me, as she rests her elbow on the bench and puts her chin on her knuckles, holding her up.

"Your parents?" I ask, knowing a little about them from rumours at school.

"Yeah. They're still as controlling as ever."

"I heard stories about them at school. Are they really that bad?" I ask.

"Probably worse. They were the ones who set me up with Mitch," she tells me, which has me raising a brow in question. "The cheating ex," she clarifies.

"Ahh, I see."

"I haven't told them we've broken up either because I know my parents. I will get a lecture ending with them either telling me to beg Mitch to take me back or they'll blame me and say it's my fault he cheated," she huffs out. This time she grabs the tequila herself, pouring it quickly into the glasses and shooting it back before I realise she's doing it.

"Do you always care what your parents think?" I ask, genuinely curious to get an in-depth look into her world.

"I was raised to care what they think. They made it so hard to disappoint them that lately I go along with whatever they say without trying to defy them. I think tonight is the first time in a long time I've done something for myself," she blurts, before she drops her forehead against the cold bench. Her wild hair fans down her back. I long to reach out and stroke her head in comfort, to touch her beautiful locks but I rein myself in.

"What would happen if you did defy them?" I ask. I hear a distinct groan come from where her face is buried before she lifts it.

"Nobody defies Holden and Kennedy Philips."

"There's always a first time for everything," I tell her, as I pour us another shot each. She takes it and tips her head back before I've picked mine up. "You know I'm starting to think I should have asked you if you're a puker when drunk because the way you are drinking now, you are gonna be getting well acquainted with my toilet."

Her eyes meet mine and again we both crack up with laughter.

"I wouldn't know. I've never been this drunk before," she confesses.

"Like ever?" I ask, bewildered.

"Never. Back in high school I didn't go to many parties and when I was away at college, I never wanted to drink. I'm starting to think that had more to do with Mitch though as he always made rude remarks about girls who drank."

"You know this Mitch guy sounds more like a douche with every new thing I hear," I tell her, leaning my arms on the bench.

"I blame my parents for that. They thought the sun shone out of his ass. It might have something to do with the dollar signs they could see from his family connections," she says.

She leans down and starts unzipping the side of her boots then kicks them off one at a time. I catch a glimpse of the bright purple socks she has on which make me smile.

"That's better," she says, as she tucks one leg under her butt as the other one dangles down. I can feel the alcohol starting to take effect. The warm feeling rushing over my body and my head feeling lighter.

"Is that all your parents want for your future? Money?" I ask.

She lifts her shoulders before she adds, "I don't know. Most of the time it feels that way. I guess it doesn't matter now as I'll probably die as an old spinster woman unless they demand I get back with Mitch."

"I hope you don't get back with Mitch," I blurt, before I can take it back. The nerves I feel around her are starting to show themselves.

"Don't worry, there is no way in hell I'm getting back with that cow turd. I always told myself growing up if someone cheated on me, that would be it. No second chances. I think I'd rather take my chance as a spinster," she giggles, and I can tell the alcohol has kicked in for her.

"You will not turn into an old spinster," I shake my head, as I pour us each another shot.

"It's highly likely because who in their right mind would willingly put up with my parents as in-laws. The other option is someone who likes my parents and I think that might be worse."

Now I blame the next words out of my mouth on a brain snap. I also blame it on the fact that at that moment in time, Gramps' face pops into my head telling me second chances must be grabbed by the horns. And grabbing them by the crazy horns is exactly what I'm about to do. Or at least try to get and keep the girl of my dreams.

"You know what, I'll make you a deal. If by the age of thirty, we are both single, then I'll marry you. I'll save you from having to die an old spinster," I blurt into the universe. I watch as her eyes widen before she throws her head back laughing. I'm too shocked at myself to laugh and she soon realises she's laughing alone.

"You're joking, aren't you?" It's her turn now to be shocked.

"Is marrying me that funny?" I ask, wondering what she really feels about the idea.

She vigorously shakes her head before saying, "No, marrying me is the funny part. Why would you want to marry me and become a part of my crazy family when you could get any girl you wanted?"

I don't want to admit my feelings to her because she's only gotten out of a relationship and she needs to figure a way to get out from under her parents, so I say, "Maybe at thirty, you'll be the girl I want to marry."

"I highly doubt that," she says, as she crosses her arms and leans her chin on them as they rest on the bench.

"Well, it's eight years away. A whole lot can change in that time. By then, we could both be married to other people and be extremely happy. But if not, what have we got to lose?" I try to persuade her.

"You're serious?" she asks.

"Why not?"

"Because it's a bit crazy. Well, a lot crazy."

"What's so crazy about it? We know each other and we like each other's company. Well, I do, at least. People have arranged marriages every day. It'll be like we are arranging our own. Wouldn't you rather be stuck with me than a guy with a stick up his ass your parents picked out for you?"

Her head tilts to the side as her eyes pierce me in concentration before whispering, "So it would be like a real marriage?" She says it so quietly, I almost miss it.

"What do you mean by real?" I prod.

She wrings her hands as her gaze drops to the bench.

"You know, like I would be your actual wife in every way. You wouldn't just be my husband on paper and then have a girlfriend waiting in the wings?" she asks, and it makes a smile spread across my face.

"Soph, are you talking about sex?" I tease, which has her blush returning. Every time she blushes, it lights up her neck, which I find fascinating.

"Cheating is a hard line for me so if you're a cheater, then it won't work," she blurts, causing my nose to scrunch up.

"Is that what you think of me?"

57

"Well, there were a lot of rumours about you when we were at school. It was hard to know what was real or not," she confesses.

"What rumours?" I ask, more curious than anything.

"Mainly that you were a ladies' man and were bouncing from one girl to the next every other week. Plus, the threesome story but you cleared that up back then. People still probably believe that's true though," she says, her words rushing out.

I can't help it. The look on her face is so serious, I throw my head back letting out my loudest laugh yet. Once I gain control over myself, my eyes find Sophia. She sits there waiting patiently while I finish my soft chuckles.

"Firstly, I wasn't a ladies' man. I never hooked up with any of the girls from school. I kept to myself and barely talked to anyone. Cheating is a hard line for me too. Plus, I had bigger issues outside of school to worry about so I couldn't care less what people at school were saying about me."

She stares at me so I say, "I promise if I marry you, you would be the only woman in my life and in my bed."

Her blush deepens as she slowly nods.

"It'll probably be awkward at first but I'm sure we can get through that."

"What do you mean by awkward?" she asks, her brows pulling together.

"You know. Penis shock," I say, with a straight face, before turning to the fridge and grabbing two bottles of water, sliding one across to her.

"Why would it shock me? What's wrong with it?" she asks, her eyes drifting down towards the front of my pants like she can get a look at it with her imaginary x-ray vision.

"Ah ah ah, it's a secret you will learn only if we get married. So maybe you'll find out and maybe you won't," I say, while smugly smiling at her.

"That's not fair. What if I don't like it after we are married? Does your warped penis give me grounds for divorce?" she asks, crossing her arms over her ample chest.

"Don't worry, I have no doubt you will like him," I state, while copying her stance and crossing my own arms over my chest. "Should I write up a contract, just to be safe?" I suggest.

She nods, so I walk over to my buffet table in the entryway, open the drawer and take out a notepad and pen then take a seat next to her when I return.

Sitting down, I start writing and reading out loud as I do, "We, Sophia Philips and Lorenzo Moretti, agree that once we have both hit the ripe age of thirty that we will marry each other if we are both still single. We agree to the following terms:

1.No cheating on each other. If one of us cheats, that is grounds for divorce.

2.If Sophia isn't completely satisfied with Lorenzo's penis, then she is free to divorce him, but only after she has taken him for a test drive."

"Oh my God Lorenzo, you can't write that," she shrieks. She grabs my arm, pulling it away from the notepad to see I have in fact written the exact words I read out loud.

"Don't worry, it's for our eyes only." I laugh at how serious she is taking all of this.

"Okay, well add in you can't divorce me because of the headache my parents will cause. I have warned you about them and you still think this crazy idea is a good one."

I turn my body, looking her in the eyes when I say, "Honey, when I marry you, it's for keeps. Nothing in this world could make me divorce you, least of all your parents." Holding her gaze I watch as she gulps and receives the message loud and clear. I mean business. If my plan works, I could finally have the girl of my dreams. It will be a hell of a long wait for the plan to play out though but that's a risk I'm willing to take. I now need to hope and pray some other douche doesn't come along and steal her away when she is within reach. As I'm contemplating asking her to marry me then and there, she nudges my arm to get my attention.

"You looked like you were away with the fairies," she laughs, as I shake my head to clear the fog.

"Sorry, I think the tequila is kicking in," I lie.

"Oh, I thought it kicked in when you made this crazy offer," she laughs, before looking at me, her eyes drifting shut, telling me the tequila has set in for her.

"Anything you wish to add to our list?" I ask, showing it to her. Although I'm not sure she can read a word of it with the number of shots she's had.

"Sundays, no matter what, will be for the two of us. We can watch a movie or go out to dinner, but they must be spent together," she suggests.

"Sounds like a good suggestion," I say, as I write down what she said. I quickly write out another copy of the contract, word for word then sign both. Sliding the notepad her way I say, "Here, sign these."

She lazily grabs the pen from my fingers, scrawling a signature across the paper. I rip one copy out of the book and fold it up. I hold it out to her between two of my fingers. She takes it grazing my hand. As she stares me down, she tucks it into her bra, right over her heart.

"For safekeeping," she whispers. My eyes drift to her pink luscious lips. I wish I could kiss her, but fear of wrecking things holds me back.

"I'm out of tequila. Wanna watch a movie?" I ask, instead of lavishing her mouth like I want to.

"Sure," she replies, sliding off her stool and walking over to my comfy grey couch like she owns the place. She tucks her legs up underneath her as I grab the remote off the coffee table and turn the T.V on then flick to a random movie on Netflix.

"This okay?" I ask, regarding the action movie I picked.

"Yeah, that's fine," she says, a yawn catching her off guard, as she covers it with her hand.

We settle in to watch the movie, but I can't focus at all with her sitting so close to me. There are many questions I want to ask her, but I bite my tongue, so as not to scare her. It's the first time I've seen this girl in years, I don't want her running for the hills already. Lost in my thoughts, I don't notice we are halfway through the movie until I focus back on the T.V. Soft snores next to me pull my attention her way.

Her head is turned towards me as it rests on the couch, her fringe hanging down across her forehead while the rest of her fiery hair surrounds her face. Before I can stop myself, I reach up with my pinkie and gently move the hair of her fringe to the side to get a better glimpse of her. Her smattering of freckles spread out across her nose and cheeks, making my finger itch, wanting to trace them.

I've always been a man who believes in fate. Things happen for a reason, whether good or bad, but they happen to direct you on the path you are meant to go down. In this moment, I believe fate led Sophia to this bar to find me and I've got to believe in eight, hopefully fast years, it will bring her back into my life again. If it doesn't, I may have to make fate happen myself and go and find her.

Her head starts sliding forward until it hits my shoulder. In her slumber she rubs her face against my arm, getting comfortable. Finding the right spot, she stills, and her snores return. I sit like that, barely daring to breathe so as not to wake her for a few minutes and relish the feeling of her snuggled up against me. As I feel my own eyes starting to drift, I make the decision to take her to my bed.

Gently so as not to wake her, I slide my hand under her legs, pulling her to my chest and stand up straight. Her head rests against my chest as I walk, and I can't help but think I could spend the rest of my life carrying this girl wherever she wanted if I got to call her mine.

Once I reach my bed, I manage to pull the covers back and wriggle her in before covering her up. Peacefully her snores return, unaware she was moved at all. I glance at Ally and she's still fast asleep in the same position we left her. Her own snores fill the quiet room.

With one last longing look at Sophia, I push myself up to stand and stumble out of the room. I plop myself back on the couch and kick off my shoes. Grabbing the blanket off the back of the couch, I throw it over me and as soon as I'm settled, my eyes close and I'm out for the count.

Chapter Ten

Sophia

Stretching my arms above my head, I point my toes in the opposite direction feeling a satisfied smile cross my lips at the pulling sensation. Curling back into myself, I roll over pulling the fluffy bedspread under my chin. The strange feeling of the blanket has me peeking one eye open to be greeted with two big brown eyes staring back at me. Ally's own smile stares back at me.

"So, do you want to explain where we are, Missy? Because this bed belongs to neither of us," she says, as she lifts the blanket to prove her point. I push up to my elbows and the fast movement has me grabbing my forehead and flopping back down on the pillow as my head throbs. Looking around, I examine my surroundings. It's a plain room with a pure white bedspread over us, two wooden bedside tables on either side of the bed and an open door shows an ensuite behind Ally. There are no personal touches anywhere around the room, signalling who the mystery room may belong to.

Closing my eyes, memories fill my mind of us line dancing, then the creeps from the bar and of Lorenzo coming to the rescue.

"Lorenzo," I whisper, which has Ally raising a brow at me.

"Who's Lorenzo?" she whispers, snuggling down in the blanket and facing me, pulling it up to her chin like I had a minute ago. I snuggle down and face her.

"He's a guy I went to school with," I whisper to her, keeping us in a secretive bubble.

She pulls the blanket over both our heads before whispering back, "Is he cute?"

I cover my mouth to stop the giggle from escaping. She pinches me, knowing it'll make me laugh harder and I swat at her. After fending her off she settles back down, placing her hands under her head watching me.

"You have no idea," I tell her, my smile stretching wide across my face.

"Tell me, tell me," She whispers.

"You know the cool guys that don't try to be cool, they just are. That was him. He had this mysterious bad boy vibe dripping off him and all the girls secretly tried to get his attention. Well, some were not so secret about it," I inform her, reliving memories of him in my head.

"Ugh, those are the dangerous ones. I likey," Ally says, which has me giggling.

"You would think he would seem dangerous but not Renzo. I've always felt, you know, safe around him. It's hard to explain," I tell her.

"Soph, I don't mean actually dangerous. I mean dangerous for your heart. He sounds like the ones who will have you falling madly in love with them and then you're fighting for breath like you're underwater, not knowing which way is up or down," she sighs, looking lost in her own thoughts.

"You sound like an expert on this topic."

"Liam Waterson," she sighs again. "The bad boy from my school who stole my heart. Well stole is not the right word because I

64

stupidly gave him my heart willingly. There was no way to deny him. And if he walked back into my life right this second, I would be a pile of mush. Right back where I started," she admits, with a shimmer in her eyes. "This Lorenzo sounds like him."

"Well, he doesn't make me turn to mush but I had the biggest crush on him. I don't think he knew I existed back at school. We never hung around the same friends or talked much back then." I keep the fact I would pack extra lunch for him every single day a secret. I don't want to divulge the information for some reason.

"If you had the biggest crush on him, then why on earth are you in bed waking up with me and not with him?" she demands.

"Ally, you know what I'm like. I can't jump from guy to guy. Even if one of them is as hot as Lorenzo."

"Ugh, Mitch the asshole does not deserve your sympathy or loyalty. And you know what they say, the best way to get over someone is to get under someone else," she winks at me. My palm slaps across my mouth to cover the laughter as Ally does the same.

"I was trying to build up the courage to jump his bones and was shooting the tequila to give me liquid courage, but I think the tequila got the better of me. I don't remember how I got in here. The last thing I remember is sitting at the kitchen bench talking with him." I close my eyes like it'll help clear my foggy brain and fill in the gaps of what happened last night.

"You've still got time to jump his bones now, you know," she teases. I start to laugh before I stop, my eyes widening. Grabbing her wrist, I check the time.

"Damn it, I didn't realise it's so late. I've got lunch with my parents. And I don't need the third degree with this headache about why I'm late," I say, panicking. I fling the covers off us, knowing Ally will start to get up now too.

"Have I told you lately how much I hate your parents?" she asks.

"Not today you haven't. But I'm sure you will on our way home."

It's always the same with Ally. We've known each other since college where we shared a dorm so she knows how bad my parents can be. They don't approve of Ally either as they claim she is too much of a wild card to be my friend. They would have a fit if they knew Ally and I were on the other side of town and not wrapped up safely at home. They still don't know Mitch and I broke up so I will have to drop that bomb today too.

Ally pulls her phone out of her bag which was sitting on the bedside table. Lorenzo must have taken it off her when he placed her in the bed.

She presses buttons before saying, "Our Uber is ten minutes out, so let's get a wriggle on." Placing her bag over her head, she finds her boots and slips them on. I look around the floor for my own before I realise they are out in the kitchen probably where I left them.

"You ready to make our getaway?" she asks, smiling at me.

"Do you think he's awake out there?" I whisper.

"No idea. But what do you want to do? Be quiet and sneak out or say goodbye?"

I contemplate it for a minute but as much as I want to stay and talk to Lorenzo, the old Sophia takes over and makes up my mind.

"It's better if we sneak out," I huff.

"One day, you'll start living for yourself Soph. I can only hope that day comes sooner rather than later." Her sad smile stares at me and I can't help but feel my happy little bubble from a minute ago pop.

"Let's go," I say, walking towards the door. Quietly as possible, I twist the doorknob and pull it towards me. Darkness from the living room greets us and I take in the room. Large windows cover one side of the room, covered by dark curtains, blocking out the sun. A wide L shaped couch sits in the middle facing the T.V. I catch sight of a tanned muscled arm dangling over the end of the couch. I point it out to Ally and press my finger to my lips, to remind her to be quiet.

I glance to the kitchen seeing my favourite boots, lying haphazardly on the floor where I must have left them. Tiptoeing over to pick them up, I dangle them from my fingers not wanting to put them on in case they make too much noise and wake him before we can escape.

My feet slide around in a pivot to tell Ally to hurry but when I catch sight of her, I nearly yell. She's standing right behind the couch, staring down at Lorenzo. She turns to me with wide eyes then she puts the back of her hand against her forehead pretending to faint from his looks. I pull my lips in to try to contain my giggle but she's making it hard. She then makes a heart shape with her fingers and starts moving it over where her heart is as if it is thumping out of her chest. I slap a hand over my mouth as my laughter gets louder. Forgetting to be quiet I quickly step over to her, grab her arm and push her away from the couch towards the door.

She quietly laughs at me, but my eyes get drawn down to the figure on the couch. A shirtless Lorenzo lies there. His quiet breaths go unheard as his peaceful face is directed at me. With his eyes closed, he's still so gorgeous. More so now. Growing up, Lorenzo always had hard eyes. It was as if the weight of the world shone through them. Well, that was always the impression I got. I think others saw a leave me alone attitude, but I always thought there was more to him than he allowed others to see.

I can't help my gaze dropping to the tattoo of the wolf that covers one side of his muscular chest. Lorenzo wasn't this bulked up at school. He was a bit lankier, but he's filled out more since then. His jet-black hair, shaved on the sides but a lot longer on the top, hangs down across his forehead.

I have what I call a brain fart moment and my finger slides the hanging piece of hair out of the way so I can get a perfect view of his face. His stubble looks as if it's grown since last night and I ache to run my fingers over it, to feel it against my skin. My parents would never let me be with a man with facial hair. Clean shaven is the only way in my parents' world. Like a clean face determines the worth of a person. I shake my head at the silliness of their ideas.

Wanting to break free of their control over my life, I bend forward. For once I want to take something for myself. For me. I want to do something because I want to do it. So, before I can second guess myself I slide further down, wanting to press my lips against his cheek in a silent goodbye.

Centimetres away from his cheek I reach my lips out, so close. Before I touch his cheek his face turns, a firm, strong hand pulls my head in and before I know it his soft, full lips are pressing ever so gently to my own. A stark contrast to the strong grip he holds my head with. My eyes don't have time to close and enjoy the sensation before he's pulling away, his now open eyes staring back into mine.

Seconds tick by with neither of us saying a word. The silence stretches as I feel the familiar heat of my cheeks. Something in the way his brown eyes gaze into mine has my heart speeding up. It looks a lot like longing. But that can't be right.

"I wanted to say goodbye," I whisper. I don't know why I whisper when he's obviously awake now so there's no need for me to carry on being quiet.

"And I couldn't let you walk out of my life again without kissing those lips that have featured in my dreams countless nights," he whispers back, and I become aware of how close we still are. I'm still draped over the couch with his tight grip in my hair. I don't know what to say to his confession, so I lean back, putting much needed distance between us.

I catch sight of Ally whose eyes are bulging out of her head, but she silently stands there, not knowing what to do either. I drop my gaze from her but increase my steps to where she stands. The rustle of Lorenzo's movements alerts me that he's getting up from the couch and worry flits through me at the thought he might try to convince me to stay. I think I'm more afraid of the fact I don't want to leave.

"Thanks again for last night Lorenzo. It was so good to see you again," I stutter, as I turn towards him as Ally and I reach the door. Now it's my turn to stand there with my eyes bulging out of my head. Lorenzo stands there in all his gorgeous glory wearing nothing but tight black boxer briefs. His muscular legs match the rest of his body and have my mouth watering. What training must he do to have a body like that?

Ally must sense I need to get out of here because she opens the door and tugs on my arm before she says, "Yes thanks for your help last night Lorenzo. Sorry we have to run."

"It was my pleasure, Ally. And it was nice to meet you," he says, sending a genuine smile her way before his gaze flits back to me.

"And Sophia, I'll be seeing you in eight years," he says, his smile widening as he shows off his perfect teeth, crossing his thick arms over his chest. It makes my brows pull in together in confusion. Ally gives another tug on my arm and I'm nearly out the door before he slides a hand through his hair pushing it back. "Don't worry, I'm sure it'll come back to you eventually," he says, as he brings his hand over his heart, tapping it there.

"I don't...." I start in confusion, before he cuts me off saying.

"Let's just say I hope fate is on our side," he says, as Ally pulls me through the door and closes it behind us. Lorenzo's laughter can be heard from the other side as Ally grips my wrist and practically drags me down the stairs. We manage to find our way out the front of the bar to our waiting Uber.

"Ally, what the heck? Why are you in such a rush?" I demand, after I come to my senses and the Uber driver is driving us away from the bar.

"Girl, I've never seen that look on your face, but I know damn well what that look means. It was the look where you are about to blow your life up. And I couldn't let you do that. Even though that man is sex on a stick," she says, as she fans herself.

"What makes you think he would blow my life up?" I ask, a defensive note to my voice. Ally's sad smile looks at me as she drops her head to one side before taking my hand in hers.

"Sweetie, I never said he would blow up your life. I said you would blow up your life because the way he looked at you was as if he would move heaven and earth to be with you. And you and I both know your parents have way too much control over your life. There is no way they would let you and him be together with a happy ending."

I shift in my seat and lean my head against the glass of the door window. Her words swirl in my head. She's right. We both know it. I've never stood up to my parents and I don't think I have the courage to do it. And that alone is why I can't drag Lorenzo into my world. Even if it was for a night. I'd be kidding myself if I believed a night would be enough for me. There's no way I want my parents' poison to taint Lorenzo in any way. So that's where he must stay. A memory. One I can look back on, remember fondly and smile. Far away and hidden from anywhere they would be able to reach him.

"We're here," Ally says, as she wakes me from my nap on the car ride home. I must not have gotten enough sleep or else the excess alcohol I drank is making me sleepy. I rub my eyes to wake me up and look out the window. A sigh escapes as I take in the house the driver pulled up in front of. My prison AKA my parents' house where I currently reside.

"Thanks Ally, I'll message you later," I say, pushing my buckle to release it and leaning over to give her a quick hug. Once I close the door, the driver wastes no time and pulls away from the curb. I wish it was taking me away with it.

I'm too hungover to care what my parents will say if they see me with my cowboy boots dangling from my hand or the fact my unbrushed hair is out in public where someone important could see me. I know I will regret it if they catch me, but something about having to walk away from Lorenzo has me wanting to lash out. I have the start of something burning in me, ready to be defiant for the first time in my life. Let's hope it lasts.

So, I casually walk through the front door like I don't have a care in the world. I make no attempt to be quiet as I waltz through the house and make my way to my living quarters. Yes, I have quarters because our house is outlandish and it's just the three of us. I can't believe my luck when I reach my door unscathed but then dread fills me and sweat drips down my back as I hear my mother's voice behind me.

"Sophia? Are you just getting in now, young lady?"

I turn to face her before nodding.

"What will Mitch have to say about this?" she asks, but before I can answer she continues with, "Never mind, hurry up, shower and get presentable as he and your father are waiting for us."

That stops me in my tracks, and I shout at her, "What do you mean he and father?"

"Mitch rang this morning, and I invited him to lunch," she casually tells me. The look on my face has her adding, "I didn't think you'd mind."

"Well, I do mind," I state, turning my handle, walking in my room and closing the door. I lock it for good measure because my mother will not tolerate that behaviour from me. As predicted, she knocks on the door, but I pay no mind to her words, dropping my boots on the floor. I head towards the ensuite, relieve myself, then start to undress for my shower.

Before I unclip my bra, I notice a scratching in one cup. I run my fingers inside my bra finding a folded-up piece of paper. I start to unfold it before my mothers knocking draws my attention back to her. My eyes roll in annoyance, though she can't see me, and I place the paper on the vanity telling myself I'll come back to it later.

Jumping in the shower, I soak my hair. I take my time washing it, wanting to prolong the time before I must meet my parents. And Mitch. Bloody Mitch.

What the hell is he thinking? He can't seriously think he can act all chummy to my parents and I'll take him back. Who does he think he is? I don't care what my parents have to say about this either. They can't force me to be in a relationship with someone who has no respect for me and who cheated on me of all things. That's a deal breaker for me and I'm about to let it be known. Hell hath no fury like a woman scorned.

As I dress in my immaculately pressed dress, I can't help but feel restricted. As soon as the material is against my skin, I itch and want to rip it from my body. I've never felt like this. I've always been numb, going along with the motions, never fighting the control my parents have over me. Last night was the start of something changing in regard to the relationship I have with my parents.

Once my hair is perfected into a chignon at the nape of my neck, I smooth my hands over my dress, take a deep breath then exit my room. My small black heels click clack against the wooden floor as I make my way to the dining room where my parents and that cow turd of a man are waiting for me.

Before reaching the room, I hear their laughter on the other side of the door. I can't help the eye roll it causes. I stop, take a deep breath and plaster on a fake smile for my parents because anything less and I would be reprimanded. It's right about now I'm regretting not popping painkillers for my worsening tequila headache. Or the intensifying pain is from the sight of Mitch sitting there calmly and casually as if he didn't cheat on me. I don't know what I ever saw in him to begin with. He did me a huge favour by cheating on me. I should send him a thank you basket.

"Mother, Father," I greet them, as I slide into the seat opposite Mitch at our ridiculously sized oak dining table. The table can seat twenty people, which I find utterly absurd since only three people reside in this house. We hardly ever have ten people seated at this monstrosity, let alone twenty. Another example of appearances taking over my life. I would take a smaller rickety kitchen table with a home cooked meal on it than this lavish pristine table with food made by our chef any day. Don't get me wrong, our chef is an amazing cook and person but what I wouldn't give to feel some love in my food. If only I knew what that tasted like.

"Aren't you going to acknowledge Mitch?" my father asks, drawing me out of my thoughts.

Mitch's smug smile shines my way and I wish I could wipe that look off his face. I reach out for the glass of sparkling water, taking a sip. Yes, sparkling water. This house can't be seen drinking normal tap water like everyone else. I lower the glass before setting my eyes on Mitch when I would like nothing more than to throw the glass of water on him and ruin his Italian loafers that cost more than Lorenzo's motorcycle.

"No, I don't want to acknowledge the man who I broke up with a few days ago because he's been cheating on me for a year," I calmly say. My response makes the smile on Mitch's face grow bigger which has the hairs on the back of my neck rising. Where does this jerk wad get off?

"I'm sure it's all a big misunderstanding," my mother tries to interject, and my hard gaze turns to her.

"I think I understood perfectly fine. I walked into his office on Monday to surprise him for lunch and I ended up the one surprised. He looked like he rather enjoyed having his pants down around his ankles and his receptionist bent over the desk. Or maybe it was her moaning I misunderstood Mother."

"Enough," my father yells from the head of the table, as he slams his now empty glass down. It's a bit early for alcohol but that's never stopped Holden Philips. His love of whiskey is the one thing that managed to rub off on me. I rarely drink but when I do it's my drink of choice. "Sophia, you need to learn that a husband has needs and sometimes his wife can not fulfill them. It is your job as a wife not to question his actions."

My head whips towards my mother in response to my father's words. Is he talking about their relationship? I receive my answer from the slight nod of acknowledgement from my mother. My hackles rise further as his words cut deeper.

"It's a good thing I'm not his wife then, isn't it?" I argue, moving my focus back to my father.

"Well, we were discussing that matter before you arrived. Mitch here has asked for my blessing to marry you and I have given it," he states blandly, as if he's ordering steak for lunch.

"Sophia," Mitch tries to talk, but I cut him off.

"I will not marry him, and you can not make me."

"As my daughter, you will do what I say," he states.

My last hold on my control snaps and I yell, "I will not marry him." I push my seat back, the screeching against the wooden floor makes my father angrier before I swiftly walk away, heading to my room.

"Sophia. Get back here right now," my father yells, making me pick up the pace as I hurry to get to the safety of my room where I can lock my door at least.

Once in my room, I slam my door and click the lock into place. Not feeling safe enough, I carry on through to my ensuite and lock that door for good measure too. Leaning against the vanity, I face myself in the mirror. I can't stand the sight of tamed hair, so I vigorously start yanking out the pins holding it in place, throwing them down haphazardly.

My fiery wild hair surrounds me reflecting my mood. Taking forceful breaths I exhale loudly, to lower my heart rate. I can't believe they expect me to marry him and to be happy with him cheating on me for that matter. My head sags forward as I close my eyes until my breaths have slowed.

The white folded paper from before my shower catches my interest when I peel my eyes open. I stand up straight, snatching it up and unfolding it. The paper is filled with scratchy handwriting but still readable. As I read the words over, a glimpse of a memory from last night pushes through. Lorenzo and I seated at the kitchen bench in his apartment taking tequila shots. It becomes a bit hazy after that, but I do remember him writing in a notebook.

A pact to marry when we are thirty if we are both still single? And from my signature I clearly agreed to this. I slap my hand against my forehead because I've gone from no marriage prospects to two in a matter of minutes. The first is not an option I would consider for all the money in the world, but the thought of Lorenzo has me pausing.

Did I only agree last night because of the alcohol or was it for another reason? Try as I might, the memories remain fuzzy, and I can't for the life of me remember anything else. It clearly states on this little piece of paper that cheating would be grounds for divorce. I wonder if I told him about what Mitch did to me.

Reading over the pact again, I can't help but think thirty is a hell of a long time away. Eight years. A lot can change in that time. And with the way Lorenzo looks, I doubt he will stay single for long. Underneath all his bravado it's his tender and caring nature that would have any woman falling head over heels for him. He has shown me nothing but genuine kindness which is sadly something lacking in my world. Who am I kidding, he will get snapped up in no time. Anyone who got him would be crazy to let him go. With a realisation

75

and an exhale, I take one final look at the tiny shred of hope I hold in my fingers before folding the notebook paper back up. I walk defeated into my room and on tiptoes I push the folded piece of hope to the back of my closet along with any defiance I felt burning.

Chapter Eleven

8 YEARS LATER / PRESENT DAY

Lorenzo

"Renz, I say this as your friend and not your employee but what the heck has crawled up your ass lately? You turned thirty a few months ago and you were the happiest I've ever seen you. Then come this week, you're snapping at everyone within a ten-kilometre radius of you," Niko, my best friend says.

I'm currently busy on a backboard working on the underside of a car so he can't see my face. He's right, I have been short with a few people lately but the weight of the date happening in two days has gotten to me. It's Sophia's thirtieth birthday. It's make or break time. I've never told anyone about the pact I made with Sophia. I guess if we did go through with it, I didn't want people knowing how we started off. Plus, I like sharing a secret with only her.

With a huff I slide myself out from under the car. Niko holds out his hand for me to grab so he can help me up. I pull the dirty rag from my back pocket and wipe the black grease from my hands.

"Got a lot on my mind," I tell him, after spending way too long staring at my fingers.

"You want to talk about it?" he offers.

"Nah, I'll be sweet," I say, shaking my head.

"Well, I'm here if you ever wanna unload. Stop biting everyone's heads off and we'll be fine," he tells me, as he punches my shoulder chuckling to himself.

"I haven't been that bad, have I?"

"Well, I'm not sure if Mrs. Carrigan will be back. You yelled so loudly about her dog yapping, she hightailed it out of here, dragging the poor mutt behind her. The poor sausage dog was choking on his lead with how fast she took off," he informs me, before bursting out with laughter.

I laugh along with him at the thought of Chester dragging behind her. I'm sorry to have missed it. Thankfully losing Mrs. Carrigan's business won't be too much of a loss as I couldn't stand having the town busybody talking about everyone constantly.

In need of a drink, I walk over to our small work fridge and pull the door open forcefully. There's a lot of grime in the seals so it gets stuck from time to time. Grabbing two bottles of water, I throw one to Niko who catches it effortlessly. The seal of the lid breaks as I unscrew the cap and tip the bottle to my lips, letting the cold liquid cool my throat as it runs down it. Before turning to Niko, I screw the cap back on and place the half empty bottle on my work desk. The work desk that is currently covered in overflowing stacks of papers. I need to sort out a new receptionist.

"Can I ask you something?"

"You know you can ask me anything," Niko replies, widening his stance.

"Have you ever done something crazy in the name of love?" I ask, tilting my head to the side.

He laughs lightly before saying, "So it is a girl making you bite everyone's head off. Who is she?"

I should have known if I mentioned something to Niko, he would see right through me.

I let out a sigh shaking my head, "Forget it."

"Hey come on Renz. It's me. You know I'm just pulling your chain."

Dropping my head to my chest I say, "You're gonna think I'm crazy."

"Well probably not any more than I already do," he replies, with a smirk. His teasing eases me so I gesture for him to take one of the chairs we have for customers while I lean my ass on the edge of the desk.

Crossing my arms over my chest, I settle in and tell him the whole story about the girl who stole my heart back in school. I tell him about the night eight years ago and then I wince when I tell him about the pact we made and again when I admit I've been holding on to it for all these years, patiently waiting for my chance with my dream girl. Of course, there have been women but I've never let myself get serious about any of them because I've been waiting for this day to come. Now it's here, I'm freaking the fuck out because I may have waited all this time for nothing.

As I finish telling him everything, I stare at him waiting for him to reply. He takes a minute before he throws his head back in laughter.

When he settles himself down, he looks me in the eye and says, "I always knew you were a crazy son of a bitch but this, this is next level."

"Hey, if you were this crazy about a girl, you'd do questionable things as well," I defend.

"Why on earth did you not just ask this girl out? You know, like a normal person?"

I wince because I don't want to admit I've never felt good enough for her. Instead, I try to divert.

"You wouldn't understand."

"Try me," he pushes, not budging.

I push off the desk and turn my back on him as I walk back to the car I was working on. I can hear his footsteps following me. Knowing Niko, he won't stop until I explain, so I turn, which halts his steps.

"Her name is Philips," I tell him, staring him down, waiting. His eyes crinkle before widening.

"As in Holden Philips?"

I give him a single nod which makes him laugh hard.

"You really are crazy."

"I didn't claim not to be," I defend.

"The mayor's daughter though?" he asks.

"She wasn't the mayor's daughter when we were at school. He hadn't been elected yet."

"Are you guys talking about the big party this weekend?" Howie, one of my other mechanics butts in.

"What party?" I ask, raising a brow.

"The mayor's daughter. The mayor is throwing her a big thirtieth birthday party," he casually says, before turning back to the hood of the car he was working on.

"How do you know that?" I ask, as my palms start to sweat.

"Did you not read the paper today?" Howie asks, which causes me to shake my head. He walks over to his tool station and grabs the newspaper lying on top, before smacking it against my chest. "Front page and everything," he says, before going back to his work.

I unfold the paper as Niko comes to look over my shoulder. There on the front page is the girl who I've dreamed about for years. Her parents each stand on one side of her smiling, while Sophia stands front and centre with a small sad smile on her face.

"She is gorgeous, so I'll give you that."

"She's more than a pretty face," I say, while staring at the picture of her. She looks more like a woman now instead of the young girl I used to know. Her hair is still perfectly slicked back from her face. I wonder if she hates it like that. I bring the memory of her from years ago to the forefront of my mind. Her wild hair I wanted to run my fingers through.

"Look, it says her dad is throwing her a masquerade party. You could go and assess the situation without her knowing you are there," Niko says, as he points to a section of the article.

I start reading from the beginning and it's obvious this party is for all Holden's political friends and connections. I haven't kept tabs on Sophia these last few years, wanting her to live her life without any outside pressure from me. If she chose a life without me then so be it. All I wanted was for her to be happy. Something that would make her truly happy. But seeing her in this picture, I see I was wrong. Others may not see it, but I've secretly studied the face of this girl for so long I can tell a fake smile when I see one a mile away. The one she shows to the camera is the fakest of them all.

I should have said to hell with the pact and gone and got my girl earlier. I won't admit fear has held me back. I may seem like a man who takes risks and has a don't care attitude but that's all different when it comes to Sophia. She's the only one in this world who makes me doubt myself. I don't know whether that's a good thing or a bad thing. But I do know after all this time, I still can't get her out of my mind.

Gramps would have loved her too. He always said a beautiful soul trumps a pretty face any day. Looks will always fade but a beautiful soul will always be there as it's the very essence of the person. If you can find someone with that essence, who loves you above all else then you have won the lottery.

"So, what are you gonna do?" Niko's question draws me out of my thoughts.

I turn to him with a wide grin saying, "I'm gonna get my girl."

His laugh fills the air as he shakes his head saying, "Yeah, you're one crazy S.O.B. Tell me, Romeo, how are you going to get into this party? It says it's by invitation only."

I shrug my shoulders, "I'll figure something out. I've got a couple days to work on a plan."

"Do you really think the man who keeps trying to buy this place and who you keep knocking back is going to let you run off and marry his daughter?" Niko queries.

I squeeze my forehead with my thumb and index finger, feeling a headache beginning. Holden Philips has been trying to acquire my business for years. He doesn't want this run-down mechanic shop for his own. No. He wants the land it resides on as it's the only thing stopping him from building his pretty new shopping mall.

This business belonged to my gramps. Between this and the house, they were the only things my grandparents left behind for me once they passed. The house isn't much. A small three-bedroom villa on a quiet street. I live there when I'm not working at the bar and crashing at the apartment.

Gramps left me with a small mortgage I'm still paying off on the house. I had to remortgage it at one stage to help keep the business afloat. The thought of selling has never crossed my mind. It's where I grew up and I haven't been able to part with it. It's the same with the business. I didn't want to part with it as it was Gramps' hard work that went into this place, building it up from scratch and I can't bear to see it demolished. I know I could always relocate to another site, but I've never felt the need or desire.

This is the leverage I need to make sure Holden won't stand in my way when it comes to Sophia. I know I'm not what he'd want for a husband for his daughter. I'm gonna need all the help I can get to convince him. I know Gramps said if I get a chance to take it. I hope he understands it's going to cost me his business.

Looking up at Niko I say, "If the price is right, I would sell."

Niko's wide eyes stare back at me unblinking. Grabbing me by the bicep he drags me further away from Howie before he starts talking.

"Renz, I think you have officially lost the plot here man. You can't sell your Gramps' business to what? Buy the mayor's daughter? You're sounding a lot more than just crazy."

"You don't understand," I huff.

"You're damn right, I don't. You think because you made some pact nearly a decade ago you should sell your business to her dad so he will let you marry her? A business you said you would never think of selling. How well do you know this girl? It's been eight years, she may not be the same person she was back then," he pleads.

I close my eyes and roll my neck from side to side. One part of my brain understands he's talking sense but it's putting up a good fight with the other part that won't listen to reason and could care less about how crazy I sound right now. I made a pact with Sophia and I'm going to follow through with it. I peel my eyes open and stare at Niko for a moment without saying a word.

"Ah damn it Renz. Fine. If this is what you want to do then fine, I'll support you. But when it all turns to shit, I'm gonna look you in the eye and you are gonna be able to read my mind because it's gonna be a big, clear 'I told you so'," he huffs out, which makes me smile. I knew my best friend would have my back. We may not always agree on things, but we have each other's back regardless.

"Thanks Niko," I say, patting him on the shoulder.

"So, what's the plan?"

"I'm gonna go talk to Holden about marrying his daughter," I tell him.

"For the record, I want it known that this is the craziest idea I think you've ever come up with."

"Yeah, I heard you the first time," I reply, laughing as I walk off to finish up on the car I was working on and give myself time to think through this plan. I know it's crazy, but I can't seem to stop myself from getting off the train.

Chapter Twelve

Lorenzo

Smoothing my hands down my white t-shirt under my leather jacket, I try to wipe off the sweat on my hands as I sit patiently waiting for my meeting with the devil himself.

"He'll see you now, Mr. Moretti," his receptionist tells me.

"Thanks." With a slight nod her way I make my way to the double oak doors and open the door to my possible future. Closing it silently behind me, I walk into his enormous office. I guess no expense was spared when it came to decorating the place. Sleek oak wooden bookshelves matching the doors line both sides of the room. Filled with books, all perfectly aligned with nothing out of place. I must stick out like an eye sore in this room. I wore my Sunday best, but when the rug on the floor costs more than my mortgage, I know I have an uphill battle in front of me.

His wide desk sits in the middle of the room with a large window behind him, which lets in the sunshine from the early morning. I rocked up here first thing this morning and told his receptionist I wasn't leaving without seeing Mr. Philips. It didn't take long for her to squeeze me in. I can only guess I intrigued his curiosity and he wanted to see what I had to offer. Maybe he thinks I have finally agreed to sell to him.

Seated behind his desk, with a smarmy smile on his face, "To what do I owe the pleasure of your company on this early Thursday morning Mr. Moretti?"

I stand my ground, with a widened stance putting on a relaxed front when I can feel the sweat trickle down the back of my neck.

"I came here to make you a proposition," I tell him. My voice surprisingly coming out strong and steady.

"Have you finally come to your senses and are ready to sell your business?" he asks, with a greed-filled gaze.

"I'm open to negotiations. I'm willing to sell for the last offer you gave me of a million dollars along with something else."

"A million dollars is more than your business is worth and we both know that," he replies, as he sits forward with interest.

"It still isn't enough for me to sell, that's why I want something else as well," I tell him.

"And what is that?"

"Your daughter's hand in marriage," I say.

His mouth drops open while he stares at me before speaking, "You've got to be kidding."

"I'm quite serious."

"Why on earth would you want to marry my daughter?"

"Why not?" I ask, not wanting to show my hand too much. I have a feeling Mr. Philips here has no idea that I know Sophia or that we went to the same school.

"So what? You're trying to buy my daughter's hand in marriage?" he says, his voice raising.

"Don't act like you haven't been trying to use your daughter as a pawn in your political games. I'm sure you already have a few people lined up who you could gain from if they married her. I'm just here throwing my hat in the ring," I tell him.

"Apart from your shop, what would I gain from you marrying her?" he asks, confirming what I've always thought. He'd sell his own daughter to whoever could give him the best offer.

"You'd win. You would get your shopping centre, more money to add to your ever-growing bank balance and last but not least, a happy daughter. But who knows if her happiness is important to you," I reply, crossing my arms over my chest.

Laughing, he stands from his desk before replying, "I must say Mr. Moretti you either have the biggest pair of balls or you're the dumbest idiot ever to walk into my office and accuse me of such things."

I stand watching him, waiting for him to continue. He glances down at the photo on his desk of a much younger Sophia. She sits upon his lap, looking up at him like he placed the sun in the sky for her. I wonder where it all went wrong for them. He tilts his head as he looks back at me, clenching his jaw.

"I'll make you a counteroffer, Mr. Moretti. The same I've offered several others, shall we call them contenders," he says, as he places his hands behind his back.

"And what is that?" I ask, my brows scrunching.

"Have you heard I'm throwing Sophia a masquerade party for her birthday on Saturday?"

"Yes, I have."

"Good. I'll take your deal to sell the business for a million dollars."

"What about marrying your daughter?"

"Well, that is up to you. Or should I say, it's up to Sophia. You see I've given this deal to the other contenders too. If you can find Sophia at her birthday party and you can convince her to accept your marriage proposal, then I won't stand in your way and you can marry her. But if you don't find her or she doesn't agree then I get the business regardless and you don't get my daughter." The twinkle in his eye should tell me something about his deal isn't as straightforward as I think it is, but I don't pay attention to it. I'm too busy trying to tamp down the excitement building inside because my plan might work.

"Deal," I say, before I can stop myself.

"Great. I'll have my lawyer draw up a contract today for you to sign. Now if that is all, I have other meetings to get to," he says, dismissing me.

"Thank you for your time," I politely say, as I turn to leave.

"Oh and Mr. Moretti, good luck finding your needle in a haystack," he says, his boisterous laugh following me out as my brows scrunch harder together. What does he mean by that?

Chapter Thirteen

Lorenzo

"How does this one look?" I ask, holding my hands out to the side as I wait for Niko's response.

"It looks as good as the last five you tried on," he murmurs.

"Yeah, but which one looks like the best proposal suit?"

"How would I know? Isn't a suit just a suit?"

"It's gotta be perfect man," I say, as I turn back around to face the floor-to-ceiling mirror.

"I think you're making it weird. In fact, I think this whole thing is dead set crazy but because I'm a good best friend, no scratch that, an amazing best friend, I'm telling you to wear the first grey suit you tried on. It made your butt look great," Niko says, his brows lifting as a smile appears on his face.

"Why on earth are you checking out my butt?" I laugh.

"Didn't you know girls like tight buns on a man? If you wear the grey suit and showcase your umm assets, then I'm sure she will say yes. Well, if she's as crazy as you are, then she'll say yes but that suit will help sweeten the deal," he says, shrugging his shoulders my way.

"Grey suit it is then," I agree, choosing to ignore all his crazy comments. "What are you gonna wear?" I ask.

"Wear where?"

"Wear to the party. You're gonna be my wingman, aren't you?" I say, giving him my best puppy dog eyes.

"Ugh okay okay. I'm sure there will be other girls for me to hit on while you propose to the girl of your dreams," he relents.

"Thanks bud. I couldn't do this without you. I'll pay for this and then the next stop is ring shopping," I tell him.

"Oh man Renz. A ring? Really?"

"I can't propose without a ring. It will make me look like I'm not serious. I need Sophia and her father to take this very seriously," I tell him.

"Maybe you should. You know in case she says no. It will save you money in case it doesn't work out."

"You doubt my skills that much? I don't want to ask her in some lame, half-assed attempt. I can't go in there thinking she might say no. If I start doubting myself then I have already lost half the battle."

"Shall I ring all this up for you sir?" the sales assistant asks, halting our conversation.

"Yes please. That would be great," I say, offering a genuine smile. He gathers up the grey suit we decided on and heads to the sales desk while I turn back to Niko.

"I know you think I'm crazy and this whole idea is a bit bonkers but if you had the girl of your dreams within your grasp, would you not take a giant leap of faith and hope you don't crash and burn?"

Releasing a breath Niko replies, "Okay. I'll try to be more supportive."

"Thanks. If you ever get crazy over a girl, I promise to bust your balls over it as payback. It's only fair," I say, slapping him on the back.

Laughing he says, "I guess we will be needing a ring then."

After paying for my suit, we walk through the shopping mall until we locate the local jewellers. Before I enter the store Niko grabs my arm, halting me. I raise my brow in question before he winces.

"I'm being supportive, I promise. A word of advice. Don't spend thousands on a ring please. If it all works out, you can always come back and buy her a fancier ring later."

I pause for a minute considering what he's saying. I know my friend is only looking out for me and I want him on side with this plan so to ease his worries I agree.

"Yeah okay. I won't go crazy," I tell him. If this plan works and she does marry me she can choose whatever she wants, the sky's the limit. Knowing what I know about Sophia though, I doubt she'd want something ostentatious, so Niko has nothing to worry about.

"Come on then. Let's get this over with," Niko says, pushing the door open and holding it for me to walk through. Glancing around, I notice the three staff who work here are all busy with customers, so I decide to browse through the see-through cases instead. Looking at what they have to offer, something might jump out at me. I've never contemplated buying a ring in my life. I've never bought any type of jewellery for a woman before so this whole experience is a bit daunting.

"Over here," Niko calls, from a couple of cases down.

I walk over to him and look in the direction he's pointing. Rows of different rings stare back at me. There are gold ones, silver ones, diamond ones and rings with coloured gems. Taking my time, I start at the top row and work my way along, studying each ring and asking myself if it's something I think Sophia would like. After about the twentieth ring, I start to lose hope I will find anything that calls to me. Shouldn't there be like a magic moment where the ring jumps out at me and I think 'aha, this is the perfect ring, destined to sit forever on her finger'?

"Why do there have to be so many choices?" Niko whispers to me, as if reading my mind.

"Tell me about it. None of these rings are calling to me either."

"Is that what they're supposed to do? Call to you?" he asks.

"Shouldn't I feel some kind of connection to the ring?" I ask him.

"How would I know? I thought blokes walked in and picked the first ring within their price range that looked more expensive than what they actually paid," he tells me. Maybe he isn't the best wingman for this job.

"My gramps always told me the story about the ring he bought for my nana. He had to travel to a few different stores and even some that were a few towns over because nothing was calling to him. He happened to drive past a jeweller when he was coming back from his brother's place a couple hours drive away and he thought why not, so he stopped. He said as soon as he laid eyes on the ring, he knew in his bones it was the one," I tell Niko.

"Well, what did the ring look like? You could get her something similar," Niko suggests, and a light bulb goes off in my head.

"Niko! You genius," I all but shout.

"I am?"

"Yes. I know the perfect ring. Let's go," I tell him, turning and walking towards the exit.

"You aren't gonna buy one?"

"No, I already have the perfect ring. It's at my house."

"You do?" he scratches his head, as he replies.

"Yeah. I'll show you," I tell him, as he follows me out of the store.

"How do you already have a ring at home? Did you forget you had it?" he asks, as he moves into step beside me.

"It's the ring. The one my gramps bought for my nana," I tell him, smiling.

"Oh, jeez Renz. Now you're going to give this woman a family heirloom?" he questions.

"Yep," is all I say.

"What if it all gets messed up and you end up losing one of the only heirlooms you have?"

I stop in my tracks and turn to him.

"I'm serious about marrying this woman. If she agrees to marry me, even though we both know it's about the craziest thing in the world, I don't plan on letting her go. Ever. She's it for me." I look him straight in the eye waiting for him to realise how serious I am about this girl.

"Okay then. I was just double checking to make sure you were deadly serious, you know. It's what a good friend would do."

"I know man. To clarify, you're not a good friend, you're the greatest."

"Well come on then, let's go look at this ring and get the girl of your dreams," he says, with a smile on his face and a pat on the back.

Chapter Fourteen

Lorenzo

The night of the party has arrived, and I've changed my shirt several times today due to the sweat patches under my arms. It feels like I have run a marathon, and nothing is helping me to cool down and stop sweating. Niko has arrived at my place so he can give me a ride to the party. I had to go into Holden's office yesterday and sign the agreement. His smug smile confused me. I know he's up to something, but I have no idea what. He looked like the cat who got the canary and a whole bowl of milk. I wish I could wipe the smug look off his face, but if this is the way to get my chance with Sophia, I'm not backing out.

There was no mention again of me finding my needle in a haystack but if he's referring to Sophia, wouldn't it be the opposite? The woman couldn't blend in if she tried. It's as if she was born to stand out, especially with her fiery red hair. Anyway, I've pushed the thoughts of his words to the back of my mind while I've gotten changed into my suit. Well, half a suit. I only have my pants on as I didn't want to sweat through yet another shirt before we left my apartment.

"I'm sure any woman would fall to her knees and accept a proposal from you topless, but I think you're gonna have to put a shirt on so we can leave. We are going to a classy joint and you might get arrested for indecent exposure," Niko jokes.

"I know. I'll finish dressing and then we need to leave in case my white shirt suffers the same fate," I tell him, as I walk into my room. The newly ironed shirt sits on the hanger. I grab the towel I used for my shower and dry my back and chest one last time, to be safe. The towel lands in my laundry basket with a thud then I shrug into my pristine crisp shirt and button it up and finish off the look with my grey suit jacket.

Checking myself over in the mirror I say, "You've got this Lorenzo," before snatching the black velvet box off my bedside table. My thumb pushes the lid up to glance over the ring one last time. It's a slim gold band with a single ruby sitting in the centre, surrounded by a row of diamonds down each side. My nana loved it and never took it off. I hope Sophia feels the same. With a snap, the box closes, and I push it into my front pocket before joining Niko at the front door.

"Let's do this," I say, as he raises his hand for a high five. My palm slaps his and I add, "You're gonna need to drive with the windows down so I don't sweat through this whole suit. I've never been so nervous in my life." I grab the two invites to the party from the kitchen bench as we leave.

"You've got this boss," Niko says, with a hint of a smile on his face. He knows my nerves are getting to me.

I think that's why he isn't voicing his doubts about my crazy plan anymore.

Once in his car, he winds the windows down as soon as the car starts. We drive in silence to the fanciest hotel in town. It has a big ballroom situated in it which is the destination for tonight's festivities. As we pull up, the valet takes Niko's keys so we can head in without worrying about having to find a carpark.

"Where is everyone?" Niko asks. It's at that moment I take in my surroundings and realise we are the only two around. I check my watch on my wrist and see we are about twenty minutes late. I thought people would be waltzing in at all times of the night but that isn't the case.

"I'm guessing the party has already started," I tell him, as we make our way through the foyer, following a sign that says Sophia Philips thirtieth birthday. At least I know we are in the right place. Two huge security guards stand on either side of the double doors. Niko hands over our tickets he grabbed from the car. Luckily, he did as I'd forgotten all about them.

"Did you two forget it's a masquerade party?" One of the guards says, and my heart sinks as I did in fact forget. He must see the wince on my face, so he points to a box behind his friend on a small table off to the side. "You've got to wear a mask to enter. You can grab one of those each and then you're good to go," he tells us.

We step around his friend and inspect the contents of the box. All sorts of different masks fill it to the brim. Niko and I try on a few, laughing at how they look on each other before he settles on a green one.

"Wear that one," Niko says, pointing to the one in my hands I'd picked up.

"You don't reckon it's too much?"

"Nah it covers more of your face. That way you can observe her before she realises it's you," he tells me.

"Good idea," I say. Taking the cool metal mask, I place it on my face, and it fits perfectly.

"It's fitting really with all your talk about grabbing horns and holding on," Niko says, which has me reaching up and stroking the horns of the bull atop my head.

"You sure it's not too much?"

"Nah. Come on, seize the day. Now quit stalling and get a move on," Niko says, as he places the green lace mask across his eyes and ties the ribbon at the back of his head.

"I already feel claustrophobic," I tell him.

"It'll all be worth it if you get the girl, right? Just try not to faint," he laughs, as we turn back to the security guards. Giving us a nod, they let us through the doors into the darkened ballroom. The lights are dimmed so low it's hard to make out any of the people filling the large space. Light chatter fills the air. "What's the point of the masks if we can't see anyone anyway?" Niko whispers from my right.

"Well, I won't be able to find Sophia if it's like this the whole night," I tell him.

"Maybe."

"Good evening, Ladies and Gentlemen," Holden's voice cuts off whatever Niko was about to say. "I bet you're wondering what is going on tonight. As you know it's my darling daughter's thirtieth birthday." The lights still haven't come on so we're all standing in the dark, facing in the direction of where Holden's voice is coming from.

"My wife and I wanted to do something different for Sophia's birthday. I know it's a masquerade party, but we've added a twist to it. You'll see what I mean when the lights come on," he says with a laugh. "Sophia didn't want us making a big fuss but if you'll bear with me and all join us in singing happy birthday to her before the lights come on, I think she'd really appreciate it."

The off-tune crowd starts belting out happy birthday, so Niko and I join in with them. I strain my eyes trying to catch a glimpse of the people around me but it's no use. The heat inside my mask added on top of the darkened room is not helping my feelings of claustrophobia. I can only hope the lights will come on soon. Cheers and clapping start as the singing finishes.

"I guess this is what he meant by finding a needle in a haystack," Niko's voice sounds from beside me.

97

I'm about to reply when Holden's voice comes over the microphone again.

"Thank you everyone. Now please enjoy the rest of your night at our masquerade ball with a twist." Holden's voice bounces off the walls, as the bright lights flash on and I'm blinded for a second, as is everyone else around me. As my eyes adjust, laughter rings out and I notice what everyone else does too.

"I think this is the haystack he was talking about," I tell Niko, as my eyes bounce around from woman to woman. All dressed in different types of black gowns, all with long black hair that runs down their backs. Obviously, some are wigs and they all wear different types of masquerade masks concealing their faces. Niko's laughter booms next to me.

"Oh, mate well isn't the mayor a right old cunt then."

"Too right he is," I fume. I thought I had it easy. With Sophia's hair being so distinct, I thought I would notice her easily in any crowd. I'm starting to doubt my abilities and my whole crazy plan.

"How the hell am I supposed to find his daughter now?" I hear a man say. He's wearing a black suit and a white mask, similar to the outfit worn by the phantom of the opera and is standing a few feet away from me.

"There was no way he was going to make it easy for you," I hear his friend reply.

"Let's split up and try to find the stuck-up cow so I can get this proposal over with," the white masked man says, before they part ways.

"Shit, how many others do you think are trying to find your dream girl tonight?" Niko whispers, having heard what I did.

"I'm not sure, but he did say there were other contenders. I don't like this at all," I confess.

"Well, we already knew the mayor was a prick. Let's kick him where it hurts by finding Sophia and hope and pray she says yes."

Niko's light-hearted pep talk spurs something inside and my eyes start searching the crowd. There's easily over three hundred people here tonight. Half of those are women. This is going to be an amazing feat if I can pull it off.

"Champagne?" a waiter asks, as he passes by juggling a tray with champagne flutes on it.

"Thanks," I say, carefully taking two and handing one to Niko.

"Here. You go enjoy yourself. I'm gonna walk around for a bit and see if I can't feel her out or something."

"Well, if you insist. Let's hope you don't find me kissing your girl when you see me next," he laughs.

"Don't kiss anyone until I find her," I grunt, which increases his laughter.

"I can't promise anything," he taunts, as he takes a sip of the fizzy liquid and stalks off in the opposite direction.

I take in my surroundings as I walk slowly through the ballroom. The low hanging chandeliers give the room a magical ambience. Black hair and dresses surround me everywhere and the chatter between different groups of people passes by me as I step around them, making my way through the crowd.

When the lights blinded me, they distracted me, so I didn't manage to get a look at where Holden's voice was coming from. I don't know what mask he is wearing but I would love nothing more than strolling up to him so I can give him a piece of my mind.

My heart sinks a bit at the thought that my night isn't going to turn out the way I envisioned. Every woman I pass seems a replica of the one before her. Slight differences are there in the details. Different shades of skin colour are the main one as well as a distinction of different lip colour shades. The different masks add another layer of confusion along with the jewellery their skin is adorned with.

I manage to make my way around the room twice within the next hour but I'm no closer to finding her as I was when I first entered, and we stood in the dark. I've spotted Niko a few times, mainly at the bar getting a refill. I've grabbed myself a few champagne flutes as the waiters have passed by me on my endeavours.

Without seeming too obvious or getting too close to random women, I've tried to inspect them as closely as possible. They are all starting to blur and roll into one so I'm not making much progress. The black velvet box is starting to feel like a weight pulling me down. This is my one shot to get her, and I feel it slipping further through my fingers as the clock ticks on.

Music plays as people dance but I haven't taken notice of those people, assuming she wouldn't be one of them. But maybe she is, and I need to change tactics. I've tried homing in on some Spidey senses to see if I can feel her presence, but that's not the case. I think the harder I try, the more I feel like she's not in the room.

Deflation fills me as I round the room for what I think is the fourth or fifth time but then fate steps in to help.

"Ally, come and dance with me?" The man's voice has me spinning so fast I nearly knock over a lady walking past me.

"Sorry," I tell her, steadying her before I release her arms and follow the man.

"One dance and that's it Eric," Ally says, and I can't be sure but it faintly rings a bell. I wonder if this is Sophia's best friend from that night eight years ago. I've got nothing else to go on, so I watch as Ally dances with Eric. My eyes don't leave her because I'm hoping wherever she goes, she will eventually lead me to Sophia. I doubt she would listen if the mayor told her she couldn't hang out with Sophia tonight. I wouldn't put it past him not to tell his daughter to keep her friends away even though it is her birthday.

The song finishes but they keep dancing, so I keep watching, not moving an inch in case I lose the only lead I've had all night. It isn't until a few songs pass that she kisses him on the cheek and they part ways. I've memorised her black lace mask. It has white flowers outlining the eyes so I know if I lose her, I should be able to find her easily enough. Well, I hope that's the case.

I keep a safe distance but follow as she moves through the crowd and heads towards the bar off to the side. Niko has moved on so isn't there now. Hopefully he hasn't found my dream girl and disappeared somewhere with her. Ally takes a seat at the bar and orders from the bartender. I'm too far back to make out what she orders but she sits there with empty seats on either side of her, tapping her fingers against the bar top.

I don't want to encroach on her space, so I sit a few seats down and wait until the bartender serves her before I order myself a glass of water. I need to clear my head, plus it's starting to get sweaty underneath this mask. Glancing at Ally, I notice two drinks in front of her. One looks like a colourful cocktail of some sort and the other is a neat brown liquor. My heart pounds in my chest because I feel it in my bones this is Sophia's friend.

That's when I feel it. A lightness radiates from the top of my head down to the back of my neck and it's at that exact moment, a woman takes a seat a couple over from Ally, missing a seat in between them. Ally slides the tumbler with the brown liquor along the bar and the woman catches it effortlessly, before she picks it up and takes a sip. Her long black hair shields her face so I can't see her features or get a good look at her mask from this angle. I don't know how to explain it, but I know it's her. It's Sophia.

Ally doesn't say a word. She stands with her cocktail in hand, sipping on her straw before she turns and walks away. Not even a backwards glance to her friend. It's then I realise I was right. Holden would keep his daughter's friends away from her tonight. It's her birthday for fucks sake. All that does is make me vow to not leave here without this woman saying yes to me. Who cares if it's crazy. I must get her away from the selfish prick. She deserves the world and I intend to give it to her.

Out of the corner of my eye I notice she finishes off her drink, studying the now empty glass as she turns it back and forth in her hand. Her bright red nails catch my attention. An act of defiance, I'm sure. And a way for me to find her again if I lose sight of her. Placing her glass on a coaster, she pushes her seat back about to leave but I stop her.

"Can I buy you another drink?" I say, making my voice deeper so she doesn't recognise it, hopefully. My question at least halts her movements, and she sits and turns to me face on. Looking at her now I don't think I've passed her at all tonight.

Seeing her close I catch sight of the freckles she tries so hard to hide with her foundation. Her black wig is well done and if I didn't know her hair was red, I would think this was her natural hair. Her eyes shine brightly at me from behind thick black makeup that flows into the mask covering the upper half of her face. It's beautiful. A bird. Its beak covers her nose then feathers fill the rest of the mask around her eyes until they fan out into wings that flutter around her face and head.

Her lips pull up in a slow seductive smile, drawing my attention.

"You do know the bar is paid for, so technically you can't buy me a drink?" she says, and with that I know it's her. I recognise the voice. I can't stop the smile she pulls out of me.

"Have a drink with me then?" I ask, moving a seat closer but leaving a couple empty between us.

"And why would I do that?" she asks, her head tilting to the side.

"For no other reason than you want to," I push.

"Who says I want to?"

"Don't you, little bird?" I tease.

"Little bird?"

"The mask," I tell her, pointing to my own face fully covered by my mask.

"One drink won't hurt," she tells me, settling back in her seat.

"Same again?" I ask, moving another seat closer but still leaving one between us.

"Sure," she replies. I signal to the bartender which has him stepping over to us. "Whiskey neat," she tells him.

"Make that two," I add, which makes her lip pull up in the corner. The bartender pours our drinks, placing them on coasters in front of each of us. I take a generous sip before placing my glass back. I enjoy this type of drink a lot more than the fizz of the champagne.

Out of the corner of my eye, I catch sight of her taking a drink herself before copying my movements and placing her glass down. I don't know what to say now that I have her focus, so I start with small talk.

"Are you enjoying the party?" I ask, not wanting to give anything away that may suggest it's me.

"Between you and I, it's very uppity, don't you think?" I choke back a laugh.

"That's one way to put it, for sure," I reply, taking another sip.

"It's a bit much with all the theatrics," she says, nodding her head towards my mask.

"I'm enjoying the mystery of it. Aren't you?"

"I like to know who I'm talking to, is all," she replies, before she raises the glass to her lips.

"Would it make you feel better if I removed my mask?" I offer.

"Didn't you hear? That's against the rules," her voice lowers, and I hear the pain through it.

"Oh, I don't think I received the memo about the rules. Were there any others I should know about?" I tease.

"Let me see," she says, tapping one of her sharp red nails against her chin in thought. "All the women, as you can see, had to wear black, along with a black wig if they didn't already have black hair. Everyone had to wear a mask which they aren't allowed to remove for the entirety of the party. You aren't allowed to use your real name. So, if you don't know anyone, you are out of luck," she tells me.

"Is that all?"

"Yes, I think so," she says, before she swallows the remainder of her drink.

"So, I can't give you my name and I can't remove my mask?" I ask, turning towards her.

"That's right," she says, turning to face me too.

Looking her dead in the eye I say, "So is there a rule that says this stranger with a mask on can't fuck you up against the wall over there?" I gesture with my chin to the side of the bar that's hidden from view of the party.

Her pupils dilate and she visibly swallows before she answers, "No. There's no rule against that."

I want to grab her in my arms right then and there, but I can't because it's not part of my plan, so I force myself to stay seated. I laugh lightly, smiling at her which makes her smile in return.

"Another drink?" I ask.

"One more won't hurt," she says, so I signal the bartender again. Before I can order two whiskeys again, she speaks and tells him, "Two tequila shots."

I throw my head back laughing but trying to contain it at the same time in case she recognises it.

"Are you trying to get me drunk, little bird?"

"I doubt one tequila shot would do much to you," she says, looking me over which has me blushing under my mask at her obvious perusal.

"Well, you don't need to get me drunk to have your wicked way with me," I state, making her eyes shoot to mine.

The bartender places the two shot glasses in front of us along with a saltshaker and lemon slices. I pick up one of the glasses foregoing the salt and lemon and she copies me.

"Shall we toast?" I ask, looking her in the eye.

"Sure. What would you like to drink to?"

With the small glass raised I reach out and say, "Here's to growing back your clipped wings and setting you free, little bird." I tap her glass and tip the liquid down my throat before I notice she does the same, only slower.

She places her glass down before she replies, "Who says I'm not already free?"

I stand, walking around the chair so I'm right next to her. She turns her whole body in her chair to face me. I can't help myself and reach out my finger to trace it slowly along her jaw from her ear to her chin where I tilt her head. As I lean into her, I hear her breath hitch the closer my lips get to her ear.

My voice lowers to a whisper, "Little bird, can you not see you were caged when you were born but you are destined to fly? Besides, if you were already free, then I wouldn't be here." I deliver a kiss to her neck, below her ear, letting my lips linger for a second before pulling away. I turn and walk from her without a backward glance, hoping my plan is going in my favour.

I head to the men's bathroom, walk into a stall and lock the door. The mask is suffocating so I slide it off my face and suck in deep breaths. A sheen of sweat covers my face, so I unroll some toilet paper and dab it across my skin before running my hand through my hair. My heart pounds in my chest so I draw a few more breaths in to calm myself.

As my heart rate lowers, I realise Holden is a bigger prick than I predicted. Part of the contract I hastily signed said I wasn't allowed to break the rules of the party or else I would forgo my chance of marrying Sophia and Holden would be able to purchase my business for a third of the price he is offering. There's no way in hell I'm letting him get away with that. So, I can't take my mask off or tell Sophia who I am. How the heck am I supposed to get her to agree to marry a complete stranger. I don't know if she would accept my proposal knowing it was me. She seems further away now and the dream of marrying her seems next to impossible.

With another deep breath, I place the hot metal mask back in place. I relieve myself then unlock the door and walk to the basin to wash my hands. While at the sink the phantom of the opera man and his friend walk in talking, so I zone in on their conversation while seeming inconspicuous.

They walk over to the urinal with their backs to me, so I keep my eyes on my hands, but my ears on their conversation.

"Have you found her yet?" I hear the friend ask.

"I think I've narrowed it to a couple of women out there. I think I'm going to have to pick one before the night is over and hope like hell it's the right one," Phantom guy says.

"You aren't losing anything if you pick the wrong woman. You just lose your connection with Holden," his friend says.

"That's true. The risk is worth the reward. I'll show you my options and you can help me decide." They finish up and move to the basin. I pull out some brown paper towels, dry my hands and leave while they continue chatting. The door swings shut as I exit the bathroom. I don't move too far away but stay out of sight as they exit then I follow them without them realising.

There is no way I'm letting this idiot marry my girl. It's obvious he wants her to have ties to Holden where quite frankly I would cut those ties to save her in a heartbeat. Why did life have to be so cruel and give this kind sweet woman a horrible father?

Following dumb and dumber, I see him pointing out a few women to his friend. None of the ones he has chosen have any resemblance to Sophia so at least this is one problem I don't need to concern myself with. Feeling better I don't have to worry about him proposing to the real Sophia, I scan the room in search of Niko.

I should have known I'd find him back at the bar. He's there talking to a woman, so I stand a few seats down until he looks up. I tilt my head to gesture for him to come talk to me. I didn't want to interrupt his flirting game. I order another water while I wait for him to finish up then he comes over and takes a seat next to me.

"Enjoying yourself I see," I say, as he sits.

"I might have to wear this mask all the time. It's attracting women like honey to a bee," he tells me, ordering a vodka with sugar free red bull. "Did you find her?" he asks, lowering his voice.

"I did," I reply, taking a sip.

"And?" he prompts.

"And I laid some groundwork. Well, I think I did."

"Groundwork? You don't particularly have time for groundwork," he tells me, before taking a big gulp of his drink.

"I know you're right. I'm unsure what to do now. Apparently, there are rules to this party that I wasn't aware of."

"What rules?"

"You can't remove your mask or tell anyone your real name if they don't know who you are," I tell him. I see the exact moment he clicks.

"Ah, well you're screwed then, aren't ya."

"Thanks for the boost of confidence mate." I take a sip of my water, as the feel of sweat forms at my temples.

"You and I both know this was always a crazy plan. Right now, the odds are heavily stacked against you. Unless you can get your girl to accept a proposal from a stranger. No offence but from what you've told me about her, I don't think she's the type to go out on a crazy whim like that."

"What do you think I should do then?" I ask. Running his hand over his beard in thought, he takes a minute before he responds.

Glancing my way, he lowers his voice, "You know I've known you a long time and I've never seen you want something as much as you want her. So, I say fuck it. Go all in and grab the bull by the horns or whatever it is you keep chanting at me," he says, before knocking back his whole drink and slamming the glass on the bar. I stare at my best friend, my brain warring with my heart, before my heart decides.

"I can do this." I take one last drink of my water before standing.

"Go get your girl," he says, as he lands a smack on my back.

"Thanks man," I reply, walking off in search of my future.

Chapter Fifteen

Lorenzo

It doesn't take me long to locate her now I know what mask to look for. Her red nails help a lot in my search too. She sits off to the side of the dance floor, seated at a table. Alone again. It makes my heart drop to think this party is supposed to be for her, but she seems to have spent the majority of it on her own. She sits there watching the people on the dance floor move, while she eats a slice of what I assume is her birthday cake. Watching her, she takes the tiniest bites like a taste is all she's after and not wanting to eat the whole slice.

She barely eats half of it before placing her fork on the plate, eyes glued to the dancing bodies. I see my chance to get her attention again. I'm moving towards her before I can talk myself out of it. Walking up beside her, she doesn't see me until I'm right next to her then she turns her head my way.

"Little bird," is all I say. I see the hint of a smile she tries hard to hold in.

"Well, if it isn't the bull in a China shop."

"Are you accusing me of being awkward or clumsy?" I ask, my brows pinching.

"Neither. You're reckless and seem like you throw caution to the wind," she replies.

I laugh lightly before replying, "I'll take that."

Her eyes move away from me and back to the dance floor.

"Dance with me?" Her eyes shoot back to me, a slight tug of her lips.

"First a drink and now a dance, isn't someone being greedy?" she taunts.

"Something about you brings out that side of me. I'm usually the opposite. I'm very much a giver," I tease, holding out my hand, hoping she will take it.

Her eyes drop to my outstretched hand before she places her soft fingers in mine. I close my warm hand around her delicate one, holding on tightly. I pull her to stand and lead her onto the dance floor.

Guiding her through the heated bodies, I spin and pull her body into me in one fast movement. I wrap my free hand around her waist and pull our joined hands behind my neck where I let go, leaving her hand there. She follows my lead, bringing her other hand up to wrap around my neck and I pull her closer. Swaying our bodies to the music, we don't talk, just move. The first song finishes, and we still dance, neither of us letting the other go.

She breaks the silence between us saying, "I feel like you are trouble."

"You have no idea," I whisper in her ear.

"Can I ask you something?" I hear her faintly say over the music.

"Anything."

She locks her eyes with me, saying, "What brought you here tonight?"

I gulp, reach up and grab her hand and spin her out before bringing her back in flush against me. She laughs before I reply.

"I came to claim something that belongs to me." I know I'm being cryptic, but I have no other option than to hope she remembers our words from eight years ago. She blinks but there's no confirmation in their depths. She still doesn't realise who I am or that it's her I came for.

"The mayor's daughter's party is a funny place to be retrieving something, don't you think?" she laughs, and I join her.

"No. It's the perfect place," I reply, my hand slowly moving lower down her back.

"Why is that?"

"You really don't see it, little bird?" I ask, taking a deep breath, realising it's now or never. I'm grabbing the bull by the horns and going for it.

"See what?" her voice wavers.

"It's you. You're what belongs to me," I whisper, pulling her closer. Her body freezes and my heart rate picks up speed because I know I've said the wrong thing. I'm scaring her off and it's the complete opposite of what I want to do.

The DJ comes over the microphone at that moment, stopping the music.

"We are going to have a short fifteen-minute break then we'll be back to party the rest of the night away," he says, before chatter begins around us.

I literally feel her slipping through my fingers as she pulls back, her now hardened eyes staring up at me.

"I belong to no one," she spits out, through clenched teeth. She turns to rush away but I grab her hand and hold on.

"Please give me a chance," I soften my voice, hoping she can hear the sentiment in it.

All the dancing people head back to the bar or tables since the music stopped. While she stares me down, the dance floor empties and the two of us are left standing there alone. I can feel eyes on me, but my eyes are only on her. I don't know how to make it right, but I feel if I let her walk away right now, she will be walking away for good.

"No," she abruptly says, pulling her hand and trying to leave. I don't let go though. Instead, I push my other hand into my front pocket, covering the small box with my fingers.

"Marry me?" I softly say, so only she can hear. Watching her I see her eyes widen and it takes a second for her to start pulling her hand again, trying to free it from my grasp. I pull the velvet box free from my pocket and release her hand to open it. Her eyes follow my hands, seeing the box and I hear her gasp for air, before I drop to one knee and say loud enough for most of the room to hear, "Marry me?"

Other people gasp but my eyes never leave the girl in front of me. If this is what my gramps meant about grabbing the bull by the horns, then I'm grabbing them and holding on for dear life. This is by far the scariest, craziest thing I've ever done.

It feels like a lifetime passes as we stand there, looking at each other. Her with her wide-eyed expression and me holding open the box with my grandma's ring. She hasn't looked at it. Her eyes haven't left my face. Then I feel it. There's a shift in the air. Her face drops and her eyes close. When they open again, she breaks the thread I'm hanging on to.

Shaking her head she says, "No," before turning to rush away from me.

I don't think, I react and yell out, "I'll give you all of my Sundays," for everybody to hear. The silence in the room is deafening. But it has the desired effect, and it makes her stop dead in her tracks. She hasn't turned around yet but I wait. She's got to remember this if nothing else because I wrote it on the list. A list I've looked over at least once a week for the last eight years.

Slowly she turns, her eyes scanning me as if she's trying to decipher some code she didn't see before. Does she remember?

112

"What did you say?" she whispers.

"I'll give you all of my Sundays. From now until forever. You and me. Every Sunday," I gently tell her. Hell, I would give her all my Saturdays too if it would make her say yes.

She lowers her gaze to the ring in the box. I'm holding it out to her still and her breath hitches again at the sight of it, and I know I've made the right choice. I'm not sure she's aware but she's slowly walking back like an invisible force is pulling her towards me. Her eyes have a glassy sheen over them now, like she's holding back tears.

I remember when we made the pact that the Sunday thing was a big deal for her. I have no idea why but if that's what she wants, she can have it.

Her eyes are back on me so I softly coax, "Marry me and you can have all of my Sundays."

The faintest hint of a smile pulls the corner of her mouth up as she replies, "Okay. I'll marry you." My heart gets sucked into my throat and I nearly choke before it starts thundering like crazy in my chest.

"Really? You'll marry me?" I ask, dumbfounded.

"Yes," she replies, which sends everyone around us exploding into cheers. My body on instinct moves and lifts her in the air, swinging her around. Her laughter surrounds me and brings the biggest smile to my face as she wraps her arms around my neck, squeezing. I squeeze her tightly back.

"I can't believe you came back for me," she whispers right into my ear, so only I can hear.

"I told you I was coming for what belonged to me," I whisper right back, kissing her neck before swinging her around again. Placing her feet on the ground, I take my grandma's ring from the box and slide it onto her finger. It's big but we can get it resized.

Her body draws flush against mine and I whisper in her ear, "Happy birthday," before I pull back, smiling at her. She returns my smile, but before we can get lost in each other's gazes, our happy moment is broken by Holden's voice booming through the room.

"I think congratulations are in order for the happy couple. I would be honoured if they would join me and my wife for a celebratory drink," he says. I follow the voice to the DJ's booth where Holden is holding the microphone. He wears a black and red mask that covers his eyes. I must say it's fitting; it makes him look like the devil.

There's tension around his fake smile, but I'm unsure if anyone else notices.

"I guess we can't tell him no, can we?" I whisper to her, behind a fake smile of my own. She pulls me along behind her as she leads the way to her parents. People congratulate us on the way and for a second we are consumed by the crowd. I take this opportunity while we are hidden from view to talk to Sophia.

"You have to act surprised when it's revealed it's me," I tell her. She must hear the serious tone in my voice as her head whips around to mine. I search her eyes and see the slight nod she gives me, not asking any questions but understanding. It takes us another five minutes to manoeuvre through the remaining crowd to reach Holden and his wife, whose name I can't seem to recall.

They are at a table situated apart from the rest of the room. Four chairs surround it. Holden holds out his hand for me to shake so I take it.

"Congratulations," he says, as I squeeze it firmly.

"Thank you," I reply, moving to hold out Sophia's chair for her to sit.

"So should we get straight to the point then?" Holden asks, and I feel a tense energy coming from where Sophia sits next to me.

"Sure," I reply, as I slide my hand under the table and onto Sophia's knee, giving it a gentle squeeze in reassurance.

"Well, I know who she is. I'm not entirely sure who you are," he admits, and I chuckle. How many suitors did this man have coming for his daughter tonight?

"I can rectify that easily if you would let me remove my mask," I tell him.

"Very well but before we do that, I have a question for your lovely lady. Why did you accept his marriage proposal if he's a complete stranger to you?" he asks Sophia, and I feel the sweat drip along my neck. The waiter walks over then and delivers a glass of champagne in front of each of us.

Holden and his wife take a sip when Sophia replies, "Oh because he promised to fuck me up against the wall with his mask on." Holden's wife spits her champagne out in shock, her jaw dropping as she looks at me and I can't help but smile widely at her. Holden's face reddens and matches the mask he's wearing, and I can't help the glee I feel at my fiancee's little act of defiance. Fiancee, now that's an amazing word.

Sophia and I each take a sip from our drinks, sink into our chairs and wait for Holden's next move. He thought he would catch me out at breaking his rules. I haven't removed my mask, and I haven't voiced my name so technically I haven't broken his rules. If he had an inkling I'd secretly hinted at her who I was, he would use it in his favour.

"I guess you can remove your masks and then I can announce the happy couple to the party," he tells us, clenching his jaw, clearly unhappy someone outsmarted him at his own game.

I take a deep breath playing my part, then slide the mask up and over my face, running my hand through my hair. Holden's nostrils flair the moment he sees who I am, and I can't help but smirk and wink his way before facing Sophia. She gasps as her hand covers her mouth in shock, playing her own part believably well. She takes a second before reaching up and untying her own mask from her head and pulls it off her face. Her heavy black eye makeup has smudged all around her eyes, but it brings out the blue magnificently. I don't think she could look any more beautiful than she does. No scratch that. If her own fiery hair was showing, she'd look perfect.

"Lorenzo?" she asks, pretending still.

"You know him?" Holden asks, shock lacing his own voice and I'm glad I kept that bit of information to myself.

"We went to high school together," she tells him.

"Hey Sophia," I say, taking in every inch of her face to remember this moment.

"You had no idea it was him when he proposed?" Holden's anger seeps into his voice.

"No none," she lies. His hard eyes flicker back and forth between us in thought.

"Very well, let's introduce you to the party, shall we?" he says, pushing his seat back with a screech.

We all stand as Holden walks back over to the DJ's booth, grabbing the microphone.

"Good evening, ladies and gentlemen. I know we had rules tonight where you couldn't remove your masks but I've allowed the happy couple to do that so we can give them a big congratulatory round of applause. To the happy couple Mr. Moretti and my beautiful daughter Sophia." There are a few gasps at the mention of Sophia's name but we step back into view of the party as the attendees face us. With linked hands I raise hers to my lips, delivering a kiss to her hand. The crowd applauds and I hear a loud cheer from the back corner. I have no doubt it's coming from Niko. He will be proud I sealed the deal and got the girl. Finally getting what I came for, I realise I don't want to stay here any longer.

"Do you want to stay or leave?" I quickly ask Sophia, and her eyes widen.

"Leave," she tells me, smiling. I raise my voice above the crowd to get their attention.

"Thank you very much everyone, you are too kind. If you don't mind, my fiancee and I might leave the party to start our own celebrations." The crowd laughs and cheers and I glance at Holden again. He stares back at me with his lips pursed and I wave in farewell.

"Lunch tomorrow at the house please. Make sure you're both there," Sophia's mother tells us, before she hugs Sophia and gives me a timid smile. I take Sophia's hand and we exit the party swiftly through a side door.

"Let's get out of here," I tell her, and she nods before realisation hits her.

"Can I text Ally to come too?" she asks, and it's then I remember Niko was my ride.

"Yes of course. I'll text my friend Niko as well, then we can get out of here."

We both pull out our phones and quickly send texts. It takes a few minutes before they emerge from the doors, rushing to us. Niko's smile beams at me as he pats me on the back, not saying anything in front of the girls. Ally wraps Sophia up in a hug and doesn't say anything either.

We start walking outside and Niko hands his ticket to the valet and he pulls his car around. We gather in and Niko starts driving.

"I'm Niko."

"I'm Ally and this is Sophia," Ally says.

"To the bar?" Niko asks.

"Oh my gosh is that the same bar from all those years ago?" Ally chimes in with.

"The one and the same," I tell her, a smile in my voice.

"I'm down," Ally replies. "Sophia?"

"Yeah, I'm in," she timidly says. I glance back at her from the passenger's seat, my brows pulling in for a second. I hope she's not having second thoughts.

"We've gotta go celebrate your birthday properly," I say into the car, and the three of us start singing happy birthday to Sophia which makes her crack up laughing, loosening the worry in my gut.

Chapter Sixteen

Sophia

Twirling my gorgeous new engagement ring around on my finger, I sit in the back seat of the car in shock. How on earth are the last few hours of my life real? Ally nudges my arm, pulling me from my thoughts. Lorenzo turned the music up so there's not much talking going on. The guys are both focussed on the road ahead so don't notice the rolling eyes and panting faces Ally is making next to me in regard to Lorenzo. I choke on the laugh I'm trying to contain, catching Lorenzo's attention causing him to turn to me with a raised brow. I school my features and my fingers fiddling with my ring draw my attention to how loose it is.

"Lorenzo, can you hold on to this for me please? I don't want to lose it," I say, and I don't. It's beautiful and I hate to think what he spent on it. On me.

"Of course," his smooth voice says, and the sound of it makes me melt. How did I not recognise it was him with his mask on? I slide the ring off and reach out, placing it in his hand. I pull my hand back, but he lightly grazes my index finger with his which has me gazing into the depths of his rich brown eyes. Slowly his lip pulls up on one side, a dimple appearing and heat rushes to my cheeks. I stand by my earlier statement. He is trouble with a capital t.

I spend the rest of the drive staring out the window. It isn't long before we pull into the dirt parking lot. I glance at the bar. It looks exactly as I remember, if not a little run down and the wooden exterior weathered from the years. My eyes drop and I can't help but feel overdressed in the black satin cocktail dress. Ally catches me inspecting my dress and grabs my hand.

"Who cares Soph. It's your birthday for a few more hours so let's go in there and get drunk and celebrate you turning dirty thirty," she says, poking her tongue out at me.

"Dirty thirty, I like the sound of that," Lorenzo says from the front seat, and I can't help the blush I'm sure covers my whole body.

"You two can get a room later. Let's go party," Niko says, opening his door and slamming it shut. Walking into the bar, heads turn our way at our fancy attire before someone yells out to Lorenzo.

"Well don't you clean up well lad," the old man behind the bar says to Lorenzo.

"Thanks Ted. Can I get a round of tequila shots?" he says, making me smile.

"You know I hate shots but since it's your birthday, I'll suffer through," Ally whispers in my ear, which has me laughing loudly.

"Just the one then we can get you your fancy cocktail things you like to drink."

"Sure. One I can handle, I hope. Stop me if I try to dance on the bar or do anything embarrassing," she pleads. I wrap my arms around her waist pulling her into my side.

"Thanks for being my friend and sticking with me all this time Al," I tell her, right before our shots arrive.

"Pfft you couldn't get rid of me if you tried," she says, squeezing me back. Lorenzo passes out the shots to us so we each take one.

"To the birthday girl. Happy birthday," Lorenzo says, and Niko and Ally add in their happy birthdays as we clink glasses and throw our heads back, downing the liquor.

Slamming her glass on the bar Ally's eyes light up as she says, "Ooh I love this song. Come dance with me my new friend," as she grabs Niko by the hand and pulls him on to the dance floor.

"Order me my usual Renz," Niko calls out to Lorenzo, as he watches Ally's butt sway into the crowd.

"I hope they don't hook up and make things awkward," I say to Lorenzo, as he stands at the bar and orders a whiskey and a vodka with sugar free redbull before turning to me.

"What do you and Ally want to drink?"

"I'll take a whiskey and get Ally a fruity cocktail." He adds those to the order before he turns his whole body to me.

"I don't think things could get any more awkward than they already are."

I laugh and he joins in, his dimple showing. It makes me want to stick my finger in and turn it to see how deep it goes. The bartender places our drinks on a tray for Lorenzo and he pulls out his wallet.

"The shots and this round are on the house since it's the pretty lady's birthday. Enjoy your night sweetheart," Ted says.

"Thank you," I reply, as Lorenzo carries the tray like it's the most natural thing and leads me to an empty booth. He places the tray down then scoots into a seat and I sit opposite him. We have a perfect view of the dance floor and can see Ally and Niko moving along to the music, although a bit too close for my liking. I don't want any more weirdness about this situation if we can help it.

"Don't worry about Niko, he's harmless. Well mostly," Lorenzo says, trying to ease my worries. He must have caught me watching them.

"It's more Ally I'm worried about. She can be a bit of a man eater," I confess, which has him throwing his head back in laughter.

We both take a sip of our whiskeys, watching them dance. Neither of us says anything else. I don't know what I want to say to him. He was only a fantasy this morning and now he's my fiance.

"You know you don't have to marry me, if you don't want to?" His soft tone grabs my attention.

"What?"

"If you've changed your mind. I know tonight has been crazy and the pact we made eight years ago was pretty crazy so if you've changed your mind, that's okay. I won't hold it against you or anything. When you think about it, it all is a bit..."

"Crazy," I finish his sentence, smiling at his overuse of the word.

"Yeah," he says, laughing.

"Can I ask you something?"

"You can ask me anything, anytime. No need to ask permission first," he softly says, and I nod.

"There's no one else you want to marry? I mean, shoot, that came out wrong. I mean there hasn't been anyone else you've wanted to spend your life with?" I blurt, because I can't understand why he hasn't been picked up by someone yet. He's quite the catch.

"No. There's no one else I'd rather marry," he slowly says, looking into my eyes. My cheeks heat and I'm starting to hate how easily my skin reddens because it's a dead giveaway the effect he has on me.

"What about you? There hasn't been a man you've wanted to commit to?" he asks.

I stare into the brown liquid before tipping my head back and swallowing it all in one big gulp. Twisting the now empty glass out of habit I then place it on the table. Looking up at Lorenzo he has a small smile on his lips.

"The only men who have been in my life have always had a hidden agenda. They want to get in favour with my father. So, I hope this doesn't sound harsh but if I marry you, at least I'm choosing someone on my terms and not on his, you know?" I say, feeling my skin heat again at my confession and for speaking my truth.

His smile fades before he replies, "It makes perfect sense."

His understanding makes my worry ease.

"We don't have to rush anything either. We can have a long engagement and get to know each other properly first," he suggests.

"No," I blurt. His raised eyebrows stare at me while he tries and fails to hold back a smile.

"In a hurry to tie me down, are ya?" he asks, humour lacing his voice. I can't help the smile he brings out of me.

"I want to get it over with. Shoot, that's not what I meant either. I mean if we're only engaged, my father will try to intervene and have me marry one of his little minions he can easily manipulate. I'd rather we got married so at least he couldn't use me like that," I say, my gaze dropping to the table. I hear the squeak of the vinyl chair as Lorenzo moves then I feel his body warmth as he slides into the seat next to me.

"Come here Soph," he softly says, as he pulls me into his arms. His large hand cradles my head against his chest as the other one wraps around my waist. I wrap my own arms around his waist, noticing how hard his body is underneath his suit. "I won't let him cause you any more hurt. That's a promise."

"Thanks Lorenzo," I say, enjoying the feel of being in his arms. We stay like that for a minute before he speaks again.

"I do want a real marriage with you though. I know it will be awkward at times but I'm sure together we can work through it all. We have to communicate if something is making us feel awkward," he says.

"I want that too," I say, quietly against his chest.

"We'll take it slow," he says, and I squeeze him tightly in agreement.

"Did you mean what you said about all your Sundays?" I ask, wanting to know if he meant it or if it was a line. He unhooks my arms from his waist pulling me back so he can look into my eyes.

"I meant every word Sophia. From now until forever, I'll give you all of my Sundays." My eyes flicker back and forth between his eyes, looking for any deception but I see none.

"Thank you," I whisper, and he leans forward delivering a chaste kiss to my cheek which has me closing my eyes. Too soon he's pulling away before smiling at me. I'm starting to think with the way my body reacts to him, I may have trouble taking this whole thing slow. I guess that's a good start though, wanting to jump your fiance's bones.

"Another drink?" he asks.

"Sure. Can we get a round of tequila shots? I want to celebrate my birthday properly," I tell him, feeling excitement bubbling inside of me at the prospect that this marriage may work.

"I'll be right back," he says, leaning forward and kissing me on the forehead. He pulls back and looks at me. He slides his fingers along a section of hair. "Can the wig come off? I miss your red hair."

"Not easily. I'll have to do it tomorrow because everything I need is at home," I tell him, chuckling. I'd forgotten I was wearing the wig until he mentioned it.

"Tomorrow it is then," he says, before standing and walking to the bar. With his back turned, I check out my fiance's tight butt. Hot damn, those pants make it look amazing. I sigh out loud which makes Ally laugh opposite me. In my ogling, I hadn't realised she'd joined me at the booth.

"Checking out your soon to be hubby I see," she teases, making us both laugh.

"Well, he isn't sore on the eyes. That's for sure," I tell her, as I continue to watch him. Seeing Niko join him at the bar. I turn back to Ally.

"Please don't sleep with Niko and make things weird," I tell her honestly.

Rolling her eyes she says, "Fine. Only because it's a weird enough situation as it is. But damn the way that man moves, I'm sure he'd have me singing in the sack in seconds." We both laugh loudly at her words but I'm starting to think the same about Lorenzo.

"Be honest, do you think it's weird we are gonna do this? I know we laughed and joked about it over the years after I told you but now it's happening, is it weird?"

"Yeah, it is but it doesn't mean it can't also be right. People get married every day for all sorts of reasons so why can't this be another reason? The way you two look at each other, I don't think you'll have many problems," she says, wiggling her brows at me.

"What do you mean the way we look at each other?"

"Seriously, you both look at the other like they are your favourite meal and you're starving," she chuckles, as my mouth drops open. "Don't look so shocked, you know it's true," she whispers, and I realise why she dropped her voice when the guys return with more drinks. Lorenzo holds a tray, two whiskeys for us, a vodka for Niko and another cocktail for Ally while Niko holds four tequila shots between his fingers. I glance at Ally and see her eyes widen as Niko places one of the shots in front of her.

"How about I take your one too. It is my birthday after all," I tell her, wrapping my fingers around her shot glass and sliding it my way.

"Thanks," she says, offering me a small smile. We both know Ally is a lightweight when it comes to alcohol so the cocktail she's drinking will probably be enough for her for the night.

"Here's to new beginnings," I say, grabbing one of my shots and clinking the glass with the three of them. We drink our shots while Ally takes a big sip of her cocktail.

"Let's dance some more," Ally says, looking in my direction.

"Yes, let's," I tell her, as I quickly tip my head back taking my other shot and then grabbing my glass of whiskey. Lorenzo stands up so I can slide out of the booth, and I take my glass with me to the dance floor as Ally links her arm with mine. The guys stay behind at the booth drinking and chatting, while I hold hands with Ally and sway to the music. The fuzzy feeling from the alcohol is taking effect and making me a lot more relaxed than I was earlier in the night.

We hold hands and dance while sipping from our drinks. We continue like that for a few songs until both our drinks are finished. I'm about to ask Ally if she wants another when I feel a warm body pushed up against me. I instantly step forward until I hear Lorenzo's voice.

"It's me."

I relax, peeking over my shoulder to double check it is in fact him. Niko steps up in front of me and loosens my empty glass from my hand taking it and then does the same with Ally.

"Do you want another drink, Sophia?" Niko asks and I nod. He looks to Lorenzo and silently asks him before he turns to Ally.

"I'll come with you. I need a break from dancing," Ally says, letting go of my hand.

Lorenzo pulls me back into his front, swaying us gently as he holds me by the waist. He rests his chin on my shoulder, and I can't help but feel safe in his embrace. I don't know if it's from the alcohol or not, but I'll go with it.

We continue dancing like this as Niko hands us each a drink and then he and Ally head back to the booth. I can see Ally has switched out her cocktails for water now. She probably doesn't want to get blind drunk but tonight, I don't care if I do. I want to celebrate my birthday how I want to, on my own terms without my father's interference.

That drink turns into a couple more and before I know it, I'm stumbling and laughing all over the place.

"This is the best birthday ever," I tell Lorenzo who I now face, my arms wrapped around his neck.

He switched to water a few drinks ago but told me he would look after me if I wanted to keep drinking. He mentioned he still lives above the bar and said we could all crash there when we have had enough partying. I close my eyes and he sways us to the music letting any remaining worries drift away.

"Get it out Sophia. It's okay," I faintly hear Lorenzo's voice.

My heavy eyes peek open, and I take in the porcelain toilet I'm currently bent over. Vomit sits in the bowl making me gag again, adding more.

"That's it," Lorenzo says from my side, as his hand rubs circles on my lower back while I hurl into the toilet.

My hair flings forward as my stomach lurches.

"Shit," Lorenzo swears, and moves around me. Then he's pulling my hair back from my face gently and holding it out of the way while I vomit so it doesn't get in my hair. "Damn it, the wig is gonna need to get thrown out cos I wasn't fast enough," he murmurs.

I can't answer, but in my head I think it's okay, it's a wig. Not like I was gonna wear it again. I stop for a minute, and he flushes the toilet, taking the horrid smell with it.

Releasing my hair he says, "I'm gonna get you a glass of water. I'll be right back. Will you be okay?"

I nod. Well, I think I do as my head feels heavy. The door squeaks open, and his retreating footsteps fade as I close my eyes again. My head gets heavier, and I want to lay down.

"No, no, no." Lorenzo is back again, lifting my head from the cool surface. "You can't rest on the toilet. I've got you," his soothing voice tells me. My eyes are too heavy to open now, and I want to sleep. "Have a sip of water before you sleep," his voice tells me.

I feel the cool glass pressed against my lips so open my mouth as he tips the cold liquid in. I take a small sip, swallow then the world goes black.

My head feels heavy against the soft surface I'm lying on. Throbbing behind the eyes keeps me from opening them straight away. I groggily peel them open; the bright light forces me to squint to adjust to the brightness before fully becoming aware of my surroundings. White tiled floor and white walls with a door. I crane my head to the side, catching sight of the toilet behind me and realise I'm in a bathroom.

I push myself to sit up and realise my pillow is a pair of legs covered in grey suit pants. I scan the body all the way to the face. Lorenzo's soft snores fill the air as his head rests against the bathroom cabinet. A strand of dark hair has fallen across his forehead, so I gently reach up pushing it back into place.

Running my eyes down my dress I see there's vomit on it. I guess that answers my question about how we ended up here. My movements must cause Lorenzo to wake because he runs a hand over his face before turning to me, his eyes opening. I watch as he wakes and the realisation, I'm awake too has his eyes widening.

"Hey. You feeling okay?" he asks.

"Yeah," I croak, my throat feeling rough, making me wince. He glances at the watch on his wrist.

"It's still pretty early. If you're feeling okay, how about you get some sleep in the bed. Ally's already in there and Niko's on the couch," he tells me.

"Okay, but could I shower first?" I ask, looking at the vomit on my dress.

"Of course. I'll grab you a t-shirt to sleep in," he says, as he pushes himself to stand. He holds out a hand for me and pulls me up. My body shakes and he raises his eyebrows at me.

"Will you be okay in the shower?" he asks, holding my forearms.

My stomach lurches and I turn, emptying the contents into the toilet. It's not much, my stomach is mostly empty from previously vomiting I'm guessing. Lorenzo stands behind me, my hair gathered in his hands. I stay like that for a few minutes making sure I'm not gonna vomit again before standing upright.

"Could you hang around to make sure I'm okay? Don't look though," I ask, my body shaking a bit more now.

"Anything you need," he says, a small smile gracing his lips. "Sit down and I'll grab you something to change into and a towel." He lowers the toilet seat then helps me sit on it. He quickly exits the door and I hear the light banging of drawers before he returns.

He places some clothes by the sink before opening the shower door and turning on the water for me. He throws a towel over the top of the shower glass, so it's easy for me to reach. He steps back to me, helping me stand.

"Can you undo the back of my dress please?" I ask, because my mother had to do up all the hooks for me as it's a corset top.

"Sure," he says.

I slowly turn and he starts unhooking them all the way to my lower back.

129

"All done. I'll stand by the door and face it until you're finished," he tells me and I nod, which has my head throbbing. He moves away towards the door like he said and turns facing it.

I use the sink to hold on to for balance and I step out of the dress. My shoes are already missing which makes it easier. I unhook my bra and remove my underwear then step into the steaming water.

I pump some of his body wash into my hand and wash the best I can while still shaking and feeling weak. Worry settles in my stomach from my run-down state so I splash my face, rinse my mouth and body before shutting the water off. Running the towel over my body at a slow pace I then wrap it around myself before pushing open the door and stepping out.

True to his word, Lorenzo is facing the wall, waiting. I quickly grab the t-shirt he left, pulling it over my head. It falls to mid thigh so it's a perfect fit for a nightie. He's also left a pair of boxer shorts, so I carefully step into them and pull them into place.

Picking up the towel, I dry my hair the best I can while I say, "I'm decent," to Lorenzo. He turns around smiling.

Holding out his hand he says, "Come on, let's get you to bed. Drop the towel on the floor, I'll sort this all out later."

I take his hand and he leads me to the far side of the bed, pulling the blanket free for me to get in.

"I'll get you some pain relief and water," he whispers, before leaving to head into the kitchen. He comes back with a glass of water before going into the bathroom and coming back with two Advil.

I take them, swallowing them with a couple sips of water.

"Get some sleep, Sophia," he whispers, which has me resting my head against the pillow.

I hear him moving around but when it goes quiet, I peek open my eyes. He's placed a blue bucket right beside the bed for me, just in case. He's also grabbed a pillow and blanket so he can make up a bed on the floor to keep watch over me. Glancing at him, I see he's changed out of his suit and now wears a singlet and boxer shorts before he pulls the blanket up to cover him.

His eyes find mine and he whispers, "Sleep," while smiling at me.

"Thanks Lorenzo," I whisper back, before closing my eyes and drifting off to sleep.

Chapter Seventeen

Lorenzo

"Renz?" I hear whispered, which has me opening my eyes into the semi-dark room. Glancing around I locate the voice near the door. "Where's your good pan with the heavy base?" Niko asks.

I wipe the sleep from my eyes before flicking the blanket off me. I stare at the bed, seeing Sophia and Ally are still fast asleep so I let them be and walk to the door, shutting it behind me. "It's in the cupboard next to the oven," I tell Niko, as I let out a yawn. I shake my wrist to check the time on my watch. It's already 7.00am. I didn't get much sleep as I kept waking to check on Sophia to make sure she wasn't vomiting again, but every time she was fast asleep in the same position as she is now.

"Gonna cook up some eggs and bacon. That should fix the girls' hangovers," Niko tells me, as he bangs around the kitchen gathering all the ingredients he needs. He's over here as much as he is at his own place so knows where everything is, well except his so-called favourite pan apparently.

"Hopefully Sophia can keep it down," I tell him.

"Was she still vomiting after I crashed out?" he asks.

He helped me get the girls upstairs before he crashed in the lounge. Ally passed out in his arms as soon as he picked her up and his foot hit the first step. I picked up Sophia as she was stumbling around and the rocking motion of me carrying her up the stairs wasn't great for her stomach and that led to her bent over the toilet most of the night. Well, that and all the tequila and whiskey. Note for future reference: get her to stick to one type of liquor instead of mixing.

"Yeah, most of the night," I tell him, as I take a seat at the kitchen island while he places bacon into the sizzling pan. "Can you grab me some water?" I ask, so he opens the fridge and throws me a bottle.

"I still can't believe your brain haired plan worked and you got the girl," he says, his back facing me as he laughs.

"Me too. I nearly lost it when I saw all the women wearing similar black dresses and wigs," I admit.

"That mayor of ours is a prick, isn't he? How many other guys do you think were trying to find her last night?"

"No idea. There was the phantom of the opera guy who seemed like he'd have his lips permanently stuck to Holden's ass, so I'm glad he didn't find her," I tell him, scrunching my eyes as my head throbs from alcohol and lack of sleep. Niko's boisterous laugh fills the room before he turns to me, pointing the tongs at me.

"You, my friend, are an idiot. That girl wouldn't have said yes to just anyone. It doesn't matter if they had found her or not. They wouldn't have gotten a yes. That is one thing I'm sure of," he states, before he turns back to tend to the bacon.

Mulling over his words I can't help but think he's right. I don't think Sophia would have said yes to just anyone. Niko's chuckle draws my attention to him.

"She's as crazy as you are for going along with this pact you guys made. You're both abnormal in my books," he says, as his laughing continues.

133

"Normal is overrated," I tell him, taking a sip of my water.

That makes him laugh more before he says, "Too right, my brother."

The creak of the door has our heads whipping in that direction.

"Hey," Sophia says, as she squints an eye.

I take her in, standing there in my black Metallica t-shirt that falls over my boxers she's wearing. My heart rate increases, and I must say I enjoy seeing her in my clothes. It's like a primal part of my psyche has awoken at the sight.

"Morning. How are you feeling?" I ask, pulling out the stool next to me as she slowly steps towards me.

"Just peachy," she says, before lowering her cheek to the kitchen island. She closes her eyes and sighs at the cool marble against her skin. I let out a chuckle at her misfortune because she looks cute even though she probably isn't feeling the best.

"Is that bacon I smell?" Ally asks, as she waltzes through my bedroom door with her black gown still on like she hasn't got a hangover at all.

"Sure is. You want some with eggs?" Niko asks her.

"Yes please. A man who knows the way to a woman's heart," she says, patting Niko on the back as she passes him to come sit on my other side.

"Isn't that the way to a man's heart?" he asks.

"I eat like a man so po-tay-toe, pa-ta-toe."

Niko finishes cooking the bacon then cracks eggs into the pan.

"Anyone want a coffee?" I ask.

"I'll take mine black," Ally responds.

"Yeah, I'll have one," Niko says.

"Sophia?" I prompt, as she still rests with her cheek pressed against the cool black marble.

"I guess I can try it and see if I can keep it down. I'll have one with two sugars and a splash of milk please," she says, her eyes never opening.

"You got it," I tell her, pushing my stool back and walking around the kitchen island next to Niko. I fill the kettle to boil and grab four mugs, making their coffees as they like. I already know Niko's which is coffee and cream. He hates white sugar and will add the artificial stuff which I don't keep in the apartment. He follows the keto diet, so he is currently making bacon and eggs without toast. I prefer mine like Sophia's, so I make ours the same. One less thing for me to remember.

Handing out the mugs once I'm done, Niko slides plates of bacon and eggs in front of everyone. Sophia raises her head and I watch as her nose scrunches.

"It might make your tummy settle a bit," I tell her.

"I've never been this hungover before. Is this a normal thing to eat greasy food after you've been vomiting?" she asks quietly, not wanting the others to overhear.

"Yeah, people reckon it helps soak up the alcohol in your stomach. I don't know if it's correct, but it usually does the trick for me," I say, stabbing my fork into my scrambled eggs and enjoying the first mouthful.

Sophia tentatively takes a smaller forkful and lifts it to her mouth, chewing before swallowing.

"Take it slow. There's no rush," I tell her, nudging her arm. Niko takes the remaining seat next to Ally and silence falls over us as we all dig into our food.

Niko and I finish quickly, and Ally isn't too far behind. She wasn't kidding about eating like a man. I pick up my coffee holding it in two hands and let the warmth flood into my palms before taking a sip.

135

I glance at Sophia's plate, and she's eaten about half of what Niko gave her, which is more than I thought she would with her queasy stomach.

"I can't wait to get this wig off," Ally says, flinging the black hair over her shoulder.

"Me too," Sophia says, and I can't help but think the same.

"What time will your parents be expecting us to show up?" I ask, remembering what her mother said about coming over today.

"Probably around ten," she says, reaching both arms above her head as she yawns. She then picks up her own mug taking a small sip of coffee. "Remind me never to drink again," she says, causing everyone else to crack up with laughter. Her puzzled face looks at us. "What's so funny?"

"That's what they all say babe," Ally tells her, smiling at her.

"Well, I mean it," she says, which makes us all laugh harder.

"They all say that too," Ally replies, and Sophia shakes her head at us.

Finishing my coffee, I start rinsing off the dishes and placing them in the dishwasher so I can run a cycle while we are out at her parents.

"I'm gonna jump in the shower and get ready," I tell Sophia.

"I might shoot off Renz," Niko says, as he grabs his discarded suit jacket from the back of the couch where he left it.

"Sweet man. I'll catch you at work tomorrow," I reply.

"Ally, do you want a ride home or are you gonna hang around waiting for these two?" he says to Ally, as she finishes drinking her coffee.

"Are you going by Kingfisher Place by any chance?" she asks.

"For you I can. It's not too far from where I'm headed. Come on."

"Okay. Soph, I gotta love ya and leave ya but I hope you had a great night last night. You deserved it. Don't listen to whatever your parents say today either," Ally tells Sophia, as she pulls her in for a hug. "Bye Lorenzo. I guess I'll be seeing a lot more of you now," she laughs, which has me smiling.

"I guess so."

She and Niko leave, waving goodbye as they exit. I see Sophia hasn't finished her food but she's managing to drink her coffee which is something, I guess.

"Okay, showering now," I tell her.

She offers a small smile behind the rim of her mug which meets her eyes. I return it before walking through my room to my ensuite. I run the water at my usual cooler temperature and quickly wash my body along with my hair before hopping out and drying myself off. Sophia's discarded clothes I said I'd take care of catch my attention.

I throw on my best shirt and jeans wanting to look somewhat presentable for her parents.

Not knowing what to do with the dress, I walk out to the kitchen to ask Sophia. "Hey, do you want me to get your dress dry-cleaned for you?"

"Oh no that's fine. I'll take it home with me," she rushes to say.

"It's honestly no trouble. I'm dry-cleaning my suit, so I'll send your dress along with it."

"If you're sure."

"I wouldn't suggest it if I wasn't Soph," I tell her. Laying the dress across the back of the couch I sit next to her in the kitchen, taking her hand in mine. "I need you to know I mean what I say, and I say what I mean. There's no hidden agenda behind my words," I say, looking straight into her eyes.

Her eyes drop to her lap, but I place a finger under her chin, raising her eyes back to mine. Something shimmers in their depths.

Uncertainty maybe. But she nods her head slowly anyway, accepting what I've told her.

Wanting to lighten the mood I add, "So fiancee, shall we get this lunch with your parents over with?" A smile lights up her face before she hides it behind her hands.

"Are we crazy to do this?"

"I always thought life was more fun with a little crazy." I shrug my shoulders at her, making her laugh. "You don't have to marry me if you don't want, Sophia. I will never make you do anything you don't want to," I tell her again, making sure she is a hundred percent okay with marrying me.

"No. I want to do this. I want to marry you." Her skin colour deepens with her admission.

"It's settled then. We are doing this. It may not be how we thought this would happen, but we can make it amazing." I lean forward kissing her on the cheek, before standing and placing the rest of the dishes in the dishwasher and setting the cycle to run.

"Why don't we go the whole hog and get married today?" she blurts. My wide eyes face her as I turn around.

"What now?"

"Let's get married today."

"You're serious?" I ask, stunned.

"My dad has drilled it into me about not living with a man before marriage," she says, her eyes dropping to the kitchen bench.

I walk around and pull out the seat I was seated in before. Turning her whole chair around to face me, her eyes lift to mine.

"Is that the only reason you want to rush us to the altar?" I stare into her baby blues.

She nibbles the side of her bottom lip, and I can't help the glance I make to them, wondering if they are as soft as they look.

"Actually, I want you to make good on your promise to fuck me up against the wall with your mask on," she deadpans and after a beat of shock, my boisterous laughter fills the room.

"Honey, I don't need to marry you to make that happen. If you want, I can make good on that right now," I tell her. I watch as she gulps, a deep tinge of pink sets her skin on fire.

She releases a huff before she says, "I don't want you to change your mind okay."

"What?" I ask as her eyes drop to her fingers that pull on the opposite index finger.

"I don't want you to wake up one day and realise you don't want to spend the rest of your life with me," she meekly says.

"Look at me," my soft voice says. I wait until her eyes raise on their own before I continue. "There is nothing I want more than to be your husband. I mean it. I do want a chance to win your heart before we get married though. So, if I promise I won't change my mind will you promise to give me a chance to capture your heart?"

Her eyes flicker back and forth as they search mine for the lie in my statement.

"All right. As long as you don't change your mind."

"Cross my heart and hope to die," I say, crossing my fingers over my heart.

She laughs as her hand lightly swats at me.

"Plus, I saw you puking your guts out last night and I'm still set on marrying you, so I don't think there's anything that will change my mind if that couldn't," I say while laughing at the shocked look on her face.

"Ugh I wasn't that bad, was I?"

"Worse," I joke. I lean forward kissing her cheek as she sits in shock.

"You are trouble," she admonishes.

"With a capital t. Now should we do this?" I ask.

She looks at herself before she says, "Umm I think my parents are going to have a heart attack with me rocking up in your clothes." Which makes us both laugh before my face drops.

"Shoot. We'll have to order an Uber as I have the bike and I don't think that outfit is bike friendly." I raise a brow at her.

"I've never been on a motorbike before," she softly says, her eyes lighting up at the prospect.

"Safety first, love. I'll have to get you a helmet. Plus driving around in my clothes on the back of my bike is not how I want my first impression with your parents as your fiance to go."

"Fair enough. It's already going to be an uphill battle with them," she huffs.

"Well, no time like the present. Let's get this over with then we can enjoy the rest of our first Sunday together," I tell her, which has her smile growing.

"You meant that?"

"Absolutely. Now come on. I'll order the Uber," I tell her, heading back to my room and grabbing my phone.

Chapter Eighteen

Lorenzo

Twenty minutes later, we are on our way across town to the mayor's house. The driver pulls in through the gate after security sees Sophia in the back and lets us through. Slowly inching up the circular driveway, he makes a stop close to the front door for us to get out.

"Here goes nothing I guess," Sophia says, as I open her door for her. Closing it, I grasp her hand in mine as the Uber drives away. She leads me to the front door, opening it and we enter the huge foyer.

"I'll go get cleaned up. You wanna come with me?" she asks, turning to me.

"Sure," I say, following behind Sophia as she leads me up the stairs. Walking down the long hallway, she pushes open a door and is greeted by a kind voice.

"Hello Miss Sophia. Oh, you have company with you today. And male company at that," the little grey-haired lady says, as I step into the room.

"Patrice, this is my fiance, Lorenzo. Lorenzo this is Patrice," she says, introducing us.

"Fiance?" she asks, clutching her chest.

"Yes, it's a long story but I'll explain later. I wondered if you have time to help me get this wig off though?" she kindly asks the older lady, who I can tell she's fond of.

"Yes of course. Let's go to your room."

I follow behind them, hearing Patrice whisper the words handsome and lucky while trying to be discreet. I can't hide the smile Sophia catches on my face when she turns my way to check if I've heard Patrice.

Entering her room, my heart drops as I take in everything. This is her room and it's huge. Bigger than half the size of my gramps' whole house. She has a huge king-sized four-poster bed and a huge walk-in wardrobe that I think is bigger than my kitchen. How do I have anything worth offering her when she has it all already?

Patrice directs her to sit at her large white dresser, staring into the mirror that sits atop it. I stand silently watching as Patrice gets to work applying products then manoeuvring the wig off after the glue loosens. It takes a while, but she gets it off.

Sophia's hair is braided underneath so they both get to work undoing them as fast as they can.

"My hair is a mess now. It needs a wash," she says, looking at herself in the mirror while Patrice puts everything away they used.

I walk up behind her and place my chin on her shoulder, staring at us in the mirror.

I softly whisper, "I like it like this," causing her cheeks to redden. I push her hair to the side and deliver a swift kiss to her cheek before standing straight.

"I'll leave you two to it. Have fun," Patrice says.

"Thanks for your help, Patrice," Sophia says.

The little old lady smiles at us as she leaves the room.

"I'm gonna shower quickly and then we can get this meal over with," she tells me.

It doesn't take Sophia long to shower and change and then I'm following her back down the stairs.

"He'll be fine with me if you would join your mother in the dining hall. We won't be a moment," Holden Philips' voice cuts in before I can follow her.

"Go on. I'll be okay," I say, lowering my voice for only her to hear.

She glances at her dad before wincing at me then nods. She releases my hand before rushing back up the stairs.

"Let's go to my office, shall we?" Holden suggests, turning on his heels and walking away without waiting for an answer. I run my hand through my hair before following behind him.

Entering the huge office that is like his one in town, he walks towards the small cart that has a glass decanter with glasses next to it.

"Whiskey?" he asks, as he pours some into one glass.

"No thank you," I tell him. He turns with his drink in hand, gesturing for me to take a seat in the big brown leather armchair while he walks behind his big desk, taking his own seat.

Taking a sip, he lets the silence stretch between us before he says, "So," and nothing else.

"Soooo," I drag out, waiting for him to add more.

"I don't know how you managed to get Sophia to agree to marry you, but I must say I'm surprised. You're adamant she didn't know who you were before your proposal?"

"Not a clue. Must be my awesome power of persuasion," I tell him.

"Hmm. Well, a contract's a contract. I'll have the money transferred into a trust within forty-eight hours. You can access the trust once you've left the premises for good," he tells me before taking another sip, his eyes watching me.

"Thank you."

"I'll give you ninety days to be out of the premises," he adds, making me wince at the thought of losing my gramps' business. He tips his head back, draining the rest of his glass, before standing and placing it back on the cart. Turning to me he adds, "I'll be getting a prenup drawn up before the wedding."

"I wouldn't think anything less of you Holden," I tell him, standing myself.

Knocking on the door has us both looking when Holden says, "Come in."

Sophia's head pops in as her eyes search the room, then she pushes her way in, walking towards me.

"Mum said lunch is ready to be served," she tells us.

"Well, we don't want to keep her waiting, do we?" Holden says, gesturing for us to walk out before him. Sophia takes my hand in hers, leading the way to their dining hall.

A huge table greets us with four place settings. One down each end and then in the middle there is one on either side, facing each other. Holden and his wife, who I still can't remember the name of, sit at one end of the fancy table each. I follow Sophia's lead and sit opposite her. At least I won't have to yell to talk to her like her parents will have to.

I can't imagine what it must have been like growing up having family dinners like this. They have a personal chef and waiter cooking and serving the meal. The first course is a pumpkin soup which I must say is quite delicious.

We eat in silence and I'm unsure whether to talk at all, so I remain quiet, letting them dictate how this lunch goes.

"So, Lorenzo, my husband told me you're a mechanic?" Sophia's mum starts the conversation with.

"Yes Mrs. Philips. I work over in Cedarville," I keep my tone polite.

"Please call me Kennedy," she says.

144

Ah that's her name. I file it away to memory.

"Cedarville, is a little far. Do you live there as well?"

"I do. My grandfather left me his house when he passed, and I can't bear to part with it. I also work at a local bar on the outskirts of town here. I have an apartment above the bar I rent so I stay there on those nights," I explain, though Cedarville isn't exactly far at all, only thirty minutes away.

"So, your living arrangements aren't exactly stable then?" she politely says, and I realise my fault. She's polite but cunning. Wording things in a certain way to get you to divulge truths before striking when something isn't to her liking.

"It works for me," I tell her, my neck prickling.

"But will it work for Sophia? Do you expect your wife to spend nights without you or to go back and forth between two homes so you can earn minimum wage at two jobs trying to support her?"

"Mum!" Sophia snaps.

"It's okay Sophia," I tell her, waiting until she looks me in the eye. I see the heat in her vision wanting to defend me. "I'm thinking of expanding the mechanics business because I forgot to mention my gramps left me that too," I tell them, keeping my cool, learning to play their game.

Sophia tilts her head out of the corner of my eye while I keep my eyes locked on her mum in a silent war. They will not make me feel unworthy of their daughter, though I already feel that way. I push the feeling down as I fight my thoughts. I am good enough for her, and she deserves more than what these so-called parents have to offer her.

"So, if you expand, will you move locations then?" she asks.

The next course of chicken breasts with asparagus and some other vegetables is served. I thank the waiter as they deliver my food.

"I'm not sure. I'll have to talk it over with my fiancee and get her thoughts on what she would like to do," I tell her. My hackles rise with every sentence that comes out of her mouth.

"You know if you two are going to continue on with this charade I want you to behave as respectful members of this family," her dad interrupts our conversation.

"It isn't a charade," I state.

"Whatever you want to call it then. I won't be disrespected by you abandoning your own party we so graciously threw for you. Going forward, you will show us the respect we deserve as parents and as the mayor," his voice rises, as his face reddens.

"Well respect is earned not demanded," I state. My voice as steady as a rock. His nostrils flare as he stares me down.

"I'll demand what the hell I want. Now what you do is a reflection on me, and I won't have you tarnishing the reputation I've spent years building up. If this behaviour is going to continue, then maybe you are both too immature to get married."

"Holden," his wife says.

"Enough," Sophia yells, as she pushes her chair back from the table. "I don't care what you say or think. I'm marrying Lorenzo and, you know what, if you continue to behave like this, then you have no place in my life. So, deal with that. Lorenzo let's go," she says, as she walks away from the table.

"Sophia," her mum calls after her.

I push my own chair back ready to follow her, but Holden's words halt me.

"You will never be good enough for her. She'll come crying back to us soon when she realises there's nothing you have to offer her."

I clench my fists at my sides but don't give him the satisfaction of looking at him as I walk past him without a word. I head back the way to Sophia's room hoping that's the direction she went in. I find her there with a bag on the bed as she throws things haphazardly into it.

"Could we go look at your house in Cedarville?" Sophia gently asks, from across the room.

"Sure, we can do that," I tell her, my first genuine smile appearing on my face since we entered this house. "I was actually going to head back today."

"Okay let's do it."

"I know you don't want to stay with me before marriage so are you sure about this?" I rush.

Twisting her hands, she looks at me as I smile at her.

"Are you sure you don't want to get married? I know a celebrant who lives in Cedarville that I'm sure could squeeze us in today."

"You want to marry me that bad?" I tease.

"I'm surprised you aren't running for the hills after that."

"Nothing will change my mind about marrying you. I mean it. I need you to start believing it," I tell her, as I move forward and grasp her hands. "You know, since I promised you all of my Sundays, how about we make our first one together an epic one?" I ask.

Her lips tug upwards and her eyes light up.

"You're serious? I don't want to pressure you," she rushes.

"Soph, marrying you is not a hardship on my part. So, what do you say? You wanna get married today?"

"Yeah, I do," she squeals, as she jumps into my arms. I squeeze her hard against me before I release her feet to the floor.

"Come on, finish packing then. We have a wedding to get to," I tell her.

She kisses me on the cheek before she turns back to her packing. She grabs a suitcase out from the closest and throws things into it. I offer to help, and she tells me to shove it in and she will deal with it later. We do it all with the brightest smiles on our faces and I pinch myself because there's no way I thought this crazy plan would work out the way it has. I truly do want to win her heart but knowing she's choosing me too means the world to me. She heads into the bathroom and returns with a smaller bag, zipping it up and I'm guessing it's toiletries.

She grabs a black scrunchie off the dresser and twists her hair up into a messy bun and I'm thankful the red hair is back. There was nothing wrong with the black; it just wasn't her. She's more herself with her red.

"You ready?" I ask as she turns to me, hair up and a smile on her face.

"Yeah, I think so."

She's about to grab her bags but I say, "I got it," grabbing them instead and hoisting one over my shoulder. Her cheeks redden before she turns away, leading me out of her room. I follow her down the stairs.

She takes a sharp turn at the bottom of the stairs, heading a different direction to where we have been today. Entering another living room, her mum sits there looking through a stack of papers and pamphlets, her eyes glancing at us over the rim of her black reading glasses as we enter.

"I'm leaving with Lorenzo now," Sophia says.

"That's fine Sophia. I need you back here on Friday. We need to go through the event for the Finlay's charity and work out some details they would like changed."

"Sure. Friday it is then," she says.

"It was a pleasure to meet you, Lorenzo. I hope to see you again soon," she says, dropping her eyes back to her work in front of her.

"Same to you," I say, feeling anything but pleasure. I got grilled by her during the meal and now she is acting as if it was nothing.

Sophia walks away so I follow again. She leads me through to a large internal garage that houses five impeccable looking cars. What I wouldn't give to be able to look under the hood of these beauties.

The beep of the key fob draws my attention to the grey Audi at the end of the line, its lights flashing as the door unlocks. Sophia opens the boot for me to place her bags inside.

"Do you want to drive since you know where we're going?" she asks, holding the keys up.

I smile as I take the keys, my fingers wrapping around hers as I look into her eyes for a second before letting her go. I slide into the driver's side and Sophia tells me there's a button for the garage on the keys as well. I slowly back the car out getting a feel for it, then close the garage.

Driving through the windy town streets, we hit the long highway that will take us to Cedarville.

"Have you been out to Cedarville much?" I ask, as we drive along, the soft music humming in the background.

"I think we came out here once as a child if I recall."

"Have you ventured out of Spring Mountain often?" I ask, because from the sounds of it I don't think she has.

Her hands twist on her lap before she answers.

"Not really. I went to college in another state and that was because I argued it had a better business programme compared to what the local college had to offer. If my parents had their way, I never would have left at all," she sighs.

"Do you want to travel?" I ask, wanting to get to know her more.

"I was planning to go on an O.E but my parents kept holding me back from going."

"We could go together on this O.E if you like?" I tell her, hating the fact her parents dictate so much of her life.

"You have your two jobs, Lorenzo. Wouldn't it be hard to up and leave for a few months?" she asks.

"For you, I would make it work," I tell her, reaching for her hand and holding on to it. "How about I make you a deal? You can pick anywhere you want to go for the honeymoon, no expense spared," I say, wanting to make her happy.

"You don't have to do that Lorenzo."

"I want to. I could use a holiday too. I haven't had one before. Since my gramps died, I've had to work and support myself, so I've never had the chance for a holiday," I tell her.

"Really?"

"Yeah. Holidays weren't a priority in my life. But we need a honeymoon to celebrate this crazy life we are about to embark on," I tell her, laughing softly which she joins in with.

"I'll get planning," she says, squeezing my hand.

We spend the rest of the drive, asking each other questions and getting to know details about the other we didn't already know. I realise her parents' control over her runs deeper than I ever could have imagined. I want her to be happy, but I also wonder if what I have to offer will be enough.

Chapter Nineteen

Sophia

"Do you want to ring this wedding celebrant of yours to see if they can fit us in?" he asks, as he drives down the highway.

I pull my phone out of my handbag and swipe until I find the number I'm after.

"Hey Curtis, how are you? I was wondering if you had any free time today? Well not exactly hang out. I'm more in need of a celebrant than a friend today. Yes, I know it's sudden but please could you help one of your favourite friends out? Pretty please? Thanks, you're the best. Umm hold on." I mute the phone before turning to Lorenzo. "Do you want to go straight to his place and get married as we are, or do you want to change?" I ask.

His gaze rakes over both our outfits before he speaks, "We don't have to rush this. We can wait if you want a big wedding."

"I don't want any of that. I just want to marry you," I tell him, taking his hand that rests on the gear stick, intertwining our fingers.

"Whatever you want to do, I'm down. If you want to change, we can stop at my place." Unmuting the phone, I lift it back to my ear.

"Curtis, would you be free in a couple of hours? Yeah? Great. We will see you then. Thanks, I owe you one," I say, before hanging up the phone. "Okay so to your place to change and then to our wedding," I inform him, giving his hand a squeeze.

"We're crazy, you know that right?" he says, as he smiles at me.

"I kind of like the craziness," I reply, which has him chuckling. "Oh, and we need to ring Niko and Ally because we need witnesses."

"What's one more stop on this crazy train for them?" he jokes, making me laugh.

Lorenzo turns the Audi into a cul-de-sac and pulls the car into a driveway.

"Home sweet home," he says, turning the car off and angles himself towards me. I look out the front windscreen taking in the white cottage in front of me. The paint looks freshly done and it's obviously well maintained. The grass has been neatly trimmed as if it was done recently. I turn to Lorenzo who has been watching me the whole time.

"It's cute," I tell him, because it does look like a cute little cottage.

He opens his door, so I follow his lead doing the same. He grabs my bags from the trunk then leads us to the door. Unlocking it, he holds it open, letting me walk inside first.

I follow the beige carpet down the small hallway that leads to one bedroom on the left and another on the right.

"This is my room," he tells me, gesturing to the one on the left. "That's a spare." I nod, smiling at him. He takes over the tour, walking me down the hall. Cream wallpaper surrounds us, peeling in a couple spots. We enter a living room, which has a couch similar to the one in his apartment above the bar and a big screen T.V sits in front of it, on top of an entertainment unit. Surrounding the walls are photos of a younger Lorenzo with an older man. There are a few of an older couple as well.

"Your grandparents?" I ask, pointing to their wedding photo.

"Yeah, that's them. They raised me."

"Tell me if it's none of my business but where were your parents?"

"My mum, their daughter passed away when I was about ten from a drug overdose. It wasn't long after my nana died too so it was hard on my gramps," he tells me, looking over at a photo of a teen Lorenzo with his gramps.

I can feel the love he has for that man by the adoration he looks at the photo with. It makes me reach my hand out to link my fingers through his, giving him a squeeze. He stares at our linked hands for a beat before raising his eyes to mine.

"My gramps was more of a dad to me then the guy who knocked up my mum was. He's in prison on assault charges the last I heard, but I have nothing to do with him and it's better that way. I don't feel I missed out on anything, not with my grandparents taking over the parental role in my life anyway," he explains.

"Did you have much to do with your mum?"

"Nah. She tried to come around one time when I was little, but my nana told me to go play in the room with my blocks while she talked to her. She was high and was needing money for her next fix. She hadn't come back for me. I heard my grandparents talking about it later that night when they thought I was in bed."

"I'm sorry if I'm being nosey and opening old wounds," I tell him, feeling like it's something I shouldn't have pried into. He squeezes my hand before grabbing the other.

"No, it's fine. If we are gonna have a proper marriage, then we need to be able to talk about stuff. I haven't talked to anyone about it before. It was always me and my grandparents. I don't consider the people who gave birth to me my parents because they did nothing for me. My grandparents took custody of me when I was about a month old because my mum wasn't coping, and she was already hooked on drugs at that point."

"I'm sorry," I tell him, not knowing what else to say.

"Nothing for you to be sorry for," he says, leaning forward and kissing my forehead. "Let's finish this tour," he says, tugging my hand down the rest of the hallway. He shows me the small bathroom and then at the back of the house is the kitchen. Small white cupboards line the top and bottom of the small space. An oven sits in the middle amongst the bench space and then in the corner is a tiny square wooden table with four matching white chairs with little red flowers painted over them.

"I've been meaning to renovate but haven't had the time," he tells me, as I look around.

"Lorenzo, this house is perfect as it is. I can feel more love in this house than there has ever been in any of our houses," I tell him, meaning it. My house doesn't feel like a home; it's cold and feels like a display home, but you can feel all the love that surrounds us here. On the kitchen frame are markings showing how much Lorenzo had grown through the years. The photos are filled with happy memories. My parents' house doesn't have photos hanging up. It is decorated with art more than memories of our family.

"I know it's not much. The kitchen table is tiny."

"Hey, do you know how many times I've sat at that horrible thing my parents call a table and wished for something cozy like this?" I tell him, gesturing to the adorable table.

"Really?"

"Really. That monstrosity my parents want to eat at is horrible. You saw it. You practically have to yell to uphold a conversation." I laugh at the thought of the many dinners I've endured at that table over the years.

"Well, it was quite obscene," he says, his dimple appearing.

"That's putting it nicely." We glance at each other before both laughing.

He heads back down the hall picking up my bag he'd dropped in the hallway. He carries it back to where the doors of the rooms are and stands there. "So, I know we are gonna get married but I meant it when I said I wanna capture your heart first, so if you feel more comfortable in the spare room for now, I'm more than happy for you to do that. I want you comfortable," he says, handing me my bag, letting me make the choice.

"Thanks Lorenzo. I might take the spare room for now if that's okay?"

"It's more than okay," he tells me, pushing the door to the spare room open fully for me to enter. A perfectly made double bed lies in the centre of the room with a dresser off to the side of it. There's a small window that looks to the neighbour's property, the sun shining through it.

"This used to be my room growing up," he tells me, as he leans against the door frame, arms crossed.

"Really?" I ask, looking around the space, trying to picture Lorenzo from my past being in this space.

"Yeah. I spent a lot of nights dreaming about a certain red head back in the day," he admits, causing me to whip around, my skin heating. He winks again before standing up straight. "Settle in. I'll call Niko and be back," he says, turning and heading out the door.

I drop to the bed, taking a deep breath. This is really happening. I'm going to marry Lorenzo. I haven't taken a minute since his proposal to think it all through. I know it's crazy. It's like I'm headed straight into oncoming traffic, but my feet won't stop, propelling me forward. My brain is screaming out to take a minute, but my feet are walking me straight into the chaos.

When I think about it, I do want to marry him and get away from my parents. I'm not dumb either. My dad had other suitors trying to find me and propose last night. The phantom of the opera masked guy and his friend made it clear what their intentions were

155

when their whispered conversation was overheard so I managed to steer clear of him for the whole night. He looked to be in his early twenties so my dad mustn't have cared that we'd have such a large age gap. At least marrying Lorenzo would be on my terms. He makes me feel seen and listened to and with that hope, I'm sure we can learn to love each other.

Standing back up, satisfied with my decision, the zip on my bag squeals as it runs along. I sort my clothes into the dresser drawers before I take my toiletry bag and walk it down to the bathroom. With a pop, the small mirror above the sink releases, showing the cabinet behind it. Ally always tells me how she checks out guys' medicine cabinets and that you can find out a lot about them from what they have in there. All I see is some shaving foam, a couple razors, some band aids, extra toothpaste, a bottle of Advil and a box of unopened condoms. My lips twist to the side before my nosey fingers reach up, grabbing the unopened box and turning it over to check out the box. Magnum size. A gulp travels down my throat, as my face burns with heat. Nervous energy has my fingers juggling the box, nearly dropping it in my haste to put it back exactly as it was. My hand wraps around the Advil bottle, closes the cabinet then I step back into the kitchen. I open a few cabinets before I find one that holds the glasses, filling up the glass with water from the tap. I tip two pills into my hand, popping them in my mouth and washing them down with my drink. My head had begun pounding again. A combination of overthinking and my hangover.

I pull one of the pretty painted chairs out, taking a seat to wait for Lorenzo to return. His door closes a few minutes later.

"Sophia?" he calls.

"In the kitchen," I call back, and he appears.

"Did you get unpacked?"

"Yeah, I did. I took some Advil for my hangover. Hope you don't mind."

"What's mine is yours Sophia. You can take or use whatever is in this house and my apartment too," he tells me.

"Thanks."

"You're welcome," he says, pulling out a seat for himself. "So, I told Niko of our grand plan and I think he spent more time laughing than listening, but he said if you rang Ally and gave her his number then he could pick her up on his way."

"Wish me luck. I'll ring her now." I walk back down to the room I'm staying in and grab my phone from my bag. The dial tone sounds before she answers.

"Hey babe, how was brunch?"

"A headache. Hey, are you free?" I ask, my nose scrunches though she can't see me.

"Yeah, just lounging around. Do you need something?"

"Are you free to come to a wedding?" I ask, my eyes now scrunching as I wait for her response.

"Wedding? Who's getting married?"

"Me," I all but whisper.

"Whaaaat?" she screeches. "Sophia Marie Philips, explain yourself," she demands.

"We decided to bring the wedding forward to today," I tell her, as I hold in my laugh at her reaction.

"I left you less than four hours ago and there wasn't a wedding date set. You had only gotten engaged last night. Oh my gosh, someone catch me, I think I'm fainting," she says, as her drama queen emerges.

"Don't be so dramatic. We're set on getting married and want to do it now. Why wait?"

"To possibly think it through properly first. You've been in each other's orbits for less than twenty-four hours. What if you get married but you hate the way he snores or something or find out he hates animals. Then what?"

157

My lips twist in thought before I hop off the bed and walk back down the hallway where Lorenzo is still sitting at the table. His warm smile greets me as I walk into the room which makes my heart randomly flutter.

"Lorenzo, do you snore?" I ask.

"Oh my gosh, you're asking him. Jeez Louise girl. You're cuckoo," Ally's voice chimes through on the phone, as I hold the phone to my ear.

Lorenzo's smile grows as he watches me.

"I'm not sure if I do or not but I can't be as bad as Ally. She was snoring like a freight train last night," he yells, so Ally can hear him.

Her gasp has me covering my hand over my laugh, so she doesn't hear me.

"I bet he's lousy in bed," Ally throws back, but only I can hear her. My gaze trickles over Lorenzo before I reply to her.

"I doubt it," I say to her, which makes Lorenzo's brow pop in question as I hold his gaze.

"Nothing I say is going to change your mind. You are both as crazy as the other. Ask about the animals though to be sure."

"Do you like animals?" He chuckles.

"I've never had a pet, but I like animals. I've always wanted a dog, but never had the time to give to them but if you want pets, we can get pets. I'll get you a donkey if that's what you want," he offers.

"He sounds too good to be true," Ally says after his speech.

"Can we call him Kenneth?" I ask, which makes Lorenzo's chest shake with laughter.

"You can call him whatever you want. Now have I passed the test Ally? Can I marry your best friend today?" he yells for her.

"Fine but if it all goes belly up, you know I'll have the tequila ready," she tells me.

I give Lorenzo a slight nod to let him know she's okay with us getting married.

"Thanks Ally. I couldn't do this without you."

"I know. That's what besties are for. Now send me the address. Do you need anything?"

"No, I think I'm good, and I'll send you Niko's number. He said he would pick you up on his way."

"Great. Sounds like a plan. And Soph?"

"Yeah?"

"I'm happy for you. I hope it all works out."

"Thanks. Me too."

"Okay. Send me the number. I'm gonna go get ready and I'll see you soon," she says, before hanging up the phone.

"What's Niko's number?" I ask Lorenzo. He prattles it off, so I text it to Ally and then save it in my phone. "What's your number?" I ask. He recites his digits, so I press call once I plug them in and his phone starts ringing from his pants pocket. "That's me, so save your soon-to-be wife's number," I joke, which makes his eyes shine at me.

"Gonna save you under wifey," he tells me, which makes my skin heat at the thought that in a few short hours I will be someone's wife. "I like the sound of that," he confesses.

"Me too," I admit, which makes his dimple pop.

Chapter Twenty

Sophia

"Out of my way," Ally bellows, as she and Niko barge through the front door.

"Ally what the hell?" I call, as she stomps her way down the hall towards me with her hands full like she owns the place.

"Where is he?" she asks, as her eyes flit around the space.

"Lorenzo? He's in the kitchen."

"Lorenzo, cover your eyes. You can't see your blushing bride until she is walking down the aisle," she yells.

Lorenzo chuckles from where I assume he still sits at the kitchen table.

"Whatever you say, Ally," he replies.

"Oh my gosh Ally. What are you doing?" I ask, as she drags me down the hallway.

"Which room has your stuff in it?"

"That one," I say, pointing to my door so she pulls me past a laughing Niko as he makes his way down the hall to Lorenzo. Once inside, she closes the door and releases me. "What are you playing at?" I ask, crossing my arms over my chest.

"It may not be the traditional wedding in a sense but it's still your wedding day Soph. Hopefully it's the only one, so we are doing it right even though it's a rush. Now sit." She directs me to sit on the bed with her finger, so I do as she says but not without a roll of my eyes. She throws all the stuff she was carrying down on my bed beside me.

"Please don't tell me that is a wedding dress in there," I accuse as she grabs the zipper of the garment bag and slowly pulls it down. Gently she removes the dress out of its covering to show me.

"No, not a wedding dress but it's the nicest dress I have that I thought might work," she tells me, as she showcases it to me.

"Aww it's beautiful Ally," I gush. My fingers reach out to run them along the soft material of the cream dress.

"Well come on, let's get your makeup and hair done with all the supplies I've wrangled together and then we can sort the dress," she instructs, as she starts wading her way through a makeup bag. She pulls out products, lining them up on the bed so she can see what she has. "How about you go have a shower and then by the time you are done, I'll be ready to start."

"Yes sir," I joke, which causes her to stop and smile at me.

"Don't let Lorenzo see you," she warns, as I turn the handle on the door to leave.

"Niko?" I call from the open doorway.

"Yeah?" he calls back, as he steps into view from the other end of the house in the kitchen.

"Could you cover Lorenzo's eyes while I head to the bathroom to shower?" I ask, which makes the sound of their laughter carry down the hall.

"I'm on it. You're good to come down," Niko calls back. I step out of the room and walk down the hall. As I reach the kitchen, I shield my eyes, so I won't see Lorenzo and quickly step into the bathroom.

"Towels are in the cupboard in there," Lorenzo's voice seeps through the door. I glance around finding the cupboard he's talking about and retrieve a towel.

"Thank you," I call out. Feeling ridiculous, I shake my head. I strip my clothes off and place them in the laundry basket and step into the warm spray, careful to keep my hair from getting wet. My hands make quick work of showering and then when I'm wrapped in my towel I call back through the closed door. "I'm coming out."

"All clear," Niko calls out, so I peek through the door with my hand shielding my eyes again and rush back to Ally.

"Good timing. I'm ready," Ally announces, as I step into the room. I drop back onto the bed, and she gets to work on my face. She applies so many different creams and dabs and brushes at my skin I'm worried I will look like a totally different person by the time she is finished. "What should we do with your hair? Curl or straighten?" she asks.

"Curl, I think," I tell her, and without letting me look in the mirror to see my makeup, she gets to work on curling my hair. She doesn't want me looking at anything until I have my dress on so I can get the full effect of it in one go. She works quickly and sprays nearly a can's worth of hairspray in my hair that we end up choking on the fumes.

She looks me over when she thinks she's finished, nodding to herself.

"Alright, time for the dress," she tells me. I sift through my suitcase and manage to find a cream-coloured strapless bra and a matching pair of underwear to go with it. I should at least match on my wedding day though I don't think I will be ready to have a wedding night but it's the thought that counts. I get Ally to turn around so I can slip them on and then she helps me into the silky knee length dress. It swishes against my thighs as she ties the ribbon around my neck to hold the halter neck in place. It has gentle beading around the bust and I'm lucky Ally and I are similar in sizing so it fits pretty well.

I step up to look in the mirror that sits on top of the dresser and my mouth drops open.

"You like?" Ally asks, as her face pops up behind my shoulder.

"I look so beautiful," I tell her in awe.

"You always look beautiful; all I did was enhance it. Now give me the address of where we are going and I'll pass it on to the guys so they can head out first and we will meet them there," she says.

"Aren't you taking this a little far?"

"Of course not. I'm hoping this is the only wedding you ever have. It may have come about from some weird circumstances, but I think your soon to be husband is gonna be a keeper. Trust me I've got good feelings about this," she tells me, looking me straight in the eye.

"Here." I hand her my phone where my friend Curtis has sent the address he will be at. She takes my phone out of the room, and I assume she heads to the guys. I admire myself in the mirror. My bright hair hangs in loose curls down my back and my makeup doesn't look too heavy. It enhances the blue of my eyes and makes them pop.

"See you guys there," Niko calls out, as I hear the front door slam shut and Ally joins me back in the room.

"Slip some shoes on and then we are good to go," she tells me, handing me my phone back.

I slip it into my purse and grab some sparkly cream heels I'd luckily packed when we'd left my parents'.

"All set," I tell Ally, as I stand in them.

"Let's go get you married," she says, making my face hurt from the huge smile that shines on it.

Chapter Twenty One

Lorenzo

We pull up to the address Ally gave us. I didn't have many options for suits, but luckily, I had my trusty black one I used for pretty much every occasion. Although I don't get dressed up all that often, so it's hardly worn. Sweat trickles down my neck as we walk down the path leading to the back of a property per the instructions from Ally. Once we round the corner we are in a beautiful yard with a small canopy. A guy stands under it reading over some notes. His eyes rise when he hears us approach and an award-winning smile lights his face.

"Oh my gosh, which one of you devilish hunks are marrying my Sophia?" he squeals. I glance at Niko and see his own smile looking at me.

"That would be me. I'm Lorenzo and this is my best man, Niko." I hold my hand out to shake his after I introduce us, but he pulls me in for a hug instead.

"Lorenzo, you're gonna learn quick smart around here that I'm a hugger. No time for those old school handshakes around me. I'm Curtis " he says, before he steps into Niko who gives him a hug too.

"Nice to meet you," Niko says.

"Now Lorenzo, have you got anything you wanted to add as part of the ceremony? I'm guessing it's all very last minute as Sophia hasn't mentioned she's dating anyone, so do you have vows? You can wing it if you like, or we can do the traditional ones if that's easier?" he asks.

"I think I'll wing it but if I look stuck can you step in and help me out?" I ask, and his smile grows.

"Perfect. Now is Sophia far away?"

"No. They were gonna leave soon after us so they shouldn't be long."

"Great. Okay, well I'll get you to stand on this side and Niko, stand behind him. You guys can face that side of the house so you can see when she comes around."

We let him move us into position and then he double checks his notes before picking up a bouquet of simple white roses he has sitting on the table beside him.

"Now I usually am a great one-man band, but I wanted Sophia to have some beautiful photos because you need photos of your wedding day. So, I called my friend Vaughn, who honestly lives around the corner. He's a professional photographer and he was free, so if you'd like some professional photos to remember the day, he's already in the house waiting to be used for a fee of course. Remember you will want to remember Sophia in this moment," he blabbers, and I can't help the laugh that escapes.

"Whatever his fee is, I'll pay it. Tell him to get a lot of her."

His face lights up with glee as he claps.

"Curtis, are you sure you don't work in sales? You've got the persuasive touch there," I add, making him laugh.

"I love weddings and love love, but if I ever make a career change, I'll keep it in mind. Now I'll tell Vaughn he's good to go ahead and I'll text Sophia to wait out the front until I'm ready," he says, as he waltzes off into the house.

"This is quite a good setup for a last-minute wedding," Niko says beside me. His eyes trailing over the immaculate rose gardens surrounding us. The canopy has twinkly lights attached that could be used at nighttime to set the mood.

"Yeah, for a thrown together wedding, it sure is coming together nicely," I tell him, wiping my hands on my pants legs.

"Are you nervous?"

"Yeah. Is it obvious?" I joke, which makes us laugh.

"No need to be nervous Renz. She already said yes to your crazy plan. The hard part is over now, enjoy getting married," he says, making my heart beat faster in my chest.

"Married. Man, who would have thought?" I say, shaking my head in disbelief.

Curtis starts running back around the side of the house, a huge smile on his face.

"They've arrived. Vaughn is getting some pictures of her before she makes her entry."

I nod as I try to think of some vows to say but nothing I say in my head sounds good enough.

A few minutes later, Curtis pulls his phone from his pocket and checks it.

"They're ready," he squeals, before playing a sweet melody from his phone that is hooked up to a speaker near the house. Niko pats me on the back as I clasp my hands in front of me to keep from fidgeting as I wait for Sophia to walk around the corner.

First comes Ally whose wide smile shines our way then a few steps behind her is Sophia. The first full look at her and I blow out a huge breath as my heart thunders under my shirt. I've always thought of Sophia as beautiful but, at this moment, she's captivating. I feel it in my bones. I made the right decision waiting for her to become my wife.

Her timid smile shines at me as she steps closer and when she stops right in front of me, my fingers itch to caress her face. She hands the bouquet Curtis gave to her back to Ally and then holds her hands out for me to take. I grasp both and squeeze as my eyes wander over her face, committing it to memory. Out of the corner of my eye, I catch sight of a guy with a camera which I assume must be Vaughn, and I'm thankful Curtis had the foresight to think of photos. I can't wait to frame one of her for our house.

"Friends, we are gathered here today to witness the joining of Sophia and Lorenzo in marriage," Curtis begins. I keep my eyes on Sophia the whole time he talks until he says, "Lorenzo would you like to start with your vows?"

My eyes bug out of my head, but I nod and he offers me an encouraging smile. Squeezing Sophia's fingers again, I start.

"Sophia, I'm not sure where to begin or if this will be any good, but I'll give it my best shot. The first day I met you all those years ago when we were sixteen, I couldn't take my eyes off you. I was captivated by the girl with the wild red hair and the beautiful, freckled skin. You probably couldn't tell, but when I talked to you that day in the gym, I was so nervous. I went home to tell my gramps about you after school that day and he told me when you found a girl who made you as nervous as you made me, it meant she was worth it. He also told me not to worry about girls and to focus on my schooling," I say, which causes our small group to laugh.

"I did what he suggested, and I focused on school, but you were always there. It may not have felt like it, but I had the biggest crush on you since way back then, and now is probably the perfect time to admit it. You asked me if there's anyone else I would rather marry, and the answer has always been no. I never thought seriously about marriage until the night fate brought us back together, and since then I've never thought of anyone else except you when

167

marriage comes to mind. So, Sophia, I may not always get it right but together, I'm sure we can work through anything.

"I promise to always protect you and to keep you safe. I promise if we have bad days, I won't stop loving you. I promise to put you above all others, and we will work through everything together as a team. And lastly, I promise to give you all of my Sundays. Forever."

Sophia wipes at the tear that threatens to push over her lash line at my words. Curtis blowing his nose draws our attention.

"Sorry, excuse me. That was so beautiful," he gushes, as he wipes his own tears away causing us to chuckle. "Alright Sophia, your vows now."

"Well, it's a hard act to follow but here goes. L is for Likeable. O is for Obviously gorgeous. R is for Radiance. E is for Extremely smart. N is for Nice. Z is for Zen and O is for One of a kind."

My eyes widen as I remember the note from the rose on the day my gramps died. I never in a million years thought it was from her.

"It was you?"

Her lips twist to the side before she nods. The shade of pink colouring her skin under her makeup.

"I now know that day was probably the worst day for you, but I promise going forward if you want, we can make happy memories surrounding it instead. I promise to grow in love with you and take care of you in any way you need. I promise to be your partner in everything and build a life with you we can be proud of. I promise after this act, I will be your voice of reason because it's now clear you get crazy ideas that you run with," she says, which we all laugh at.

I feel my own emotion bubble up behind my eyes.

She squeezes my fingers before continuing, "I also promise if you want to follow any of these crazy ideas, I will follow you as your wife wherever you want to lead me. Together always."

Curtis discreetly tries to blow his nose, but he can't hide it, and we all laugh.

"Okay enough of that, have we got rings?" he asks, and my eyes widen as we didn't have time for that.

"Umm, we didn't think of rings," I say, but Niko jumps in to help.

"I've got this one you guys can use," he says, as he twists off the black ring he wears on his middle finger.

"Oooh and I've got this one." Ally jumps in, handing over a ring to Sophia. We switch them over as I hand her Niko's and she hands me Ally's.

"Well, it fits with the theme of winging it," I say, which draws a smile across her face.

"Okay. Do you Lorenzo shoot what's your last name?" Curtis whispers, though we can all hear him.

"Moretti."

"Do you, Lorenzo Moretti, take Sophia Philips to be your lawfully wedded wife? To have and to hold from this day forward?"

"I do," I say, pushing Ally's ring onto Sophia's wedding ring finger.

"Do you, Sophia Philips, take Lorenzo Moretti to be your lawfully wedded husband? To have and to hold from this day forward?"

"I do," she says, and her shaky hand pushes Niko's ring onto my finger.

"By the power vested in me, I proudly pronounce you husband and wife. Lorenzo, you may kiss your bride," Curtis says, and I glance at him before turning back to Sophia.

"Hi wife," I whisper, which makes her smile grow before she replies,

"Hi husband," she whispers back, which makes my own smile grow. My hand caresses her cheek. My thumb strokes her cheekbone

169

before I wrap my other arm around her waist and pull her in close. I tighten the grip around her and angle my face as I close the distance. Her soft as silk lips meet mine as my heart jumps about to leap out of my chest. I tease her as I run the tip of my tongue along the seam of her lips before I pull back. Sophia has other plans though. Her hands grab my face and pull my lips back to her forcing a chuckle to erupt out of me as her mouth opens and she takes the kiss she wants. I lift her off her feet, holding her to me as we share our first proper kiss, and I can't believe it's as husband and wife. We explore each other and I thread my fingers through her hair, keeping her mouth pressed to mine. When she moans into my mouth, I hear Niko's voice.

"Okay guys, you might want to get a room."

I pull away from my wife.

Her eyes twinkle at me as she shrugs her shoulders before she says, "What can I say? My husband's a good kisser," which causes me to press another soft kiss to her lips.

"Well, it's a good thing we are married. You can kiss me whenever you want," I tell her, as I watch the pink colouring spread down her neck to her throat.

"Congrats Renz," Niko says, as he pats me on the back. I place Sophia on her feet and release her. She hugs Ally and I hug Niko and then we switch. Then we both pull Curtis in for a hug as he blows his nose again then wipes his tears. He really does love love. He then directs us to the table where we sign the marriage certificate.

"Let's get some group photos," Vaughn suggests, and we pose around the canopy. Some paired up and others as a group. Curtis has a couple of bottles of wine he pulls out, saying how he wishes it was champagne, but wine will have to do.

We each take a glass before Niko makes a toast.

"Here's to these two crazy cats. Seeing you two together I'm sure this is the start of something amazing. I wish you a lifetime of love, trust and happiness. Here's to the happy couple."

"Hear hear," Curtis and Vaughn chant, before we all clink glasses and take a sip. I link my fingers with Sophia's wanting to keep her close.

"So, what's the plan for the rest of the day?" Niko asks.

I glance to Sophia and tilt my head before asking, "Home?" I watch as her eyes light up as her smile grows.

"Sounds perfect," she tells me.

"Niko, can you give me a ride back and we can let these love birds go," Ally asks.

"Yeah sure."

"I'll grab my things later Soph. I'm so happy for you," Ally tells her, as she wraps her in her arms before saying goodbye.

"Vaughn, grab your phone and I'll give you my details," I tell him.

He places his now empty wine glass on the table as Curtis and Sophia talk. He pulls out his phone and I reach forward and touch his elbow to lead him further away so they can't hear us.

"Do you print out photos as well or do you give us the collection?" I ask him.

"I can print too if you like. What are you thinking?" he whispers back.

"Could you pick the best few and have them blown up so they're a bit bigger and frame them or something?" I ask. His eyes light up.

"Yes," he squeals, and he must see my wide eyes as he tones it down before Curtis and Sophia catch on to the fact I'm up to something.

"Thanks man. Here open your phone, I'll give you my number and email," I tell him, and prattle it off for him. "Send me the invoice. Whatever the cost man and add extra for it being last minute. We appreciate it," I tell him, and he pulls me in for a hug. Guess he's a hugger too.

"Are you ready to go?" Sophia asks, as she walks over to us.

"Sure am. Send me that invoice," I tell Vaughn, and we say goodbye to Curtis and Vaughn as we head to the car.

"I'm starving," Sophia says, as I open the passenger door for her which makes me throw my head back and laugh.

"Well, there we go. My first job as your husband is to feed you. How about we grab some takeout on our way home. Do you like burgers?" I ask.

"Yeah, I could go for a burger," she says, as she sits in the car, pulling her dress in before I shut the door.

Chapter Twenty Two

Sophia

We head through a drive thru and I ask Lorenzo to order me whatever he is having as I haven't been to this takeout place before. With our delicious cargo on board, he heads back to his house, and we change into comfier clothes before meeting in the kitchen. I take a seat at the table while he dishes up the food. He places a plate with a burger and fries in front of me before putting his own food on his plate. We eat in silence. I finish all my fries first before unwrapping my burger. A moan slips out after my first mouthwatering bite.

"Oh my gosh, that is so good," I mumble, while chewing which has his smile shining at me.

"Glad you like it. It's my favourite," he admits, before he takes another bite of his own burger.

"Well, I can see why. It's delicious," I say, before taking another bite. We finish off our food and Lorenzo clears the dishes.

"Can I ask you something I'm curious about?"

"Sure," I reply with raised brows, as I wait for him to speak.

"What is it about Sundays that make them so important to you?" he asks, as he pulls his chair back out and sits down again.

My fingers wrap around my drink while I gaze into his eyes. He stares at me and patiently waits while I gather my thoughts.

"Growing up my parents were never around. I spent my weeks at school and then my weekends were mostly spent alone while my father was away on business. My mother would sometimes go with him or else she'd be at the house working so I wouldn't see her. Growing up I promised myself if I ever had a family of my own, I would prioritise a day. One day a week where we spent the whole day together. What is the point in having a family if you don't spend any time together?" I explain to him. Nerves begin to get the better of me as he sits and stares for the longest time before he stands. He steps in front of me before he crouches.

"I'm sorry you had to endure so much loneliness growing up. I meant it when I said I'd give you all of my Sundays. But I want to make you another promise. If you ever need me, tell me. If you want to spend time with me, say the word and we will. I may get carried away with work from time to time and I'm human so I may make mistakes. But if you need me, I'll be there. I don't want you to ever feel that lonely again," he says, before he takes my hand in his and delivers a kiss to the back of it.

"Thanks Lorenzo," I whisper, as the words choke in my throat from his sweet admission. How can this perfect guy exist I wonder as my vision becomes blurry with unshed tears.

"Now enough with the serious stuff, do you want to relax and watch a movie?" he asks, as he stands, grabs his own drink and takes a noisy sip through his straw.

"Sure," I tell him, picking up my own drink. He gestures with his head to follow him while he continues sipping so I do, carrying my own drink with me. I sit myself down on the couch while he grabs his remotes from the top of the entertainment unit. He sits right next to me, stretching his legs out on the matching ottoman. He moves his feet to the side, leaving space for me to place my feet next to him so that's what I do.

"How do you have such pretty feet?" I ask, making his laughter surround me.

"What?" he asks, wiggling his toes at me.

"They are quite good-looking feet for a man," I tell him.

"Please don't tell me, my wife has a foot fetish," he laughs.

"What if I did? Would that be a problem?" I ask, raising an eyebrow at him. His smile drops before he says.

"I've always wanted my toes sucked," he says, bringing his bare foot up to my face and I can't hold my straight face any longer, laughing at him.

"Okay okay. No fetish here. You've just got pretty man feet," I laugh, as he continues to wiggle his toes at me.

"Well as long as you are happy with them that's all that matters," he says, putting his feet back on the ottoman. He's closer to me as we sit with our shoulders and thighs touching now. "What do you feel like watching, little bird?" he asks, making my face heat as I turn to him.

"I don't mind. You can pick?"

He flicks through several options before clicking on a comedy and snuggling down lower into the couch to get comfortable. I take a long sip of my drink, needing the cool liquid to lower my body temperature with how close he's sitting.

"I gotta say this has been a pretty good first one?" he says, as the movie starts.

"First what?"

"First of our Sundays. Forever to go now," he says, winking at me before directing his gaze back to the T.V. I think I'm going to have to invest in an air conditioning unit with the number of times he makes me blush when I'm around him. I wonder if I can get a portable one to carry around with me.

We are not ready to call it a night so one movie turns into two. I tell him he can choose and again he chooses a comedy. I guess the way to his heart is through laughter.

"Are you hungry?" he asks, before the end of the second movie.

"No, I'm still full from the burger. Don't let me stop you if you're hungry though," I tell him. He walks down the hall to the kitchen, coming back with a ham sandwich.

"What time do you usually go to sleep?" he asks, after swallowing a bite.

I flick my wrist checking the time. It's a little after 9.00pm so it's still early.

"Usually about ten so we've still got time to hang out," I tell him, which makes a smile appear.

"Do you want to play a board game or do a puzzle together?" he asks, finishing off his sandwich.

"I haven't done a puzzle in forever if you have one," I ask, as flutters stir in my belly.

"You're in luck. Gramps and I used to spend our down time in the evenings doing puzzles together after my nana passed," he admits, as he heads into his bedroom and comes back carrying about five boxes in his arms. He places them in front of me on the couch for me to look through.

"Let's do this one," I say, holding up the box with the safari animals on it.

He grabs the rest of the boxes and takes them back to his room. He picks up the ottoman and moves it to the corner of the room and then walks into the spare room and comes back out carrying a rolled-up cylinder in his hands. Laying it down on the carpet he unrolls it to show me it's a puzzle board.

"That's so cool."

"Yeah, my gramps found it after we had done a few puzzles on the kitchen table and then realised the table wasn't big enough," he tells me, smiling as he sits on the carpet and pulls the puzzle box down. I sit down next to him crossing my legs. He opens the box and says, "Me and my gramps would find all the border pieces first. Unless you have another way you like to do puzzles?"

"No, that's how I like to start too," I tell him, smiling as he pours half the pieces into one half of the box for me to sift through. We fall into a comfortable silence, searching the pieces for flat edges and pulling them out. It isn't long before we have the border complete for our thousand-piece puzzle.

I release a yawn. I try to cover with my hand, but Lorenzo sees.

"How about we finish for the night and get some rest? It's been an eventful twenty-four hours," he says, glancing at my face.

"Yeah, sleep sounds good," I tell him, letting another yawn loose. "I'm gonna brush my teeth and then head to bed."

"Whatever you need to do. It's your house now too," he adds, shrugging his shoulders.

"I like it here," I tell him.

"I'm glad. Go get ready for bed, we can sort everything else later. You need some rest," he tells me, moving aside so I can walk past him to get to the bathroom. I run through my usual bathroom routine before heading back out. I hear Lorenzo in the kitchen, so I head that way. "Do you want some water?"

"Yes please."

"Here. There are bottles in the fridge, help yourself. I thought you might like some more Advil before bed as well," he says, holding out a bottle of water for me in one hand and the Advil for me in the other.

"Thank you," I say, taking both and washing the pills down with my water.

"I'll be leaving early tomorrow to head to the garage. Did you want to come with me? I've left my bike at the apartment, so I'll have to take the Audi if it's okay with you?" he says, facing me but leaning his hands behind him on the kitchen counter.

"You can take the car. I'll hang around here. Might go explore. The strip mall isn't too far from what I saw when we drove up here," I tell him.

"Yeah, it's not far in the car but might be about a twenty minute walk."

"That's fine. A little walking won't hurt," I tell him.

"Okay first things first, you've got my number so if you need me for anything, ring. I don't care what it is, call me. If I don't answer, ring until I pick up as sometimes, I can't hear my phone in the garage when it gets a bit loud," he explains, looking at me seriously.

"Harass you like a stalker until you answer. Okay got it," I say, laughing when his smile appears.

"Well, you're the only one allowed to stalk me, so that's fine. I might have to save you on my phone as stalker instead."

"You will not," I gasp, grabbing at his phone as he types away. He holds his phone above his head, as I jump trying to reach. His smug smile looks down at me while I try hopelessly to get his phone. He relents, handing my phone over.

"Two, one, nine, three," he says, causing me to raise my brows. He tugs my forearm as he spins me around. My back presses up against his front as he shifts the phone, so both my hands hold it while he unlocks it. "Two, one, nine, three, my passcode," he tells me, as he taps in the numbers unlocking it. His chin rests on my shoulder as he goes to his previous call list and there sits the most recent call, little bird. "I've got nothing to hide. If you ever want to use or check my phone, the code will never change. There are no other girls or anything. I want to be clear. I meant it when I say I want a real marriage with you and to build a life with you Sophia. No one else, just you," he says, softly into my ear. He wraps his arms around my waist, and I place his phone on the kitchen counter, running my hands on top of his. "People may call us crazy, but I don't care. I care what you think. We'll make decisions as we go. Together," he tells me.

"I feel the same," I agree, which makes him squeeze me tighter before he kisses my temple then turns me around to face him.

"Now I've got a spare key I keep up here," he says, releasing me and reaching up into the cupboard above the fridge. He moves his hand back and forth, feeling around until he hits what he's looking for and then pulls the set of keys down to show me. One is a green key while the other is blue. "Green is for this house and the blue is for the apartment," he tells me, as he pops the keys into my hand and folds my fingers around it with his.

"Thanks."

"I leave for work at about seven thirty and then I finish at five so depending on traffic I usually make it back here around six," he tells me, and I nod taking in all this information.

"Got it."

"Is there anything else we need to go over for tonight?" he asks, but I shake my head, not thinking of anything. "Oh, the address. Do you want to take it down, so you don't get lost," he asks.

"Yes, good idea," I tell him, pulling up my notes app on my phone. I look at him expectantly waiting for him to tell me the address.

"Fifty-four Rutherford Crescent."

"Fifty-four Rutherford Crescent and save," I say, as I type it into my phone and save it. Knowing me getting lost is a definite possibility tomorrow.

"There's food in the fridge but if you want other stuff, we can go to a supermarket tomorrow when I finish work if you like," he tells me. I nod along, sure whatever is in the fridge is fine.

"I'll be fine. I might head to bed now."

179

"Yeah sure. Good night, Sophia," he softly says. I step in closer, leaning forward and give him a gentle kiss on the cheek before leaning back.

"Good night, Lorenzo," I whisper, before turning and walking down the hall. I push the door for my room open. Finding the light switch on the wall, I turn it on and head over to my windows and pull the curtains shut. Rummaging through my drawers I find a pair of pyjamas I had packed. A plain cotton top with matching shorts. I toss them on and place my dirty clothes on the dresser, knowing I'll try to catch Lorenzo before he leaves for work to ask him where the laundry is.

I turn out the light as the room plunges into darkness. I shuffle my feet to the bed as carefully as I can without seeing. The covers are heavy as I pull them back and snuggle under the white duvet, I feel is similar if not the same one to his one at the apartment. My eyes drift shut as I try not to think about the day that's past. I can't believe how drastically my life has changed in the last twenty-four hours. I wouldn't change it for the world though and it's with that thought my tired body drags me to sleep.

Chapter Twenty Three

Sophia

The sun trickles into the room around the edges of the curtains and wakes me. The night was spent tossing and turning so instead of wasting time trying to sleep longer, I flip the covers off and walk out into the hallway bleary eyed. Flicking my wrist, I check the time seeing it's already 8.00am.

"Lorenzo?" I call out, but he said he was leaving early so it doesn't surprise me when I don't get a reply. I use the bathroom and then head to the kitchen finding he has a coffee machine I never took notice of yesterday. In front of it is a note he's left me. It says, *'Sophia, I didn't want to wake you before I left but I hope you have a good day. Ring me if you need. I have left out different flavoured pods for you. Pop one in the machine and it's good to go. Lorenzo.'* I find myself smiling at his small gesture.

Noticing the pods, I grab a cappuccino one to try. I pop it in where it needs to go and put a mug underneath the nozzle before I press start. The machine whizzes to life as it makes my much-needed coffee. I feel like I'm over the hangover from my birthday and I swear I won't drink that much again. Ever. Especially if it takes me so long to recover.

When the coffee machine finishes, I take the hot mug and sit in one of the cute hand painted chairs. Holding it in both hands I let it heat my palms as I wait for it to cool before taking a sip. My gaze wanders around the room. The little window to the side of the room with its white lace curtains shows a view out to the neighbours' house. I catch a glimpse of an older lady pruning her rose bush. Her wide brimmed sun hat and pruning shears look like they get a lot of work outside as her roses look immaculate. I wonder if we could start planting some flowers around Lorenzo's. It doesn't have many flowers around the property but I haven't ventured out the back yet, so I'll have to look at the space after my coffee.

Bringing the hot mug to my lips, I carefully blow the steaming liquid before taking a small sip, testing it to make sure it doesn't burn. It's cooled enough now I can drink it and I finish it off quickly before putting it in the sink. I open the fridge, glancing through everything to see if there's anything I can whip together for breakfast. Not finding much in there I open the bread bin, pulling out the loaf and decide toast is an easy option.

I place two slices in the toaster and lather them in raspberry jam when they pop up. A quick search of the cupboards shows me where the plates are. I move them from the chopping board to my plate and sit back at the table to enjoy them. It's nice and peaceful in this house. It was always quiet around my house growing up with my parents, but it was because I was often left alone. I find here it's a different quiet. Inviting. I could find myself happy living here.

I finish my toast and then wash my dishes leaving them to drip dry while I walk back to my room to collect my phone. There's a message waiting for me as I grab it off the charger where I left it last night.

Lorenzo: Ring me if you need anything x

My heart flutters at the effort of him leaving a note and a text. Gosh is he real? I swipe through my calls list pulling up Ally's number and ring her.

"Hey Mrs. Moretti, how's married life?" she asks, as she answers after three rings.

"It's pretty good, feels like a dream," I gush.

"So, did you sleep with him already? Tell me, tell me," She squeals.

"Calm down. No, I did not sleep with him. I slept in the spare room."

"Ugh why did you do that? Jump that McHotty husband of yours already," she jokes.

"We decided to take it slow."

"Girl slow? You've already gotten married. I don't think slow is a factor now."

"Well, we still want to get to know each other before we jump each others' bones," I explain.

"Whatever works for the two of you, I guess. What have you got planned for today? I have a client soon, so I have to get going to the salon," she tells me, and I check the time again. It's a little after 8.30am and she usually starts seeing her hairdressing clients from 9.00am.

"I'm gonna go for a walk and check out the area," I tell her.

"So, you guys will live there?"

"Yeah, I think so. It's his grandparents' house and it's so cute, I love it already."

"You sound happy," she states.

"You know what, for the first time in a long time, I am."

"I'm happy to hear that but know if you need anything, I'm here for you."

"Thanks. I'll let you get going. Check in later."

"Will do. Laters chicky."

"See ya," I say, before hanging up. I grab some clothes for the day and head back to the bathroom. I brush my teeth and shower and then step out into the backyard admiring the space. It could be a cute area if we did it up. There's a deck that runs the length of the back of the house, with two old rocking chairs. The area is fully fenced and has one side of the fence with a planter box running the length of it. I'm guessing someone once had a garden out here. Walking around the side of the house, where the kitchen window looks out, I find the older lady still pruning her roses.

"Hi, sorry to bother you. I'm Sophia," I introduce myself. She glances around finding me hanging over the fence and a friendly smile greets me.

"Hello. Are you a lady friend of Lorenzo's? I've been telling that boy for years he needs to find a woman," she tells me, causing me to blush.

"So, you know Lorenzo well then?" I ask.

"Oh yes, I've lived next to him and his grandparents since they brought little baby Lorenzo home. I'm Gladys or Mrs. McMillan, which Lorenzo still calls me," she says, shaking her head with a smile on her face.

"You might be just the person I need," I tell her.

"Oh, what do you need love?"

"I wondered if there used to be a garden out the back. I was thinking of surprising Lorenzo and planting some flowers," I tell her, and her smile grows.

"Aww. His grandparents used to tend the garden together. It was adorable how much they loved each other before his grandmother passed away. She used to love roses as much as I do. If you want some help, we could plant some rose bushes back there to liven up the space. I think after she passed, the lads couldn't keep it going," she informs me.

"That would be great. Would you be able to help me with a list of everything I would need?"

"Yes of course. I'll nip inside and grab a pen and paper and write a list for you now. Won't be a minute," she says, turning on her heels. I move back to the yard, looking around the large space and imagining what it could look like if we brightened it up with some flowers. I hope it brings a smile to Lorenzo's face especially after Gladys mentioned his grandma used to look after the garden. I wonder if it was also her who hand-painted the kitchen chairs.

Sighing, my heart feels lighter than it ever has. This whole house has so much more love surrounding it than I've ever known before.

"Sophia?" I hear Gladys's call, so I head back to where she can see me. "There you are love. Here you go. This is all you would need to get the soil in good nick to start. There's a gardening shop up at the strip mall where you'll find it all. If you have any questions don't hesitate to ask. You can use all my tools if you need so don't worry about buying any of those for now."

"Thank you so much Gladys. I'll take you up on the gardening info as I haven't the slightest clue what I'm doing."

"I'll make a green thumb out of you in no time," she tells me, laughing.

"Well, I'm gonna head off and try to find all of this. I'll see you soon," I tell her, holding up the list.

"Bye love," she says, waving as I walk back into the yard. With one last glance at the garden, I step up onto the deck, through the door then lock it behind me.

I decide against walking and call an Uber instead which takes me straight to the gardening place Gladys mentioned. Overwhelmed with choices, I end up having to ask one of the sales assistants to direct me. With some compost, soil and a few different rose plants to start with, I catch an Uber back to Lorenzo's.

It isn't until I'm standing at the front door, sweat dripping down my back, I rummage through my bag and realise my mistake.

"Damn it," I yell, I hit myself in the forehead as I realise, I've left the key to the house sitting on the kitchen table. I had pulled the door closed and the lock had clicked into place, so I didn't realise my mistake before I left. Accepting my fate, I bend and pick up a bag and haul it around to the back of the house. It takes a couple trips back and forth but then I have everything in the backyard.

"Did you get everything?" Gladys' voice calls over the fence.

"Yes, but I managed to lock myself out of the house.

"Oh no. Well how about I bring my tools over and we can get planting. You're welcome to come join me at my place for lunch afterwards if you'd like?" she offers.

"Sounds great. Thanks." With that problem solved I won't have to ring Lorenzo to come save me. Gosh, the first day of marriage and I was already going to have to call him. I don't want him realising he's married to a mess of a woman this early on. It may make him second guess this whole pact.

Gladys and I get to work, and she directs me with what to do. We fix up the soil and she shares all her useful tips about growing roses and how compost is a big help. I grabbed a couple plants, so they aren't big but it's a start.

She leads me back to her house when we are finished in the garden and makes us some tea and sandwiches for lunch. She's telling me stories about her late husband when my phone rings. The name husband flashes across the screen bringing a smile to my face.

I swipe to answer and greet him with, "Hey you," which has his light laughter reaching my ear.

"How's my beautiful wife today?" his warm voice asks, which makes my skin heat.

"I'm good, although I've locked myself out of the house," I inform him.

"What? Why didn't you ring me?"

"I didn't want to bother you and I met the lovely Gladys over the fence who has taken pity on me and invited me round for lunch."

"I did not take pity on you love. I was in need of some company if I'm being honest," she tells me, and my heart hurts for her being all alone in this house now.

"Oh, Mrs. McMillian is amazing. I am on the way though. I don't want to hear any arguing either. I've done everything I needed to anyway so it's just paperwork, but I can catch up on it later," he tells me. I hate the thought of him having to leave work for me, but I accept it.

"I will see you soon then."

"Yes, you will," he says, before he hangs up.

"Lorenzo's coming to rescue me apparently," I inform Gladys, which makes her laugh.

"That boy is a keeper; I'm telling you now. He works so hard, it's about time he settled down and had someone to share his life with," she tells me.

We finish our sandwiches and tea right before there's a knock on the door. Gladys opens it but we both know it's Lorenzo.

"Hey Mrs. McMillian," his smooth voice says as I watch him from the hallway. He leans in and delivers a kiss to her cheek.

"Hey love," she greets him. His eyes connect with mine then they scan down my body until they come back to my face. My body warms under his gaze as he steps towards me and lowers his voice.

"Hello, my wife," he says, which causes a shiver to race through me as he kisses my cheek as well. He turns back to Gladys and says, "Thanks for taking care of Sophia today. I might take her off your hands now, if that's okay?"

"Yes, you lovebirds go about your day. Sophia, please you're welcome any time."

"Thanks for today, Gladys. I appreciate your help," I tell her, as I step forward and wrap my arms around the petite older woman. She returns the hug and then we leave. Lorenzo grabs my hand and leads me to the front door as he unlocks it. As we step inside, he closes it and then pushes me gently against the back of the closed door.

"Is it crazy I missed you so much I couldn't focus on work?" he says, as his warm breath fans my face.

"Not crazy. I missed you too," I admit, because I did. I feel like my whole day revolved around him which reminds me what I was doing before I went to Gladys'. "I've got something to show you," I tell him, as his eyes flicker back and forth between mine. My eyes drop to his lips, wanting to feel them on me again but scared to make the first move. He notices my small glance and his lips widen into a grin.

"You can kiss me whenever you want to, little bird," he whispers, and I push all thoughts out of my head and instead go with my heart. I close the distance between us and it's all the motivation he needs before he has my body flush against his and pushed against the door. We waste no time, our lips greedy for the other, needing more. A deep moan travels up his throat as I pull him closer still. He threads a hand through my hair, angling my head giving his tongue the access it craves. We're so entranced when we pull away from the other, we are both gasping for air. "I will die a happy man getting to kiss these lips forever," he tells me, and I'm sure my skin burns a bright red.

"Let me show you your surprise before I get distracted again," I say, as I push off the wall and lead him to the back door. He follows me out and I show him the section we were working on. He's silent for a long time and I'm not sure whether that's a good sign or a bad sign so I stand there quietly, pursing my lips to the side, waiting. A few minutes of silence and I'm certain I've done the wrong thing until he threads our fingers together.

"My grandparents would have loved you," his soft voice says, as his eyes linger on the small rose bushes we planted. "Thank you," he adds, as he raises my hand and kisses the back of it.

"Is it okay I did this?"

"It's more than okay," he says. He leans forward and kisses me on the tip of my nose. "I'm guessing Gladys must have filled you in on my grandmother's rose bushes?"

"Yeah, I was admiring hers and then she said your grandparents used to tend to their garden together. I thought it's such a pretty space we could work on it together?"

"I'd like that. A lot. Thank you. I'd forgotten how beautiful these gardens used to be. Thank you for reminding me," he tells me, as he wraps his arms around me in a warm embrace. I squeeze my arms around his waist, breathing in his scent and let the feeling of happiness wash over me.

When we break apart, we head back inside, and I take a seat at the kitchen table while Lorenzo pours us both a drink.

"I was thinking I could take the day off tomorrow and we could hang out and go grocery shopping," he suggests.

"You aren't needed at work?" I ask, not wanting to keep him from work since I'd already kept him from finishing his full hours today.

"I'm the boss Soph. I can come and go as I please. One day isn't gonna do any harm," he explains.

"Okay then," I say.

"Yeah?" he asks, surprised.

"Yeah. It sounds good."

"How about you have a shower from all your gardening, and I'll get an early dinner on because I missed lunch?" he says.

"That would be great. Thanks." I head to the bathroom and shower before wrapping myself in a towel and walking out to head to my room to change. Lorenzo stands at the stove and his wide eyes look up when I walk past. His eyes linger as they trail from my bare legs to my face. My heart rate picks up as I shuffle into the hallway and head to my room and pull a pair of pyjama shorts and a top on. I throw my hair up into a messy bun and walk back out into the kitchen carrying my towel. Lorenzo isn't there but then he exits the bathroom with a white towel wrapped around his waist. The muscular tanned skin of his chest and stomach catches my attention and he chuckles as he walks past me on his way to his own room. The same tattoo of the lone wolf still covers one side of his chest from all those years ago. I step into the bathroom and drop my towel in the laundry basket. Drawing a few deep breaths in to calm my racing heart. By the time I exit, Lorenzo is there with his towel that he throws into the basket. He's wearing a pair of red baggy basketball shorts, his chest still bare. It does nothing to calm my heartbeat.

"Dinner should be about ready," he tells me, and all I can do is nod, my tongue feeling heavy in my mouth. His eyes light up as he watches me, his lip pulling up at one side. I take a seat at the table. He serves me a plate of spaghetti bolognese with garlic bread before taking a seat himself.

"This looks so good. Thank you."

"It's no problem. I like to cook so if you tell me what meals you like, I can cook them."

"I don't know the slightest thing about cooking so I'm happy for you to take over that responsibility," I admit, twirling my fork into the pasta.

"Do you wanna watch a movie with me after this?" he asks.

"Sure. A movie sounds good. I may fall asleep though. I'm knackered from gardening," I add.

"That's okay. You can pick this time."

"Nah whatever you want is fine." We finish our meal in silence. The food, too good to eat slowly. I take over doing the dishes since he cooked while he goes down to the living room to get settled. I join him when I'm done, and we get comfortable. He's picked out an action movie and wriggles in beside me. My head naturally falls to rest on his shoulder, and he wraps his arm around me. His body heat helps me relax and before I can relish in the feeling of being cuddled up into his side, my eyes are closing, and I can't fight it.

Chapter Twenty Four

Lorenzo

As my eyes flutter open, I'm a bit disorientated before I realise, I'm lying down on the couch. I must have fallen asleep watching the movie. The slight weight on top of me causes me to lift my head to find Sophia's sleeping figure lying on me. Glancing to the window there's no sunlight shining through yet so it's still not time to wake up. The light from the T.V still shines on, but the movie must have finished a while ago. Without waking Sophia, I reach across to the other side of the couch grabbing one of the couch cushions for my neck. I slide it under my head and wrap my arms around my wife. I should pinch myself as it's hard to believe it's real. I meant it when I told her I'd missed her.

I know it's crazy I feel this way so soon after having her agree to marry me, but I've wanted her for so long it's a relief I can let my feelings be known now.

Pulling the blanket I have over the back of the couch; I wrap it around us and deliver a kiss to her head. She wriggles, rubbing her cheek against my chest and I have to hold in the groan wanting to escape. Shutting my eyes again, I relax and fall back asleep.

Movement above me pulls me from my dreams. I peel my eyes open, and Sophia's bright blue eyes stare back at me.

"Sorry I didn't want to wake you. We fell asleep on the couch," she tells me, as she moves off me. I don't want to push her too fast too soon so I let her go when I want to pull her back down with me and drag her to my room where we could lie in bed all day.

"Yeah sorry," I apologise, sitting up and rubbing my eyes.

"You don't need to apologise, I had a good sleep surprisingly," she says, her cheeks turning red.

"Well feel free to sleep on me any time then," I tease, watching as her cheeks darken. "How about we get changed and then go out for breakfast before we get groceries?" I suggest.

"Sounds nice. I'll quickly shower. Won't be too long," she says, backing out of the living room.

"Take your time. I'm gonna ring Niko and let him know I won't be in today," I tell her, standing and walking into my room to get my phone where I left it last night. I check the time and see it's still early enough. Niko would have only gotten to work. Dialling his number, I wait for him to answer.

"Hey boss, are you on your way?" he answers.

"Nah I'm taking the day off."

"Are you all good?"

"Yeah, I'm taking the day off to spend time with my wife. Are you good if I leave you in charge today?" I ask. His chuckles vibrate over the phone.

"Yeah man. We'll be good here. Go spend time with her."

"I will. Thanks bud."

"See ya," he says, before I hang up the phone.

Knocking on the door has me calling out, "Come in Soph." Her head pops around the door.

"Sorry. Thought I'd let you know I'm ready."

"You've got nothing to apologise for. Thanks for letting me know. Niko's taking care of the shop so I'll get ready and then we can head out."

"Okay," she says, disappearing out of my room again.

Something niggles at me, so I drop my phone on my bed before following after her.

"Soph?" I call out, and she comes out of her room.

"Yeah?"

"Everything alright?" I ask, searching her eyes but she drops them to the carpet before I can figure out if something is wrong.

"It's dumb," she says, her eyes not meeting mine.

"Come sit down with me," I say, grabbing her hand and pulling her behind me to follow. I sit down and pull her, so she sits next to me, wringing her hands. "What's the matter?" I ask, worried.

"I'm feeling silly," she says.

"Hey, no feelings in this house are invalid. Tell me what the problem is, and we can sort it out," I tell her, hoping she'll open up.

"It's just I hate I've taken you away from work twice now in less than twenty-four hours and you are always paying for everything. Me not having a proper job isn't helping," she tells me.

I grab her hand to stop her fidgeting, squeezing gently.

"Do you want to work?" I ask. I guess this marriage thing is a big leap and we haven't exactly worked out all the finer details. We are both going with the flow.

"Yes. I would like to contribute to our household and help out," she tells me.

"Do you want kids?" I ask, which makes her eyes bulge out of her head.

"I guess yeah," she answers.

"Cool. I want kids too one day. So we are on the same page," I tell her, hopefully it explains my random question.

"So, if we have kids what would you like to do then? Work or be a stay-at-home mum?" I ask, feeling for a minute we are doing everything so backwards. It still wouldn't make me change it though.

"I'm not sure. Do I have to decide this minute?" she asks, as her lips pull up.

"Cheeky. I'm trying to get to know you and see what we both want for our life. It doesn't bother me if you work or not. It's up to you. Whatever you are happy doing then I'm happy with," I explain, hoping she understands I mean it.

"Well, I work for mum's charities doing a lot of the paperwork side of things and I like it but I don't think I want to do that forever. I have an accounting degree I want to make use of as well."

Then a bright idea hits me.

"You know what? I'm looking for a receptionist to sort all the paperwork and stuff at the auto shop if you want to help there and I'd pay you. You could work part time if you wanted to do something else as well?" I offer.

"Really?"

"Yeah. You don't have to decide right now. Take some time and think about it but the option is there if you want," I tell her.

"Thanks Lorenzo."

"You're welcome. And the other thing, you didn't take me away from work. I chose to have the day off today. I'm the boss so I can do that so don't feel bad for a choice I made, okay?" I hope it eases some of her worries. She nods, so I lean forward grasping her neck and pressing a firm kiss to her forehead. "I'll get ready then we can go. I'm hungry," I say, hoping to ease her worries further. She smiles up at me as I stand and I head to the bathroom to get ready.

I take her to my favourite cafe in town where I sometimes have brunch with Niko. She orders poached eggs on toast while I order mine scrambled with a side of bacon. We both order a latte needing the caffeine hit. It's nice to be out with her. We've spent most of our time together in the house and it's nice to be hanging out with her in a different environment. The more I spend time with her, the more I learn about her. All I have to do is show her I'm worthy and I can make her as happy as I know I can.

Leaving the cafe, we drive over to the local supermarket, and I grab a large trolley as the house is running quite low on supplies. Plus, now there's two of us we will need more food. Having her come with me is a bonus because I get to see what she likes and what she doesn't.

"Grab whatever you want," I tell her, as I push the trolley through the automatic gate. I watch as her lips push to the side of her face and her skin pinkens.

"I've never been grocery shopping," she whispers to me, and I stop, the trolley turning to her.

"Never?" I ask, stunned.

"No. The chefs always took care of it."

"What about when you were away at university?"

"I mainly ate at the uni cafeteria, but mum would send groceries every few weeks as well. And Ally would cook for us," she explains.

196

I try to wipe the shock off my face before I say, "Well you're in for a treat. If you see something you like or think you might like, throw it in the trolley. We've gotta celebrate this moment," I tell her, which makes her laugh.

"You might regret that when you see the bill," she teases.

"I could never regret anything when it comes to you. Now let's go shopping," I say, as her cheeks redden a bit more. I push the trolley along and she puts stuff in the trolley she may like while I grab my usual stuff. I ask her about types of dinners she may like and what meat she likes, and I manage to make a list of what I can cook for us for the week. She grabs a lot of sweet products and I realise she has a sweet tooth. I throw in a few more sugary treats I think she might like so at least she's got something if she wants it.

We go through the check out, pay and then she takes over pushing the trolley on the way out. I slip the receipt into my pocket and follow her. She pushes the trolley onto the escalator going down and I step on behind her.

"Aahh," she squeals, as the trolley wheel doesn't lock, and it keeps travelling down. I press up behind her grabbing the handle alongside her hands and hold it from moving any further.

"I've got it," I tell her, as I lower my chin resting it on her shoulder before I nuzzle into her neck. I hear her release a sigh which makes me smile.

"Thanks," she whispers. The escalator comes to an end and I push it forward firmly in case it decides to get stuck at the end, which I have had happen before.

"I'll take it if you like," I tell her, moving an arm so she can move out of the way. I push the trolley to the car while she walks beside me. We load the car up and head home. "You know, I was thinking we could go get the ring resized and get some proper wedding bands today if you like?" I ask, flicking my gaze between her and the road to gauge her reaction.

"Okay," she says, as she fiddles with her ring finger which is bare. After the wedding we both took off the rings we borrowed from Niko and Ally, and I've been thinking of replacing them.

After we put all the groceries away at home, I collect my grandma's ring from my room and we head back out to the local jewellers. He measures Sophia's finger and takes the ring saying it will be ready in a few days. We glance around the selection they have, and I tell Sophia to choose. She picks a simple band that will match her engagement ring nicely and I ask them to find me a band to match hers. I ask if they can engrave all of my Sundays on the inside of both of them which has Sophia's face lighting up. We leave them all there for us to pick up in a few days. With it all done, we head home.

"I was thinking I could cook up some lasagna if you want to help?" I ask Sophia, as we step back into the house.

"Sounds great. I'd love to learn how to cook," she says, excitement radiating off her.

"Awesome. Let's get started now," I suggest, as we head to the kitchen and pull out all the ingredients. As I talk her through the steps, I turn the oven on to preheat while we get it all sorted. I want to get to know her more, so I start asking random questions.

"What's your favourite food?"

"It might be weird, but I love any type of fruit. I could live off fruit if I had to. What about you?" she fires back.

"I love a good steak and mushroom sauce." We continue back and forth, laughing at some of the answers the other gives. I learn she loves the colour blue and prefers swimming in a pool rather than the ocean as she doesn't like deep water. She thinks she prefers cats over dogs but has never had a pet.

I set the timer on the oven once the dish is in and we head to the living room.

"There's a new mystery series out I was thinking of starting. Do you want to watch it with me?" I ask, hoping she'll say yes.

"Sure. I never had anyone to watch shows with, so it'll be nice to have someone to talk to about it," she admits.

"We gotta go over ground rules first," I tell her, looking at her with a stern face.

"Ground rules?"

"Yeah. One. Under no circumstances can you watch any episodes without the other person. That is like the cardinal sin in watching a show together," I explain, which makes her smile grow.

"Okay. What else?" she asks.

"You must go to the toilet and grab snacks before an episode starts. We don't stop an episode for anything," she nods in agreement, so I continue. "And three, phones off because we do not have time for distractions while watching."

"Are we allowed to talk while watching?" she asks, her eyes lighting up with mischief.

"I'll allow it as long as it's programme related," I tell her, keeping my face straight.

"Very serious, this series watching biz," she says.

"Yes, it is. Now do you think you can agree to all those terms?" I ask.

"Yeah. I think so."

"No thinking, you gotta know so," I tell her, keeping my laugh in.

"Lorenzo," she squeals, as she grabs the pillow behind her and playfully throws it at me, making me laugh.

"Okay, okay," I laugh louder, which has her joining in. The ding from the oven has me jumping up and she follows me. I dish up lunch and put the leftovers in the fridge for tomorrow. After we finish eating, we head back to the living room to settle in for binge watching.

"Do you want snacks? I'm gonna grab some of the chocolate," she tells me.

"Ooh yes, can you grab me one of the bags of lollies and a can of drink please," I say, sitting on the couch and scrolling to find the programme. I wait for her to come back with the treats, and she hands mine to me before sitting down beside me. "You ready?" I ask.

"Yep, I'm good," she says, wriggling back onto the couch. I want to reach out and touch her. I can't help it. Now I have her in my space, I want to show her how much I care about her, but I worry I might be coming on too strong too soon.

"Hey, can I ask you something?"

"Shoot," she says, looking at me.

"I'm not overstepping with the touchy-feely stuff, am I? That's how I show people I care through touch. I want to make sure I'm not making you feel uncomfortable or anything, so if it's too soon for all the hugs and kisses you can tell me to slow down," I explain. Her cheeks redden as she watches me.

"I'm fine with it. It's nice to get a hug or kiss out of the blue. My family isn't the most affectionate as you probably can tell so sometimes it may catch me off guard, but it isn't unwelcome. If I ever find it too much, I'll let you know, okay?" I nod in reply, glad she doesn't mind my affection. "I don't mind it. It's nice," she tells me, her face deepening in colour.

"Good to know, little bird. Okay let's start." Shuffling in beside her, I widen my legs, so my thigh presses against hers and I catch the smile that appears on her face which she tries to hold in. And that's how we finish the rest of my day off. Binge watching seven episodes of the show before we call it a night and head to our separate rooms.

Chapter Twenty Five

Sophia

I told my mum I'd be back to help with the charity work, and she wanted me there early in the morning so since Lorenzo is working at the bar tonight, I thought it would be easier if I slept at my parents' for the night. Now we are married I wanted to try to reason with them, so they know this is serious and there is no changing our minds.

Lorenzo pulls the Audi into the bar parking lot and turns off the ignition. He looks down at the steering wheel and I'm not sure what he's going to say. He looks so serious. His face turns to me, and his eyes flick back and forth between mine, searching their depths before he talks.

"If you need me, you'll ring right?"

I nod but it doesn't lighten the load so clearly showing on his face.

"I gotta go otherwise I'll be late for my shift," he tells me, unbuckling his belt.

"Go. I don't want you getting in trouble," I say. I pull my door handle and exit the passenger side to walk around to the driver's door to take his spot. As I reach him, his fingers gently tuck a stray strand of hair behind my ear, before his whole hand cups my head and he pulls me into his chest. My arms wrap around him of their own accord as I breathe the smell of laundry detergent and men's cologne. Inhaling a deep breath, I hold onto the smell and make a memory of it and its association with Lorenzo. His soft lips press a long kiss on my head, that tucks perfectly under his chin before he speaks.

"Let me know when you get there safely." He releases me, his hands lazily resting on my waist.

"I will," I tell him, looking up at his face. His eyes search mine again, waiting.

"I'll see you soon," he says, kissing my forehead and releasing me. I watch him walk away. He turns, raising his hand in a wave which I return before he walks through the door and disappears. I slide into the driver's seat, adjusting it forward so my feet can reach the pedals and then I peel out of the parking lot. I navigate the roads with ease, heading in the familiar route to my parents. A ball of emotion swims in the bottom of my stomach but I can't name what the feeling is. I just know it's unwanted.

As I ease the car into the driveway, the ball in my stomach grows. I exit and take my small overnight bag from the boot into the house. The large foyer is empty as always. I don't know what I expected. I've never gotten a welcoming committee before. I don't know why I thought this time it may be different.

The slow walk up the stairs have my feet becoming heavy. My room lies undisturbed, and everything is how I left it. I find myself glancing around the pristine space, feeling nothing. No warmth or longing. The room which has been my safe haven for so long feels hollow as I stand in the middle of it. A knock on the door shakes me out of my thoughts and I call out.

"Come in, Miss Patrice." Her grey hair pops around the door frame as she pushes it open. A bright smile greets me before she pushes the door fully open.

"Oh, Sophia dear, it's so lovely to see you back," she says, and it draws out my own genuine smile in return.

"How have you been?" I ask.

"You know me. The hips have been playing up but apart from that, I'm fine and dandy my dear. So, tell me all about this fiance of yours. You're a lucky girl capturing that handsome man," she says, fanning herself, making me laugh.

"Yes, I am pretty lucky. Lorenzo's wonderful," I tell her, my smile stretching further across my face as I keep the secret of him being my husband now.

"Gosh if he was my fiance you wouldn't be able to drag me away. No way no how," she says, making me laugh before another knock on the door stops our lighthearted moment.

My mum's head pops through the door finding my eyes.

"Sophia love. Glad to see you home. I expect you'll be at dinner?" she asks.

"Yes mother, I was about to shower and get changed and then I'll be down," I tell her, which has her nodding before she leaves my room.

"Do you want me to put away your things for you?" Miss Patrice asks, as she picks up my bag from the ground where I'd dropped it.

"No, that's fine. It's only an overnight bag I have."

"Okay then dear. I'll catch up with you later. It's good to have you home," she says, before leaving me to do my task. In my closet a blue silk dress I haven't worn for a while catches my eye and I lay it on my bed for when I get out of the shower.

After showering I slip my dress over my head. As I stare at myself in the mirror, Lorenzo's face pops into my head and knowing he likes my hair down, I leave it. The thought of a possible reprimand from my parents about it can't make me tie it up. With my head held high I walk out of my room and make my way to the dining room where my parents are already seated. The sight of the huge monstrosity makes me miss the small rickety painted table in Lorenzo's house more.

"It's good to see you home Sophia," my dad says, looking up as he shakes his napkin out before placing it on his lap. His eyes stare at my hair for a few beats but he doesn't say anything. The word home seems funny to hear in the context of this house. It's always sounded a bit off in relation to this huge mansion that is always so quiet but after the few days I've spent with Lorenzo it feels more foreign.

"Thank you. I'm only here for the night. I'll be permanently moving in with Lorenzo," is my reply. The gnawing in my gut grows as our first course of a caesar salad is delivered to the table.

As soon as I take a mouthful of lettuce my father speaks again.

"Your mother and I have been talking and we don't think this marriage is a good idea."

My back straightens as I finish chewing the bland mouthful of food.

"What?"

"Must I repeat myself Sophia? We don't want you marrying him," his voice raises.

I drop my cutlery to the table.

"That is not your decision to make," I snap back.

"When it affects our family, it's not the right decision. You're making a mistake," he scoffs.

"And who would you rather I marry? Someone who you can twist and manipulate?" I throw back at him, my body humming with rage. My mother sits there quietly not saying a word.

"At least an upholding citizen of this town would be ideal."

"Lorenzo is upstanding. He's a good person and has never done anything wrong," I defend.

"He's a mechanic, Sophia. How is he supposed to provide for you off minimum wage?"

"You know sometimes life isn't all about money and appearances."

"Don't be so naive Sophia. It's about security. How are we supposed to sleep at night worrying about your future?"

"You don't need to worry about me. I will be perfectly fine," I huff.

"I beg to differ."

"Well, your opinion is unwanted," I grunt, as I push my chair back with a screech.

"Don't be a child Sophia. Sit down and finish your dinner," he demands, as his nostrils flare from the end of the table.

"No. If you can't accept Lorenzo and I are getting married then I feel I can't be a part of this family. Enjoy your dinner," I say, as I turn to storm out of the room.

"He made me a deal," my dad says. His words have my feet stuck to the floor like they are covered in glue. I turn to him, and his lips pull up in his award winning smile as he knows he's got my attention.

"What?"

"Oh, he didn't tell you?"

"No. What deal?" I demand.

"He bought you Sophia. He told me I could finally buy his auto shop for a sum of money and for your hand in marriage," he says casually, like he's talking about the weather.

My head swims as my heartbeat picks up pace. He made a deal with my dad to marry me? That can't be true, can it? Has this all been another business transaction but this time between my dad and Lorenzo? Is Lorenzo like my dad but better at hiding it? No. No he's not like my dad and I believe the connection between us is real. You can't fake the way he's treated me. He's treated me better in the last few days than I've felt from my family my whole life. The thoughts keep lashing at me faster and faster until one sticks firmly in place. My eyes glare at my father.

"You sold me?" I yell, lashing out. His eyes widen at the fact I've chosen to focus on his part in all of this. He thought he could turn me on Lorenzo but all it's done is make me mad at the man who I call a father. "I'm done. I want nothing to do with either of you, ever again," I scream, as I turn and hurry out of the room.

"Sophia," he yells after me, but I pay him no mind, rushing up the stairs into my room. I grab the bag that still lies open on my bed. I rush from my room and down the stairs. My mother waits for me at the bottom, but I don't stop, stomping past her on my way to the car.

"Sophia, could you see it from our point of view?" she asks, following behind me. I don't reply, not in the mood to keep arguing. "Sophia please stop," she says, grabbing my forearm.

"I'm getting married to him Mum whether you like it or not," I tell her, crossing my arms over my chest.

"How much do you know about him? You've only been around him a few days," she argues.

"I know enough. He's a good man. That's all I need to know."

She releases a sigh before she says, "Sometimes that isn't enough." I roll my eyes because I can't keep having the same argument.

"Maybe if you married for love instead of money, you'd feel differently," I seethe.

"I did marry for love Sophia. That was my problem. I married the man who I loved but not one who loved me back like I deserved," she admits, as her eyes drop.

"If you know you deserve better then why stay?" I argue, as some of the rage leaves me at her confession.

"One day you'll understand Sophia. I want better for you. I don't want you making the same mistakes I did."

"He cares for me Mum. I know he does," I plead. She stares at me a few beats before releasing a long breath.

"I'll talk to your father, please don't cut us off completely Sophia," she huffs.

"I won't have Lorenzo talked down to or made to feel unwanted in this family. I don't want to see dad at the moment with what he's done but Lorenzo's going to be my husband so if you still want me in your life then you're gonna have to accept him. The both of you," I demand.

"I'll talk to your father. It'll be fine. Drive safely," she says, before turning away and walking back into the house. I unlock the car and pop the boot, shoving my bag in there. I turn the car on and peel out of the driveway, breathing deeply to calm myself down. Before I know it, I'm pulling into the dirt parking lot I left a few hours earlier.

There are more cars here than there were earlier and it's dark out now. I lock the car up, second guessing coming here. I didn't think about the fact Lorenzo would be busy with work. I drove without a plan, knowing it was him on my mind. It's a bit late to turn back now so I continue forward.

The country music blasting through the bar hits me as I walk in. I forgot Thursdays are line dancing nights. I'm surprised they still do them after all these years. The fanatics are already up and dancing like the professionals they are. Last time I was here I was amazed at how in sync everyone was. It must come with a lot of practice.

Glancing around the dim lit bar, I notice Lorenzo over by an empty table clearing glasses before he wipes the table down. He works methodically and I can't help how my heart beats faster watching him, thinking that man is my husband.

"Hey darling, are you here for Lorenzo?" the old man Ted says.

"Yeah, I don't want to bug him though while he's working. Is it okay if I hang here while he works?" I ask, taking a seat at the bar in front of him.

"He's had a scowl on his face since he walked through the door today and is checking his phone every five minutes so I doubt you could distract him anymore than he already is. I was about to tell him to call it a night as he's getting snappy," he tells me, which doesn't sound like Lorenzo at all. I watch as he pulls his phone out of his pocket, checking it. There isn't anything he sees on it that holds his attention, so he roughly shoves it back into his jeans and rubs the rag across the table harsher than needed.

Pulling my phone out of my bag, I don't see any messages from him but decide to call him, hoping the surprise doesn't put him in a worse mood. I dial his number and bring the phone to my ear. I watch him from my vantage point as his phone must vibrate in his pocket. He nearly drops the glasses in his haste to put them back down on the table. His eyes crinkle as he answers the phone.

"Little bird? You alright?" he asks, worry lacing his voice.

"I'm good," I tell him, watching as he sits his butt on the edge of the table, crossing one arm over his chest.

"Sorry I can hardly hear you over the music tonight. What are you doing now?" he asks, his foot scuffing the ground.

"I'm watching this cute guy wipe down tables," I tease, smiling as I watch him. He stands up straight with his brows pulled in.

"What did you say?" he huffs.

"Oh, did I say cute guy, I meant my cute husband," I tell him, holding my laughter in. He registers my words, his eyes looking around before they land on me. The anger instantly relaxes from his face as a blinding smile shines at me. I feel it in my gut with his smile, he cares about me. My dad is wrong. Lorenzo is nothing like him.

"Damn I gotta go little bird. The most beautiful woman I've ever seen just walked into my bar," he says, as his feet hurry towards me. He hangs his phone up, pushing it into his jeans and I hop off the bar stool as he reaches me. Lifting me off the ground he pulls me into his arms. I wrap my arms around his neck as I hear him take a big inhale. "I didn't realise how much I missed you until I saw you," he whispers in my ear, before placing my feet back on the ground. Looking at me he tucks my hair behind my ear.

"I missed you too," I admit, realising the unwanted feeling in my gut from earlier had vanished the moment I laid eyes on him again.

"There's the happy lad I know. Now if I knew all it would take to get a smile out of you was to call your lady in then I would have rung her myself," Ted chimes in, drawing a chuckle out of Lorenzo.

"How can you not smile around this beautiful face?" Lorenzo says, caressing my cheek with his thumb, making my skin heat under his touch.

"Too right kid," Ted agrees. Looking at the clock over the bar he adds, "Give me another hour lad then call it a night and you can head off with your lady. I don't want her waiting on you."

"Oh, you don't have to do that," I tell him, not wanting to inconvenience him by having Lorenzo finish early on my account.

"It's fine darling. We're quiet tonight anyway and it usually dies down soon."

"I won't be long," Lorenzo tells me, kissing my cheek before heading back to get the glasses he'd left behind on the table he was cleaning when I rang. I plant my butt back on the stool, facing Ted.

"Can I get you a drink?" he asks.

"Can I get a ginger beer?" I ask, pulling out my wallet from my bag.

"Put that away darling. Your money's no good here. As long as you're with Lorenzo, you drink for free."

"Thank you," I say, blushing again.

"I've known him since he was a wee lad. Good kid that one," he informs me, and I watch Lorenzo as he moves around from table to table, clearing them and wiping them down. Ted places a coaster in front of me before he places the glass with the light brown drink on top of it.

"Ted, can I grab two beers?" one of the patrons yells, from down the other end of the bar.

"I'll be back," he tells me.

"I'll be fine. Don't hurry on my account," I reply, which has him nodding before he walks to the guy and fills his order. I sit there and take a sip of the cool liquid as I watch the line dancers. They gracefully fall into their steps with each other. Huge smiles on all their faces as the happy vibe floats through the bar. As I drink, I keep watch, trying to learn the steps but then a new song plays and they start a different routine of steps again.

Ted gets busy down the other end of the bar with more patrons coming and asking for drinks. Lorenzo walks behind the bar to help him at one stage when it gets too much for Ted on his own and then he steps back over to me when Ted has a handle on it.

"You wanna dance?" Lorenzo asks, as he crosses his forearms across the bar top leaning towards me.

"Huh?"

"You wanna dance? You haven't taken your eyes off them the whole time you've been sipping your drink," he explains, as he nods to my now empty glass.

"They look so happy doing it." He stands up straight, glancing at the clock.

"Ted I'll be on the dance floor if you need me, but my hour is up," he says, and the old man looks between us before gesturing for Lorenzo to go. "Come on little bird. I'll show you my moves," he says, holding out his hand for me to take as he walks around the bar. I reach out grasping his hand and he leads me to the dance floor. The music changes to another country song and cheers through the crowd make Lorenzo smile and I laugh. "Don't worry, it's a favourite song they have," he explains, as he positions me next to him. "Follow me," he instructs, before he starts crossing his legs one in front of the other. Everyone else around us knows the moves so I keep my eyes on Lorenzo's feet.

He turns pulling my hand to follow him before he shakes his hips in time with the music making me laugh. I notice Lorenzo and several others place their hands on people's shoulders, letting them know they are behind them and spreading positive vibes. The crowd smiles as they jump, twirl and step in time. At one point Lorenzo ends up behind me, placing his hands on my hips to shake them in time with his. My carefree laugh fills the air, loosening me up and I lose myself to the energy surrounding us. Lorenzo's laugh joins in before the crowd is jumping in step again. He pulls my hand, turning me so I try my best to keep up with him but laugh at myself when I miss a step or fumble over my feet.

The song ends and people smile and laugh with each other, happiness radiating off them.

"Did you enjoy that?" Lorenzo asks, as he tugs my hand to pull me into his embrace.

"It was so much fun," I beam at him, as I wrap my arms around his waist.

"You can come every Thursday night if you want. You'll be a pro in no time," he suggests, smiling down at me. "You wanna dance some more?" I bite my lip before I decide to be honest.

"I was wondering if we could go home. Cedarville home?" I ask him, and his eyebrows raise before he shuffles me off the dance floor not letting me go.

"Are you okay? Did something happen?" he asks, once we are in a spot where the music isn't as loud.

"I had a fight with my parents and my dad said something I wanted to talk to you about," I explain. I watch as his eyes widen before he speaks.

"What did he say?" his soft voice asks, as he gulps.

"He told me you let him buy your gramps' business as long as you could marry me as well," I say, my voice low so no one overhears. I watch his face for evidence of what he's done.

He drops his head before his sad eyes rise to mine.

"How about we head home, and we can talk it out there?" he suggests.

I nod as it's hard to hear him over the music.

"Ted we're out. You'll be okay?" he asks the old man, as we start to leave.

"Yeah lad. I'll be fine," he tells him.

"I'll be at Cedarville tonight," he says, and Ted smiles at us before waving goodbye.

"Bye Ted."

"Bye darling," he says, as Lorenzo leads me out of the door. We walk over to the car, the cool air hitting the sweat on my skin from the dancing. When we reach the Audi, I dig the keys out of my bag as Lorenzo holds out his hand for them. His fingers linger in mine before he pulls me into his arms again and leans against the back of the car, sitting on the boot. His hands rest on my waist as I look into his eyes.

"Are you okay?" he asks again, now we are alone.

"Yeah, I couldn't stay there any longer. What's with the deal you made?"

"He's right, I did make a deal with him. I know your dad wouldn't let me marry you. So, I offered up the only leverage I had which is my gramps' business that he's been trying to buy from me for a couple years now. It might seem like the wrong way to go about it, but I was set on getting you away from them Sophia. I didn't want you to end up in some loveless marriage with one of his pawns. I'm sorry I never told you about it, but I would do it again," he confesses. His sad eyes search mine.

"I'm not mad at you Lorenzo. I'd marry you a million times over than one of dad's lackeys so I'm thankful for what you did. I wish you had talked to me before giving up your gramps' business for me and for making a deal with my dad. Going forward you need to talk to me about anything like this. I don't want you making any more deals with the devil," I tell him.

"Okay I promise. Are you sure you're not mad?"

"Is there anything else I need to know? Are you sure that's all there was to the deal?" I ask, needing to know the truth about the deal.

"That's all there was to it Soph. I sold him the auto shop so I could get a chance at marrying you." I search his eyes before I speak.

"How can I be mad when you saved me from getting pulled into one of dad's political moves for his benefit. I'm furious at my dad for selling me like I mean nothing to him," I confess, which brings tears to my eyes I didn't realise I was holding in.

"It's okay Soph. You're safe with me I promise. Let it out. I won't let them hurt you anymore," he says, as he pulls my head to his chest and lets me cry all the hurt out. It's been building up for years but to hear it from my dad's own mouth. I can't believe he sold me to gain something, it makes me feel used and thrown away like I mean nothing to him. "Did they say anything else?"

"They don't want me to marry you," I confess, watching his expression but it never changes like my words don't affect him.

"What did you say to that?" he asks.

"I told them if they couldn't accept that you were gonna be my husband soon then I couldn't be a part of the family anymore," I admit, my cheeks heating. He stares at me for so long before his thumb slides across my bottom lip.

"Have I told you how amazing you are?" he asks, and I gently shake my head, before leaning into him. His hand slides into my hair, pulling me closer too before my lips meet his. It's a soft kiss. Our lips gently pressed against the other before he pulls back. Then as if he can't bear the thought of our lips parting, he pulls me back for another chaste kiss before releasing me. "Let's go home little bird," he says, smiling at me. He releases me as he pushes off the car and I walk around to the passenger side as he hops into the driver's seat. As he pulls out of the parking lot, he links our fingers and rests my hand on his thigh where it stays for the remainder of the ride home.

When he pulls into the driveway with the small dark house sitting in front of us, I can't help but feel a weight has lifted. I breathe out a sigh of relief as we exit the car.

"Have you got your bag?" he asks, over the hood of the car.

"Yeah, it's in the boot," I tell him, moving around to the back of the car while he leans down to open the boot for me. The car ride over was quiet but a peaceful quiet. One where we didn't need to express ourselves with words as I think me showing up to his work had said it all. I push the boot up, but Lorenzo pulls out my bag and slugs it over his shoulder before I can. He unlocks the front door and flicks the light on for the hallway as we enter.

"Home sweet home," he says, heading towards my room. He places the bag in there before coming back out. "Are you hungry?"

"Yeah. I stormed out during dinner. I probably should have eaten first," I confess, making him laugh.

"Let's feed you," he says, walking down the hallway to the kitchen, turning lights on as he goes. As I round the corner my heart sighs at the sight of the little hand painted table in the corner I've come to love only after a few short days. How can it only be a few days, but I feel more at home with Lorenzo, who is practically a stranger, in his house than in my own house with my parents who I've lived with my whole life?

"We aren't moving too fast, are we?" I ask, taking a seat and watching as he opens the fridge, searching for something to eat.

Turning to me his top lip pulls up, "I've waited eight years to get you back into my life little bird. I don't care how fast or slow we go, as long as you're mine." My eyes widen at his admission.

"You've held onto that pact of ours the whole time? You didn't consider another option?" I ask, stunned. He closes the fridge, standing straight before reaching his hand behind him. He pulls his brown leather wallet out of his back pocket, flicks it open and then hands a scuffed piece of paper that's folded up to me.

I take it gently unfolding the worn page. There on the weathered page is the faded words of our pact we made all those years ago. I hardly remembered the actual conversation we had that night, but I had remembered the identical page I'd found in my bra cup and whenever I'd felt down over the years I'd hoped one day Lorenzo would come for me. I did find the longer the years went on the more it slipped from my mind. I'd thought it a silly fantasy because someone as kind and gorgeous as Lorenzo would be taken by the time we hit thirty.

"You kept this the whole time?" I ask, my hand shaking as I hold the paper.

"Little bird, can I tell you something without you running for the hills?" he says, stepping towards me and bending his knees to squat in front of me. I nod because my throat is suddenly dry. He takes one of my hands in his, inspecting my fingers before his eyes look up at me. "I've had a crush on you since back in high school and when I say crush that is probably me mellowing it a bit, so you don't run. But know there was never a doubt in my mind after we made the pact that I would come for you. I hope one day, you'll feel the same way I do about you," he says, before lifting my hand to his lips and pressing a soft kiss to the back of it.

"Lorenzo," I sigh, and he shrugs his shoulders before standing and moving back to the fridge. "We hardly know each other though."

He turns back to me before he answers, "I know enough. You're kind and sweet. You have a big heart and in my eyes you're amazing. I felt it in my bones all those years ago, there was something about you Sophia. I still feel the same way now."

"What if you're wrong about me?"

"My gut hasn't led me astray so far," he says, which makes me shake my head at him, making his smile widen. "Don't forget we need to get through number two on the list. We should alter it and have it say you can't run from your husband without fulfilling that part too," he says, winking at me before opening the fridge. With pinched brows I glance down at the paper again reading over number two. My eyes widen before I squeal.

"Take you for a test drive? Like you're a car? How drunk was I?" I blurt out, which makes him laugh loudly.

"You wanted tequila and so I gave you tequila which in hindsight probably wasn't a good idea," he says, checking the freezer. "Frozen pizza?"

"Sounds great. The pizza, not the test drive," I tell him. He turns the knobs, preheating the oven before unwrapping the meat lover's pizza and placing it on a tray. He leans back against the counter with his ankles crossed and casually crosses his arms. I glance down at the paper again before flicking my eyes up to his.

"The test drive doesn't appeal to you?" he teases, and I feel my whole-body heat under his gaze. He holds my gaze as a smile spreads across his face before he grabs the tray placing it in the oven. He walks over to the table after setting the timer to fifteen minutes on the oven. He pulls out the seat opposite me. His smile never wavering. "So?"

"So what?" I play dumb.

"Oh, Sophia you know what I'm talking about but I'll ask it again. Does a test drive hold no appeal to you?" he says, adding a wink before chuckling.

With my face probably a crimson red now I answer, "I'll be honest. It holds a slight appeal," my voice barely above a whisper.

"Well, I'm glad you're attracted to your husband," he teases.

"I never said I was attracted to you. Maybe I want to check out the goods," I tease right back, making his head fling back as laughter sounds through the kitchen.

"You can check out the goods whenever you like. They're yours now for as long as you want them," he tells me, which does nothing for the colouring of my skin.

"You mean that?" I ask, leaning my elbow on the table and resting my chin on my fist.

He takes my hand in his before saying, "Sophia, there's no other woman and there will be no other woman. I'm all yours if you want me?"

"I want," I softly reply, and I watch as his pupils dilate at my response.

He tugs on my hand before softly saying, "Come here." I can't resist, standing from my chair as he turns his around to face me, his legs wide. As I step around the table he leans forward and with the hand not holding mine, he grabs my butt lifting me effortlessly as I let out a squeal. He pulls me onto his lap, straddling him as my legs fall gently on the outside of his hips. He releases my hands to hold my hips and my hands fall to the base of his neck.

"I was in such a mood today when you left. The thought of not seeing you for a few days was horrible," he tells me, which draws out my own honesty.

"I felt the same. As soon as the car drove away, this pit in my stomach formed and it didn't disappear until I saw you again," I admit, which has him smiling at my words. He smooths my hair out of my face with his palm.

"I'll try to be the best husband Sophia," he whispers, before his eyes stare into mine.

"I know," I reply, knowing he speaks the truth. I don't need to know much about Lorenzo to know he's a good man, and in my life good men have been few and far between. His hand moves to my chin where he gently pinches it with his thumb and index finger pulling me towards him. I let him close the gap, wanting to feel his lips on mine. It starts off soft and tentative, but I want more. I squeeze my arms around his neck as my hips move forward. He releases a moan from deep in his throat as the hand on my hip tightens its grip there. His other hand wraps around my back, pulling me against his firm chest as his tongue tangles with mine. He gently bites my lower lip drawing my own moan out. The sharp ding of the oven doesn't slow us until about a minute later when Lorenzo gently pulls away.

"The pizza's gonna burn if I don't get it out," he says, his lust filled eyes staring into mine. I nod and he quickly pecks my lips before grunting from having to stop which makes me laugh. He stands with me in his arms and deposits me back on my chair, before turning to the oven. He grabs an oven mitt from one of the drawers, removing the tray and the delicious smell of cooked cheese fills the air. I stand up and grab two plates from where I've learnt he keeps them, placing them beside him. He slides the pizza onto the cutting board I set out for him too and then he digs around in the top drawer finding his pizza cutter. He slices the pizza up and places half on my plate and half on his. I take one slice from mine and add it to his which makes him smile, before he kisses my hair. Grabbing the two plates, he sets them on the table, and we dig in to eat.

We eat in silence, and he finishes before me but waits while I eat. Once I'm done, he takes both plates, placing them in the dishwasher.

"I might shower and head to bed," I tell him, needing to wash all the sweat off me from the line dancing earlier.

"Yeah, I might shower after you," he says, and I look him up and down. Something in my brain snaps or my hormones take control of the next words out of my mouth.

"You could join me? To save water?" I suggest, and I watch as his eyes widen. There's no way I can take those words back now and with the way he makes me feel, I don't think I want to.

Chapter Twenty Six

Lorenzo

"Save water?" I ask, wondering if I heard her right.

"Yeah, well there's two of us living here now, we need to think of some savvy money saving tricks. Showering together would help us save water," she explains, and I run my hungry eyes from her feet to her head as my heart rate picks up speed.

I sit there staring at her for a few minutes. Silence surrounds us but it crackles with the building tension by looking at each other.

"You know I think I'm ready for the test drive now." Her hands drop down and grasp the bottom of her blue silk dress.

I'm entranced as I watch her slowly peel it up her body and over her head before she drops it on the floor. My laboured breaths fill the air as I greedily roam her perfect body. The freckles I've always wondered about cover every inch of her and it makes my heart beat faster at the thought I get to spend forever tracing them with my fingertips.

"Is that so?" I stutter, my words stuck in my dry throat. I peel my own shirt up and over my head, discarding it. Her breath hitches as she takes in my muscled body and I follow as her gaze takes its time, drinking me in.

"Come on husband, time to show me what you're made of," she encourages, as her hands slide her arms out of her bra straps, the cups staying in place. I can't take it any longer and in three huge steps I'm in front of her. One hand cups her ass, lifting her as she lets out a yelp as my other hand clings around her body, pulling her to me. Her legs wrap around my waist, holding on as her mouth finds mine. We both moan at the connection causing us to laugh. We both want it as much as the other.

It's all lips and tongues as we fall into sync, taking from the other what we want. Her arms squeeze me to her, and my hand squeezes her ass, eliciting another moan from her. I manoeuvre us into the bathroom and break the kiss to take out my phone and wallet from my jeans.

As her eyes stare into mine I run a finger down her jawline, mesmerised.

"Fuck, you've always been beautiful in my eyes but right now you are taking my breath away," I softly tell her. Her eyes soften before her lips trail kisses down the side of my throat. I walk us into the shower and her lips suck harder right above my collar bone before she pulls back and admires her work.

"Did you give me a hickey?" I ask, laughing.

"Just marking what's mine," she says, staring into my eyes. The cool stainless handle fills my hand as I pull it forward. "Aaah, Renzo it's freezing," she cries.

"Shit, sorry," I say, turning her out of the stream. "Aaah, it's freezing," I yell, before turning it to a warmer temp.

"No kidding," she says, as she wipes her soaked hair out of her face. She throws her head back laughing and the sight makes me join her. "So much for being sexy. How's the drowned rat look going for me?"

"Little bird, even when you were spewing your guts out in my bathroom, I still thought you were the most beautiful woman in the world. A little water is nothing," I confess.

Her blue eyes hold my gaze before she leans into me again. Her smooth lips press against mine as I slow the kiss this time. We take our time exploring the other before we pull apart.

"We should get clean," she suggests. Her arms bend behind and unclip her bra then she pulls it away from her skin, dropping it to the wet shower floor. I hold her longing gaze and lower her to the floor as I unhook the button on my jeans, release the zipper and push the damp blue material down my legs. It's a bit more work now that they are heavy from the water, but I get them off. I reach down and grab her bra with my jeans and toss them out the shower door.

"Are you sure about this?" I ask, as I hook my thumbs into the waistband of my boxers. She doesn't say a word but strips off her own underwear throwing them out the door.

"Yes," is all she says.

I make quick work of removing my boxers before throwing them out and closing the door. Her eyes hold mine until she can't take it any longer and her gaze lowers. I watch the blush start at her cheeks, move down her throat and across her décolleté. When she's had her fill, her eyes come back to mine before she speaks.

"I think I'm pretty lucky to be your wife," she says, as a small smile pulls at her lips.

"Yeah, you are," I reply, as my own grin widens at her. I pump some of her cherry blossom body wash into my hand and run my hands over her. When I reach her perky dusty nipples, I swipe my fingers back and forth before holding the weight of them in my palms and giving them a light squeeze. She flings her head back as her eyes close to the sensation. My fingers trail down the centre of her body as I circle her belly button before stepping closer to her.

She gathers her own handful of body wash and smooths it over my skin, lathering me up before she lowers a hand. Bubbles light up my skin along with the goosebumps that linger from her touch. Holding my gaze, she wraps her hand around my length and that's all I can take. I scoop her back up into my arms and push her against the cold wall. She squeals out at the sensation, but my lips are on hers while her hands roam free, exploring me.

I break the kiss to swipe my tongue across her throat, leaving a trail of kisses across it to her shoulder before I find her eyes again with mine.

"So beautiful," I whisper, as I push my weight in to hold her so I can lower my hand. Finding her heat at her centre, I use my thumb to rub circles. Her own hand joins mine guiding my thumb across the tiniest fraction.

"Right there. That's the spot," she encourages, as her eyes roll back while she enjoys the sensation. "Faster and don't stop," she directs, and I watch enraptured as she gives instructions on how to make her feel good. It isn't long before she squeezes her eyes shut and a moan rips from her throat. Her body shakes with ecstasy. Her hand touches mine, so I know to stop as her lazy smile finds me.

"You're amazing," she whispers. "I'm ready for my test drive now." Her words make me laugh so loud.

"Now who's being greedy?" I tease.

"When it comes to you, I think I'll always be greedy," she confides, which has me taking her bottom lip between mine and pulling. "Now fuck me husband." Her wide smile directed at me. I kiss her lips again as I line myself up with her centre. One hand holds her hip to give me better access as I ease myself in. Our moans fill the air as I do what she asked. Our fingers glide over wet skin as the shower stream pelts down on us. Her arms hold on tight as I pick up momentum and reach down again to the spot to help her. She helps guide my fingers to the spot again and moves my fingers how she likes. A minute later and she falls apart in my arms again. I follow behind her, finding my own release.

Sated and spent, my forehead falls to the curve of her neck to catch my breath. Her own breaths slow the longer we stay like that.

"I'm going to be the greedy one," she confesses, breaking the moment and sending our laughter into the air.

"Let's get you to bed before you drain me of all my energy, little bird," I tell her, as I break our connection and lower her. We wash off quickly before we step out of the shower. I wrap her in a towel before I grab one for myself. Once dry I drop my towel and pull hers off her and lift her naked body over my shoulder.

"Renzo," she squeals, as I lightly smack her butt as I strut down to my room and drop her on my bed. With her wild hair spread out around her, my heart fills with emotion at how lucky I got. Her perfect smile stares at me with a beautiful shine in her eyes.

"Thank you for taking a chance and marrying me," I softly say, as I lift her arm and kiss the inside of her wrist.

"Thank you for thinking of me as worthy enough to marry," she whispers, as her smile drops, and her expression turns serious.

"There's no one on this earth I ever thought of marrying except you little bird," I tell her, and she lifts her head, seeking my lips. I lower myself and we spend the rest of the night exploring and I fall more in love with this woman who is becoming my everything. We fall asleep in the early hours of the morning with her head lying on my chest, her fiery hair surrounding me and a contentment inside I've never felt before.

Chapter Twenty Seven

Sophia

"Come on little bird, I've got a surprise for you for our Sunday together," Lorenzo says, as I sit at the beloved kitchen table, blowing on my coffee to cool it down.

"It's so early though," I whine, as I pull a knee up to rest my chin on it. My eyes linger on my husband's naked chest and the rumble of his laugh catches my attention.

"Like what you see?" he teases.

"Eh it's okay if you're into that kind of thing," I tease, as the blue ceramic mug touches my lips. The hot liquid hits my tongue and warms my throat.

"Well, you were enjoying it last night and the night before too." His smile widens as my face heats under his gaze.

"Hmmm I might need a reminder of what I liked. I'm quite forgetful." My words have his head dropping backwards as his laughter echoes in the room.

"I'll make you a deal, you come with me for your surprise and then I'll give you a reminder later."

"Sounds like a good plan," I say, my eyes look at him over my mug as I take another sip.

"Finish your coffee and we can grab breakfast while we are out," he tells me, as his eyes rake over my body.

After stopping at his favourite cafe for breakfast, he drives us to his auto shop. I haven't been here yet, so he gives me a tour before showing me the surprise he has in store.

"Ta da," he says, his hands held out in the direction of his motorbike I recognise. I raise a brow at him in question.

"Your bike is the surprise?"

"No, a ride on the back of my bike with your own gear is your surprise," he explains, and as excitement stirs in my belly, I leap into his arms.

"Really?" I squeak at him.

"Really," he says, giving me a quick peck on the lips before placing me on my feet. "I got Niko to grab the bike from the bar for me and I ordered a helmet and jacket for you. He told me they arrived here on Friday."

"I'm so excited," I confess. Ever since I saw Lorenzo on his bike back at school, I've had a fantasy of riding on it.

"Here, put these on," he instructs, as he hands me a black leather jacket that fits perfectly. He steps closer to me, so I get a whiff of his cologne as he stares into my eyes and zips the jacket up. He clicks the extra buttons in as well. "Might get you to wear this later," his soft voice says, which makes my cheeks burn. His finger trails the pink colouring before he grabs the black helmet with two pink stripes on either side. He pulls my hair out of its ponytail, letting it flow down my back. The helmet squeezes my face as he pushes it on and clips it underneath, so it holds.

With a flick, the visor pops open and I return his smile as his heated eyes stare back at me.

"All you must do is hold on to me and lean with me. If you need me to stop, tap my stomach," he instructs.

I nod and he grabs his own jacket and helmet and pulls them on. He hops on and then grabs my hand and helps me sit behind him. His hand pulls me closer and wraps my arms tightly around his waist.

"Hold on tight."

"Okay," I agree, and the loud thrum of the engine sends a giddy vibration through me. He eases us out of the shop and then takes off until he gets to the highway where he can pick up speed. My heart accelerates with the speed of the bike. I squeeze Lorenzo and hang on tight as he told me too. A thrill of excitement runs through me as I lose myself in the feel of wind whipping against us. Lorenzo's driving is smooth and effortless, you can tell it's second nature to him and he's been doing it a long time.

I lose track of time as he coasts along down the highway before turning back and heading to his shop. It's late afternoon by the time we get back and he turns the engine off.

"That was amazing," I scream, as my ears adjust to less sound. He laughs at me as he helps me off the bike.

"Glad you enjoyed it. We might need to start every Sunday with a ride," he says, as he shakes his jacket off and I do the same.

"That would be a dream," I tell him, as his beaming smile grows. Once our helmets are off and placed on his worktable, he pulls me into him and wraps his arms around my waist. My head tilts back to look up into his eyes. His deep brown eyes flicker back and forth between mine as he tucks a stray hair behind my ear.

"Damn I'm crazy about you," he whispers.

"I'm a little crazy about you too," I whisper back.

"Only a little?" he teases.

My smile grows as I say, "Maybe a lot." Without hesitation, his hand hooks under my thigh pulling me into his arms so my legs wrap around him. He walks us backwards as he takes my mouth and presses against the wall. Our hands fly into the other's hair pulling and tugging as he grinds himself against me. When we part, we are out of breath.

"I need to get you home now because otherwise we are about to make a sex tape on my security cameras and I am not having that," he grunts, as he carries me over to the car and puts me on my feet.

"Can you remove the tape? I think it would be hot to watch later," I admit, which has his eyes widening.

"Yeah, I can remove it," he softly says, which is all I need before my mouth slides over his. He moves us around the car, with our lips attached and lays me down on the bonnet. "I don't think I'll ever not feel like the luckiest man in the world," his voice trails off, as if it was a thought, he didn't mean to say out loud.

"I'm just as lucky," I say, as my fingers twist into his shirt pulling him down on top of me. From there it turns frantic as clothes are pushed up to gain access to skin. We caress and grab at each other, hungry. He makes quick work of removing my pants before he pushes his own down and positions me at the end of the bonnet before plunging in to my core.

Exhilaration fills me at the thought we could possibly get caught. Our movements are wild, and my hand touches the spot I need for release as he continues to thrust into me. The rushed frenzy adds to the sensation and my body explodes as my back arches. He increases his tempo and follows me with his own release after a few more pumps. His weight feels heavenly against me as we catch our breath.

His head lifts from where it was buried against my neck, a light perspire speckled across his skin.

"I'll grab the tape and then we can head home for round two," he says, as his eyes shine at me.

"Good thinking," I tell him, which widens his smile. He pulls out of me, and we gather our clothes and redress quickly. He plants a quick kiss to my forehead before he jogs away and comes back a few minutes later waving a small tape at me which makes me shake my head at the thought of what just occurred. He brings out a side of me I never knew existed and I find myself loving this new version of me. It feels as if it's a part of who I was always meant to me, and it lay dormant all these years waiting for him to awaken it.

He hops in the driver's seat, hands me the tape and then we exit his garage taking the evidence with us. As he drives us back home, his hand rests on my thigh, running up and down in a lazy pattern. He knows the effect he has on me, as every hitch of my breath brings a chuckle out of him.

He pulls the parking brake up and is around my side of the door in a flash, pulling me from the car.

"Renzo," I squeak, as he picks me up and carries me inside to our room. I bounce on the bed as he throws me onto the mattress. "What's the hurry?" I squeal, my face hurts from the smile on it.

"I'm starving for you," he states, before he whips his shirt over his head and discards his jeans. His hands are warm as they grip my ankles and slide me to the edge of the bed. In no time at all, he has me undressed and is satisfying his hunger with my body. We spend the rest of our Sunday in our own blissful cocoon in our room before passing out from exertion.

Chapter Twenty Eight

Lorenzo

It's the third Sunday since we've gotten married, and my life couldn't be happier. We've fallen into a routine that works for us. Sophia has taken up the role as receptionist at the auto shop and has been a godsend. I don't know what I was thinking, trying to do it all myself. This week has been her first week at work and to spoil her I wanted to take her out to the carnival for our Sunday this week.

"Hey man, I'm taking Sophia out to the carnival that's been going on in town. Did you wanna join us? Sophia's gonna ask Ally too," I tell Niko on the phone.

"Sounds good. I'll meet you guys there. What time are you thinking?"

"I think around three or so."

"Sweet. Text me."

"Will do," I tell him, before hanging up. Sophia walks into the kitchen where I'm seated at the table.

"Ally is in. What did Niko say?" she asks. I turn my chair towards her, holding my arms out. She walks between my outstretched legs without hesitation. It feels like everything between us is falling into place.

"He's in too. He'll meet us there around three," I tell her, as I wrap my arms around her waist, drawing her closer. I rest my cheek against her stomach as she runs her hands through my hair. Closing my eyes, I revel in the feel of her hands on me. It may not seem like much, but I can't get enough of her. I feel we are building a good foundation for our relationship and setting ourselves up for a happy life together. I want to see her face, so I turn my head to gaze up at her. She adjusts her hands and runs her thumb along my stubbly cheek.

"I've been meaning to shave," I tell her, worried she doesn't like it.

"It doesn't bother me," she says, her sweet smile meeting her eyes.

"Do you want to help me shave?" I ask, tilting my head, gauging her reaction.

"What? You want me to shave you?" she asks, as her wide eyes stare at me.

"Why not? We can make a first memory together."

"What if I cut you?" she argues.

"I'll heal. Come on," I say, as I swiftly wrap my hands under her butt. Standing, I lift her into my arms with her wrapping her legs around me instinctively as she holds on to my shoulders. Her soothing laughter sounds and drags a smile across my face. Sometimes it's hard to believe my crazy plan worked.

I walk her into our small bathroom, placing her butt on the countertop. Her legs stay wrapped around me as she hooks one ankle over the other keeping me in her space. My heart jumps knowing she wants me close. I push the mirror, so it pops open and grab the shaving foam along with a new razor. Twisting the tap to hot I let the water run for it to heat up before plugging the sink. When it reaches halfway, I shut it off. Sophia watches me carefully.

"First, we apply foam to my whole face," I tell her, grabbing one of her hands and squirting the white foam into her palm. Her glee is evident on her face by the smile shining at me. She pats the puff onto my cheek, releasing a giggle. She brings up her other hand to join in and starts massaging the product into my skin. I suck my top lip in so she can smooth it across my moustache. Concentration oozes from her as she focuses on the task at hand.

"Done," she says, staring into my eyes.

Damn, I want to kiss her right now but with all this foam on my face, I refrain.

"Next, take the razor and make gentle strokes going the same way as the hair growth. We do that all over and then can go against the grain after if we need to," I direct her, handing over the razor. She slips the plastic cover off the green and white razor and dips it in the hot water waiting in the sink. A crease forms between her eyes as she concentrates and runs the razor down my cheek. My eyes track hers as she glides the sharp razor feather light against my skin. She strokes then cleans the blade moving to the next patch of hair and repeats. I lift my chin for her to reach under it. She nicks me causing a wince.

"Sorry," she says, her own eyes crinkling.

"It's fine. I cut myself all the time. Keep going," I encourage. She shakes the blade in the water before continuing with her movements. I pull my top lip in again so she can shave the hair there and keep my eyes on hers. Mesmerised by her expression.

She smiles before saying, "You're staring."

"And you're beautiful," I say, as she finishes with that patch of skin. The rosy red flushes across her skin in a wave. She drops the razor in the sink, and I stretch behind her to grab the towel hanging there. My eyes remain on her as I wipe the excess product from my face. Her eyes flick to my lips as the towel drops to the floor. Her arms wrap around me, and I can't hold back any longer. I press my lips against hers as my eyes close. My hands find her waist as her lips part. She moans against my mouth, and it fuels me on, exploring her. Her arms pull me closer still as her legs tighten.

Her hands move into my hair, and I pull her body closer, not able to get enough of her. As I taste her a moan releases and with it the realisation my hunger for her will never be satiated. She releases my mouth and I trail open mouth kisses down her throat as she gasps for air.

"Renzo," she moans, as my lips glide against her soft skin. Her back arches, lifting her body higher into my reach. My lips trail along the silky freckled skin of her neck, lavishing her collarbone. Hooking a finger under the spaghetti strap of her singlet and bra, I lower it slowly over her shoulder, pulling another moan out of her as her thighs tighten around me seeking friction. My lips follow her beautiful trail of spots to her shoulder, kissing the skin as they lower. My hands glide up her body, cupping her breasts to bring the top of one to meet me. The supple skin draws into my mouth as I suck until the skin bruises leaving my mark.

The ringing of my phone distracts me, but I ignore it until Sophia's laugh draws my lips away from my skin.

"Answer your phone Lorenzo," she says, laughter in her voice. I pull my phone out of my back pocket, staring down at the bruise I've left on her breast feeling a male urge of possessiveness run through me. Sophia's finger presses under my chin, lifting my gaze to her amused expression. "Answer the phone," she tells me again, giggling. I press answer before placing the phone to my ear.

"You're interrupting Niko." My grumpy voice causes Sophia to laugh more.

His loud laugh rains through the phone, "Sorry to be a cock block but could you pick me up on the way, my car isn't starting. I'll have to get you to check it out on Monday at the shop."

"Yeah fine. I'll text when we are on the way," I huff.

"Well finish up whatever you were doing as it's nearly three," he says. I glance down at my wrist, cussing as he's right.

"Yeah, be there soon then," I grunt.

"Cheers mate," he says, laughing at me. Everyone seems to be laughing except me. I hang up the phone without saying goodbye, placing my phone back into my pocket. "We have to pick up Niko as his car has broken down, but I don't mind cancelling and staying home," I tell her, as my thumb runs over my mark causing her breath to hitch.

"I was looking forward to you winning me a stuffed toy at the carnival," she says, her breaths coming faster.

"I have another toy you can play with," I tease, watching as her pupils dilate before my smile widens and her mouth drops open. Her own smile spreads across her face before she laughs and swats at me playfully.

"You did not just say that," she giggles.

"I did little bird. I did," I tell her, as my hands grasp her butt lifting her back up. She wraps her limbs around me, bringing her smiling mouth down to me, and this time it's me that moans as I walk her out of the bathroom. I knead her ass with my hands as I stop to push her against the wall of the hallway, desperately exploring her mouth as she does the same. Her hands tug the strands of hair in her grasp as I press against her, needing friction myself.

"We're gonna be late if we don't stop," her breathless voice says between kisses.

"Let's be late then," I say, taking her swollen lips back between mine. I take her weight again carrying her down the hallway as we continue to kiss. I open my eyes to gauge where we are and then push open our bedroom door, walking in and laying her carefully down. She looks up at me as I crawl my body on top of hers. Her chest rising and falling with her heavy breaths.

"We don't want to keep them waiting," she whispers, glancing at my lips again before meeting my eyes.

"I don't give a damn how long they wait when I've got you in our bed," I tell her, watching the blush spread out over her skin. I lean over her as her tongue peeks out in anticipation when her phone sounds in the room this time. We both groan in unison before laughing. I roll off her, staring at the ceiling as she wiggles her hand into her front pocket, dragging her raging phone out.

Placing it to her ear she says, "Hey Ally. Yeah, we are about to leave. Yeah, sure we can come get you, we've gotta pick up Niko first. See you soon."

I roll back on to my side, leaning on my elbow as it holds my head up.

"Is it too late to tell them I'm sick? Cough cough," I joke, causing her laughter to fill the air as her eyes close and happiness radiates from her. All it does is make my hard dick harder and make me want to roll back on top of her.

"Come on you. I'm sure the carnival will heal any sickness you feel coming on," she chuckles, pushing herself up before standing and holding out a hand for me. I take it and she pulls me up and I'm tempted to pull her back into my arms again. Instead, I wrap my arms tightly around her as hers fall to my waist. I press my lips to her forehead because if I touch her lips again, I won't be making it to the carnival.

"I'm gonna go take a cold shower," I tell her, making her laugh again as she releases me.

Chapter Twenty Nine

Sophia

After picking Niko and Ally up, we pull into the packed car park of the carnival that sits in the middle of town square. They have the Spring Mountain carnival every year. I've only made appearances with my parents as part of the picture-perfect family the mayor likes to project. I've never been on any of the rides, and I can't wait.

I sit in the passenger seat next to Lorenzo, my knee bouncing from excitement. His hand clasps my knee.

"You alright?" he asks, as soon as Niko and Ally exit from the back of the car and close their doors.

"Yeah, just excited. I've never been on the rides before," I tell him.

"Never?" he asks, his raised brows looking at me. I shrug my shoulders before answering.

"Mum and Dad never took me on any. We've come every year, but we always had to present as this immaculate family," I explain, realising how much I missed out on during my childhood.

"Well tonight you are gonna go on whatever ride you want and eat whatever you want and I'm gonna win you the biggest, ugliest stuffed toy they have," he says, smiling widely at me, making me giddy.

"Thanks Renzo but can we get the cutest stuffed toy instead?"

"Nah then you might keep it in the bed instead of me," he jokes, winking at me. I roll my eyes at him, before opening my door. He does the same before he walks around the front of the car and grabs my hand. He gently sways our intertwined fingers.

"What do you girls wanna go do first?" Niko asks, as we join him and Ally.

"Oooh lets go on the Ring of Fire," Ally suggests, her excited eyes shining at me.

"Which one is that?" Lorenzo asks.

"The one where you're strapped in, and you get spun around the circle really fast. It's like a fast hamster wheel," she explains, causing my eyes to bulge.

"Umm I might skip that one," I tell them.

"Yeah, me too," Lorenzo says, squeezing my hand.

"I'm game to go on it Ally since these two are chicken," Niko tells her, causing us all to laugh.

"Well how about we split up and you two daredevils go on all the extreme rides, and we can meet up at the Century Wheel in say two hours?" Lorenzo suggests.

"Yeah, it sounds like a plan. Niko?" Ally asks.

"Yep, I'm in," he tells her. Niko steps up to the ticket booth paying for his and Ally's tickets before she can stop him, and Lorenzo pays for ours.

"See you guys soon," Ally calls out, as she runs off with Niko hot on her tail.

"Come on, let's find something less extreme," Lorenzo says, pulling me in the opposite direction. He holds my hand pulling me through the crowds of people. We come to a covered area, and he pulls me into the line, making me stand in front of him. He rests his chin on my shoulder from behind as we watch the bumper cars crash into each other. We wait behind the railing as others join the line behind us. Lorenzo sticks to my back and I find his presence relaxes me.

The buzzer sounds for the end of the round and the cars stop. People unbuckle and then quickly exit. The attendant counts us through as we pass her and rush off to find a car each. Lorenzo jumps in a green one while I find a yellow car behind him. I slip into the seat, buckling myself in. The attendant's voice calls over the sound system reminding us all to buckle up and then the buzzer sounds to start us off. I press my foot down on the accelerator in hot pursuit of Lorenzo. I thought because I chose a car behind him, I'd have the upper hand but with all his years of being around cars I'd forgotten what a skilled driver he is, even if it is a bumper car. He manoeuvres around others while I track him, but I keep getting slammed into by other people.

As I'm reversing, trying to get out of my current predicament with two cars having pinned me in, I catch sight of Lorenzo's green car coming straight for me head on. His laughing face is what I see before his car makes contact, causing me to rock in my seat.

"I'll get you for that Renzo," I yell, which makes him reverse then accelerate back into me. My own laughs fill the air as he yells to me.

"Do your worst Soph," he screams, before he reverses and speeds away. Well as fast as he can in a bumper car. I try to keep up with him, but strangers keep crashing into me and I lose sight of him. The buzzer sounds and I unbuckle as I look around for him. His smug smile greets me as he chucks his arm around my shoulders, pulling my head towards him as he kisses my temple. "That was fun."

"I thought I was gonna get you as soon as it started but you took off like your bumper car had NOS under the hood," I tell him, as we walk back outside into the open.

"Years of practice. Where do you wanna go now?"

"Could we find something to eat? I'm starving."

"Sure. Do you feel like anything in particular? Savoury? Sweet?"

"Sweet. The answer is always sweet," I tell him, drawing a chuckle out of him.

"No wonder you're so sweet," he says, pulling my head in again for another kiss.

I look up at him to see his beautiful smile as he gazes at me.

A light cough draws his eyes away and the smile drops, his hold around me tightens.

"Holden, Kennedy," he says, causing my own smile to drop as I turn around to face my parents.

"Sophia, darling. It's wonderful to see you here," my mother says, leaning in to kiss my cheek so Lorenzo removes his arm from me. I lean into my mum, but I wave my hand behind me, searching for his touch, needing it to settle me. My heartbeat speeds up now my parents are in my presence.

"We were gonna do our normal walk around the carnival. We'd love it if you could join us," my dad says, looking at me. Lorenzo squeezes my hand in support.

"We could spare a few minutes but then we want to go on all the rides," I tell them.

"Sophia, we are still a family and so should act like one," my dad chastises. I'm pulled behind Lorenzo so fast, I trip over my own feet before he rights me.

"She said she would give you a few minutes. Either take it or leave it but I won't be having you talk to my soon to be wife like that

239

again," Lorenzo says, keeping his voice low and directed at my dad. My wide eyes bounce between the pair as my mum's do the same.

"Fine. Thank you for sparing a few minutes of your time," my dad concedes, causing Lorenzo to relax his stance although his grip on my wrist remains tight.

"You're welcome," he grunts. He loosens his hold on my wrist and links our fingers together. My parents walk in front, and we follow behind. Lorenzo bends to whisper in my ear.

"Sorry about that. I don't like how he talked to you. Is your wrist, okay? I wasn't too rough, was I?"

"No, my wrist is fine. No one has stuck up for me before with my parents," I tell him, looking up into his eyes.

"You've got me now. I won't let anyone hurt you. Okay?" he asks, staring into my eyes.

I nod in reply and squeeze his hand. We continue to walk behind my parents as they play the happy couple for the townsfolk who think the sun shines out of my dad's butt. Lorenzo releases my hand and then slings his arm over my shoulder drawing me closer. I wrap a hand around his waist, leaning into him. We keep a slight distance between my parents and us but close enough people see us together. Some stop to talk to my parents, a few stop and talk to Lorenzo as well, surprising my parents. It's mostly his clients from the mechanic shop but they always have big smiles when they see him. He introduces me to them as his fiancee, making me blush. We still haven't told my parents we are married. I like keeping it a secret for now.

We spend about thirty minutes touring the grounds, which is longer than I would have liked but once we reach the stands where the carnival games are, I realise I've had enough.

"Mum, Dad we are gonna get back to enjoying the carnival now," I tell them. My dad's nostrils flare as he looks between me and Lorenzo.

"This mechanic will never be able to provide the life for you that I have, so you will show me some respect. I've had enough of this childish rebellion, and you will represent this family how it deserves," Dad hisses at me. Lorenzo's arm tightens around me in response.

"You may be my father but don't forget you sold me. You can paint it however you want but at the end of the day, you've always seen me as some bargaining chip you can use to gain favour or money. What you think you deserve and what I think are two very different things." My chest heaves as my fists clench at my side.

"So, you would choose someone who practically bought you over your own blood?" he fires back.

"Blood means nothing to me. Lorenzo has shown me more loyalty than you ever have."

"Lorenzo, how about you take Sophia and enjoy the rest of your evening. Thank you for your time tonight," my mum intervenes, as my dad and I face off. In my peripheral vision, I catch a glimpse of Lorenzo's face as he nods to Mum.

"Kennedy," he says in farewell, before pulling me away. Neither of us say anything more to my father. He will never change, and I doubt the anger I feel towards him will ever dissolve.

"Are you okay?" Lorenzo asks.

Letting out a sigh I say, "That's the first time I've seen them since the argument. Frankly, not seeing them doesn't bother me. My mum has tried to ring me several times, but I haven't answered and I haven't had any contact from Dad."

"It'll all work out," he tells me, kissing my temple.

"You think so? I don't think I'll ever come to terms with him selling me. I know you had good intentions with what you did, and I am grateful for that. I wish you didn't feel you had to make a deal with him to be with me," I confess, realising now the deal that was made is still a sore spot.

He pulls my hands in front of him so I can face him. His eyes stare into mine in the way he does like he's searching for something unbeknownst to me.

"If I'm being honest, I would do it again because it got me you and you are all that matters. You can be honest with me too about how you're feeling. Maybe deep down you do have feelings towards me about it that are not registering. We could see a couple's therapist to work through it if you like. Imagine the look on their face when we tell them our story," he says, which draws a smile from me as our story is nothing if not chaotic.

"I'll think about it. Now you promised me a stuffed toy," I remind him, before leaning forward and kissing his lips. He squeezes my hand and pulls me along.

"I sure did. Come on," he says, speeding up his steps and directing us to the ball and bucket toss. He hands over some of the small games tickets we received with the passes at the gate and picks up the ping pong sized balls. He tries to throw them at the buckets with no luck and I watch as his face scrunches up in frustration.

"Maybe this isn't the game for you?" I suggest.

He glances at me with his wrinkled forehead before looking down the row at the other stalls.

"This way," he says, making me laugh as he grabs my hand leading me to another game. This time it's balloons and darts. He again hands over more tickets and picks up three darts. "So, the more I hit, the bigger the prize?" he asks the attendant.

"Yeah, that's it. You throw three and if you hit any you can go again to try to get a bigger prize for more tickets," he tells us.

"Watch this baby," he says, making my cheeks heat as he's never called me that before. He stands back adjusting his stance like he's thrown darts a million times before.

"You play darts?" I ask, curious.

"They have a board at the bar so when it's quiet I'll throw a few rounds," he tells me, and that makes sense as he's getting into position like a pro. He aims his first one, moving his dart back and forth before letting it fly, popping his first balloon. I smile as he does his little victory. He does the same with the next two darts, popping them both too. He smugly hands over more tickets, getting three more darts and goes again. This time he pops two of them.

"What's the biggest toy prize you have?" he asks the attendant. He points his hook up to a huge stuffed alligator that hangs from the side. "How many to get that one?" he asks the attendant.

"You gotta pop six more balloons," he tells us.

"I don't want that one," I butt in. I don't find alligators cute.

"Which one do you want?" Lorenzo says.

"How much for the hedgehog?" I ask, which isn't as big, but it is a lot cuter.

"You need to pop two more balloons," the attendant tells us.

"Well get popping," I tell Lorenzo, as he laughs, handing over more tickets. He pops them easily and the attendant hands him the hedgehog which he holds out to me. Before I can grab it, he lifts it above his head, wraps an arm around my waist and pulls me into an embrace, before kissing me swiftly on the lips.

"For you, beautiful," he says softly, letting me grab it from his hands. I squeeze it tightly to my chest and give him a big smile.

"Thank you," I say, as my smile beams at him. He slings his arm back around me as he leads me away from the games.

"It's nearly time to meet Ally and Niko. Let's head over to the Century Wheel," he says. We pass through other games and some food stalls before one catches my eye.

"Ooh can we get some cherries? I haven't had them in forever," I tell Lorenzo. His eyes follow where I'm looking before he walks over and asks for a punnet of cherries for me. He swaps the cherries for my hedgehog so I can hold them.

"Here pass Harry," he says, making my brows pull in.

"Harry?"

"Yeah, I thought it would be a good name for him. Harry the hedgehog. No?" he asks, brows raised, and I can't help but fall for him a little bit more at this moment.

"Harry sounds perfect," I gush, making his lips pull up. I pop a cherry into my mouth, pulling off the stalk. Biting down through the soft flesh, the sweet taste hits my tongue with a hint of bitterness following. Chewing before I swallow, I say, "Wanna see a party trick?"

"Sure," Lorenzo says, watching me as I pop the stalk in my mouth. It takes me a bit longer as I'm a bit rusty from not having done it in a while. I push my tongue around, shaping the stalk how I want it until I manage to push it back through the loop. I grip it between my teeth as my tongue slides one edge against the roof of my mouth pulling it tighter. I smile as I hold it between my teeth and grip it with my fingers to show Lorenzo the perfect knot. His eyes light up as he stops to look at me with his mouth open.

"What? How?" he asks, stumbling over his words.

"You're drooling," I tease, laughing.

"My wife's got moves," he jokes, making me laugh harder. He takes a cherry of his own and after eating it pops the stalk in his mouth to try the trick. His cheeks flare and lips move, making me cackle at his ridiculous face and when he pops the stalk out still without a knot it makes me laugh more. "Damn that's hard. How did you learn that?"

"Ally and I spent nights in college practising. She thought it was a surefire way to get guys," I tell him, as we reach the Century Wheel and catch sight of Ally and Niko up ahead.

"Did it work?" he asks, before calling out to Niko who spots us and starts walking our way.

"Not in the slightest. I was too shy to start up conversations back then and honestly who has spare cherries lying around at parties for you to say ooh wanna see a trick?" I tell him, which makes him howl with laughter.

"I see you two are enjoying yourselves. Been on any rides?" Niko asks.

"Just the bumper cars. I was busy winning Harry here," Lorenzo says, pointing to the stuffed toy in my arms that he's proud of winning for me.

"How was the Ring of Fire?" I ask, popping another cherry into my mouth.

"It was the best. We went on it twice and we've been on a few other rides too," Niko says, as Ally walks up next to me and takes a couple cherries for herself.

We walk to the line for the Century Wheel, waiting our turn. When it comes, Ally and Niko step into the gondola first and then Lorenzo and I follow. The attendant closes the door behind us before it moves on to fill the next cart up. When the ride starts rotating faster from all the people being changed out, we get to the highest part of the ride, and it stops for us to look at the view.

"Wow," I say, as I take in the sight of our town. It's still light out as it's early evening and you can see as far as the edge of town.

"Yeah, it's beautiful," Lorenzo says, as he steps up behind me. His chin drops onto my shoulder where he loves to rest it and wraps his arms gently around my waist.

"It is. I forget how wonderful the town and people are. I may get annoyed by my parents a lot of the time, but the community and people are great. I lost sight of that though," I admit, and I feel him nod against my shoulder. We get a couple more minutes before the ride starts moving again for others to get their shot at looking at the view. He keeps his arms wrapped around me the rest of the ride as Harry sits on the seat.

"Are you ready to head home?" Lorenzo speaks into my ear from behind. I nod and he plants a kiss to my cheek before he turns to the others. "Are you guys ready to head out?"

"Yeah, I'm all carnivalled out, I think," Niko says, as Ally nods. Lorenzo grabs Harry from his perch and grasps my fingers with his other hand. After we walk to the car and pile in, we drop off Ally and then Niko.

When it's just Lorenzo and I driving home, I turn to him and say, "Thank you for today. It was fun."

"You don't have to thank me Soph. But I'm glad you enjoyed yourself. Should we grab some takeout and head home?"

"Yeah, it sounds like a plan," I agree, as I settle into my seat. I let the happiness from the day wash over me as I can't remember a day where I've had as much fun being a big kid again.

Chapter Thirty

Sophia

It's Wednesday and I'm currently seated at my receptionist desk, wading through more paperwork. I am enjoying the work. I've never had a full-time job and only helped out with Mum's charity work as it was expected of me by my parents.

I've never had a dream job I wanted to go after as the only dream I had was getting away from my parents. What a failure that was as I ended right back where I started after I finished college.

I shuffle the current pile of papers and line them up before filing them away in the grey cabinet beside my desk. My eyes glance up to find Lorenzo where he stands beside the blue Jeep he's working on. He's focused on his hands as he wipes them on his rag. I've come to learn he needs a special soap he uses to get all the oil and grease off his hands. He tells me they never feel clean for long though. The life of a mechanic.

As if he can sense my eyes on him, he glances my way, and his smile grows. He walks towards me and stops in front of my desk.

"Do you want to grab lunch?"

"Sure. What did you have in mind?" I ask, as my own smile widens as I look at him. Some days I can't believe this man is my husband.

"Lorenzo," Niko calls from across the garage, which stops whatever Lorenzo was about to say. We both look in Niko's direction and he points to the open roller door which leads to the footpath out the front of the shop. There stands my mum. My chair screeches as I stand up and her eyes swing from Lorenzo to me.

"Sophia?" she mouths, as I can't hear her over the music from where she stands. My hand lands on Lorenzo's forearm as I walk around the desk and stop beside him.

"I've got this. How about I grab some sandwiches for lunch and bring them back?" I suggest, and he nods before he delivers a kiss to my cheek.

"What are you doing here Mum?" I ask with a sigh, as I step closer to her.

"I came by to see Lorenzo to get a hold of you since you aren't answering my calls. Since you're here, could we go grab a coffee and talk please?"

"Sure. I have to be quick though." She nods in reply, and we walk away from the garage, down the street to a small cafe. Silence fills the air as neither of us speaks. We arrive at the quaint cafe, and I order two large coffees for Lorenzo and I along with a sandwich each. I step out of the way so Mum can order a coffee herself and then we walk to one of the tables outside and pull out a seat each.

"Are you working at the auto shop now?" Mum asks, breaking the silence.

"Yeah. Lorenzo needed someone and I have my accounting degree, so it worked out well," I explain, and she nods.

"I'm happy for you," she blurts, and on reflex my eyes roll. "Don't be like that, Sophia I truly am. You seem happy."

"I am," I admit. "He makes me happy Mum."

"All I wanted for you Sophia was to be happy. I know I haven't always done the best at showing that and I know I haven't always done right by you. But I'm hoping we can try to repair our relationship. I understand if it's too little too late, but I do love you Sophia," she rambles, and my eyes widen at her confession. "I know it is a lot to ask after how hard I've been on you over the years. I did want the best for you Sophia. Well better than what I had. I apologise for my own shortcomings in not having the strength or courage to stand up to your father as I should have. I hope in time you can forgive me for those faults."

We sit in silence again as I stare at her in shock. Memories from the past wash over me of times when Mum tried to be on my side but Dad would shut her down and so she'd let it slide. It happened time and time again and then the more it happened, the less she tried to voice her opinion until she became a shell of the woman I used to know when I was younger.

She has been trying to contact me since the day I walked away from their dinner. I've ignored her phone calls, sending them to voicemail and not once have I checked the messages she's left. Now here she is, once again trying to reach me, so with a sigh my heart decides.

"If you are sincere then we can try to rebuild our relationship. I'm not going to have anything to do with Dad though if that is your intention."

"No. Your father doesn't know I'm here and I'd rather we keep this to ourselves anyway," she explains.

"Do you like Dad?" I ask, as curiosity gets the better of me.

She lets out her own sigh before she answers, "When I first met him, he was a different man. Charming and successful but he was never content with that and always wanted more. It changed him over the years into someone I barely recognise. I guess I love the person he used to be, and I keep holding out hope that the man he was would reappear." Our drinks and food arrive which halts the conversation for a bit.

"He's never gonna change back to who he was Mum. He sold his own daughter to gain something for himself. That's messed up," I tell her softly. Her eyes glisten as she looks at me and nods before she wipes at her eyes and regains her composure.

"Well, I've kept you long enough Sophia, you probably have to get back to work and I need to get going as well. Maybe I could ring you sometime to see how you are doing? Would that be okay?"

"Sure Mum," I say with a small smile. Hope blooms inside me with the thought that after all these years, we may be able to repair what is broken. Small steps.

"Chat later then. Bye Sophia," she says, as she stands and grasps her paper coffee cup in her hand before she walks back the way we came. The coffee warms my throat as I take a sip, lost in my thoughts. A few minutes pass before I push my own chair back and carry our lunch and drinks back to the shop for us.

Lorenzo sits behind my desk and his eyes meet mine as I walk over.

"You wanna talk about it?"

"Later. Let's eat," I say, as I hand over his sandwich and coffee. He chats to me about the car he's working on which is a good distraction from thoughts about my mum. Once we finish eating, we both head back to work and we are so busy we don't get a chance to talk again until the car ride home.

As Lorenzo reverses the car out of the parking spot, he asks what my Mum wanted.

"She wants to rebuild our relationship."

"How do you feel about that?" he asks, as he pulls onto the highway in the direction of home.

"She seemed sincere. And it's just her. I still want nothing to do with my dad."

"That's good then. I've never had an issue with your mum so maybe she does want a relationship with you."

"I guess time will tell." My head leans against my window and Lorenzo lets the conversation drop as we ride the rest of the way home in silence as my thoughts flow through my head.

Lorenzo parks the car in the driveway and as we walk up to the front door, two large packages are there waiting.

"They arrived," Lorenzo whispers, as he looks the flat white boxes over to check they're addressed to him.

"Were you waiting for something?" I ask, as he unlocks the door then carries the big boxes in.

"These will brighten your day," he says over his shoulder, as he carries the boxes down the hall to the kitchen table. He places them gently down before he grabs the pair of scissors from the knife block and cuts the tape away with care. "Close your eyes," he instructs, which makes my smile grow at his enthusiasm. I stand there and close them while my smile grows, and an excitement builds in my belly. The sound of him cutting through the other box builds the feeling and I can't imagine what it could be that has him this excited. More shuffling sounds around me before he stands behind me and wraps his arms around my waist.

"Open your eyes little bird," he whispers right by my ear. My eyes flutter open and adjust to the light again as I take in his surprise. My breath hitches as two big canvas prints from our wedding day stare back at me. One is of me in the dress I wore for the wedding at the exact moment I walked around the corner of the house and saw Lorenzo waiting for me. My happiness shines on my face through the photo and I turn my neck to see Lorenzo behind me.

"These were my two favourite ones," his soft voice says, and I can't help the tear that drops onto my cheek.

"They're beautiful," I reply. He kisses my lips before I turn back around to the photos. The other is of us as we stand face to face holding each other's hands. You can feel our happiness through the photo as we gaze at one another and I'm glad he picked it.

"Where do you think we should hang them?" he asks, as he squeezes my waist.

"How about in the living room?" I suggest.

"Perfect," he says, as he kisses my cheek before he releases me. He picks up the two big canvases and I follow him down the hallway to the living room. We debate over the perfect spot until we are both happy and then he grabs his hammer and nails from the garage and gets to work at putting them up.

Once they are hung, we sit on the couch with his arm wrapped around me and I let the rest of the day wash away and enjoy the feeling of the moment. We may not have started out in the most traditional way of falling in love first, but as I stare at the photos, I can't help but feel the love that shines from them. I believe what we have is something that could last a lifetime.

Chapter Thirty One

Lorenzo

A new restaurant in town opened this week so I surprised Sophia earlier by telling her I was taking her on a date for this Sunday. We haven't gone on many of those, but I want to wine and dine her today. Starting full time work has taken a toll and she's been exhausted learning the ropes and falling into routine. Plus, since the conversation with her mum, she's been a bit lost in her thoughts. I wanted to do something nice for her and take her mind off that for a bit.

As we get seated at the crowded restaurant, I can't help but take Sophia in. Her long fiery hair is lightly curled today, hanging down her back. Her freckles are on full display as well which I love. We aren't dressed up just wearing casual wear as it's not a fancy dress type of restaurant so I'm glad we can eat in comfort. It didn't stop Sophia changing her purse last minute though, so it matched her outfit.

"Here are your menus," the waitress says, handing over the vinyl fold out menu for us to look through. "Would you like to order drinks and then I can come back for your food order?" I glance at Sophia with a raised brow.

"I'll take a peach iced tea, thanks," she says, smiling at the waitress before her eyes drop back to the menu in front of her.

"I'll take a lemonade, thanks." The waitress jots down our drinks before saying she'll be back and walks away.

"It's busy here. I hope that means the food is good," Sophia says. I grab the plastic in my fingers and flick through the food items. It's always so hard to choose what to order when everything looks so great.

"Do you wanna get appetisers or go straight for mains?" I ask her.

"How about we go halves on the garlic bread and share a platter and get our own mains?" she suggests, biting the side of her thumb while she looks over her hand at me.

"Whatever you want, little bird," I tell her, making her smile appear. The waitress comes back, placing our drinks in front of us.

"Are you ready to order?"

"Can we get the garlic bread and share a platter but bring everything out together. I'll also have the taco salad bowl. Does any of that have peanuts in it as I'm allergic?" she asks the waitress.

"No, none of the items on the menu have peanuts as the owner is allergic to peanuts as well so he and the chef made the menu specifically around it."

"Oh really? That's great," Sophia says, before the waitress writes all that down on her pad before turning to me.

"I'll have the sirloin steak with a side of fries instead of salad and mushroom sauce please."

"Not a problem. It may be a longer wait than usual with opening week, so if your mains are a bit further off, would you prefer I bring out the entrees first?" she asks, her gaze flicking back and forth between us.

"Sounds great," Sophia tells her. A warm smile on her face. My glass of lemonade feels cool under my fingertips as I raise it to my lips for a sip. Sophia does the same with her iced tea.

"Ooh that's yummy," she says more to herself than me, pulling a smile out of me.

"I have a present for you," I tell her, causing her eyes to meet mine with her brows raised. I dig my hand into my front pocket and pull out the two small velvet boxes. I place them on the table before pushing them towards her.

"Are these?" she says, watching as I nod before she finishes the sentence. She flicks one box open with a click and her mouth drops open at the sight. Her glassy eyes look at me before she pulls out my nana's engagement ring which has now been refitted to fit her finger.

"Let me," I tell her. Pinching the ring, I remove it from the box and slide it onto her finger where it fits perfectly now. The red ruby glistening under the restaurant lights. I flick open the other box and pull out her wedding band and show her the inscription. *All of my Sundays.* A tear drips down her face as her wide smile shines at me as I push the ring onto her finger, where it sits nicely next to the engagement ring.

She pulls out my wedding band and pushes it on to my finger for me and we clasp our fingers together over the table, staring at each other.

"I love you," I confess. I've felt it for a long time now, and this feels like the right time to voice it out loud.

"I love you too," her small voice says, before she stands from her side of the booth and joins me on my seat. Our lips meet and everything drifts away in the moment. It's just me and my wife as we kiss, and I can't help but feel my heart will burst from the happiness I feel. When we pull apart, Sophia stays on my side of the booth cuddled into my side as I wrap an arm around her to keep her close.

She holds her hand out in front of her, admiring her newest accessories.

The waitress returns with our appetisers, sliding the brown plates down in front of us.

"Enjoy. Hopefully your mains won't be too far away."

"Thanks," I say, breaking off some garlic bread and taking a bite. Sophia stabs a piece of fried chicken with her fork from the share platter and pops it in her mouth. Chewing, she smiles at me, so I grab a piece of the crumbed fish and try that. She coughs, causing my eyes to glance at her. She stares at the platter as if she's frozen. Her eyes blink but no other movement.

"Soph?" I ask, unsure what's caused the changes in mood. Her wide eyes glance at me before she coughs out the words that send both of us into a spiral.

"It feels like an allergy."

"Shit. What should I do?" I ask, freaking out inside but holding that in so she doesn't see. Her lips are already more swollen than usual.

"EpiPen," her hoarse voice says, as she runs her hands beside her.

I jump from my seat to get to the opposite side of the booth to retrieve her bag. I unzip it and hold the pen in my hand. Her breaths become wheezy, and I panic. My hand fumbles in my jeans for my phone dialling emergency services.

"Ambulance. Please hurry to Fort Street. We think she's having an allergic reaction. Anaphylaxis. I have her EpiPen here," I report to the calm woman's voice on the other end of the line.

"The ambulance is on its way. Is there anyone else there to help you?"

I look around the crowded restaurant and drop the phone from my ear. Standing on my chair, I let out a screeching whistle with my fingers in my mouth to gain everyone's attention. All eyes fly to me.

"She's having an allergic reaction. Can anyone help me?" I plead, staring at everyone around me.

"I'm a nurse," a man yells from the back table, where he sits with his family. He rushes over, takes the EpiPen from my hand and stabs her thigh. He grabs Sophia's wrist in his while he holds the pen against her leg for a few more seconds and looks at his watch taking her pulse. "Put them on speaker," he directs me, so I do that, sliding my phone across the table to him. "What's her name?" he asks me.

"Sophia," I say, looking across at her. The colour has drained from her face as my heart rate increases.

"Okay, lie her down," the operator tells us. I slide out of my seat to help the man and he gently helps me lower Sophia to the floor of the restaurant. I note someone has turned off the music and silence surrounds us.

"She's pale and her pulse is dropping. Her lips and throat look to be swelling and her breaths are wheezing," he talks into the phone.

"The ambulance is one minute out. If you could get everyone to clear the way so the first responders can reach her that would be great," the operator says.

I stand and yell out, "Please clear a path for them to get through," which sends everyone into a frenzy pushing tables back and people moving out of the way, clearing a path.

The siren from the ambulance can be heard before someone yells out, "Over here. Over here," getting their attention and showing them to us.

"They're here Soph," I say, looking at her as her breaths come a bit easier now. I reach over, squeezing her hand in mine. Her fingers are clammy and her eyes close. The first responders make their way easily through the path the patrons have created for them. The male

257

nurse hands me my phone. The operator has hung up now that help is here.

"Thank you so much," I say to the calm man in front of me. "What's your name?" I ask absentmindedly, as I stare at Sophia, lying beside me.

"Franklyn. She'll be okay now," he tells me, and I reach out to shake his hand.

"Franklyn if you ever have car trouble or need a service or anything, you come down to Moretti Motors. It'll be on the house. I own the business," I tell him.

"That's not necessary. I was happy to help, and I didn't do much," he says.

"Please. Accept the offer," I tell him, as they carefully load Sophia onto the gurney.

"Thanks. Appreciate it," he says, releasing my hand. I move behind them as they push her out of the restaurant, nodding to the patrons in thanks as we leave. They load her into the back of the ambulance, and I climb in to take a seat beside her, grabbing her hand. It's a bumpy ride as they speed back to the hospital. The paramedic in the back with us takes her pulse and checks her vitals. He gives her another shot of adrenaline before we pull up in front of the hospital.

"Did she need two shots?" I ask.

"Sometimes they need a bit more," he tells me, as the back doors open, and his partner helps him lift the gurney out and they push it towards the emergency room. Staff come out to take over and I ignore the paramedics' words as they give all the information they need. I follow the staff as they wheel Sophia through a few sets of doors before they set her up in a cubicle. They thrust a clipboard in front of me for details to fill out and I write down what I can before handing it back. Her colour returns but her eyes remain closed. They place an oxygen mask over her mouth and set up a drip as well.

I lower my head into my hands, as I suck my own deep breaths in before I raise my head and rub my hands through my hair.

"She's coming right love. We'll keep her in for about four to six hours to monitor her but she's fine. We are going to draw some blood to check what caused the allergic reaction," the nurse tells me, as she pats me on the shoulder.

"Thank you," I say, my eyes staying on Sophia. People come and go but I pay them no mind, my only thought is the woman in front of me. One nurse tells me to let her rest, so I do. I send a text to Niko and Ally to let them know what happened.

"Where's my daughter?" Holden's voice breaks through my racing thoughts, and it makes my temper rise that he's being so loud and going to wake her.

I step out from behind the curtain to catch him with Kennedy, as he yells at the receptionist asking to see Sophia.

"Where is she?" he directs my way, when he catches sight of me, storming towards me.

"Calm down. She's fine but she's resting," I tell him, holding up my palms.

"I should have stopped this silly arrangement you two had from the beginning. There is no way in hell you are marrying my daughter now, you can't even look after her," he yells at me, walking straight into my palms. I put pressure on his chest, pushing him back.

"Don't storm in here. I told you she is resting, and I won't have you waking her and upsetting her so maybe you should both leave," I tell him. He scoffs at me, and I catch sight of Niko speeding his steps towards me when he sees Holden standing in front of me. He comes up behind Holden and grabs the crook of his arm to pull him back, but Holden shakes him off.

"Don't touch me. I want to see my daughter and you can't stop me," he threatens, as his chest rises and falls with his anger.

"Actually, he can," Niko cuts in, but I shake my head at him.

"Nurse. I want these two removed from here. I'm her father so I'm in charge of her care," he demands, causing the nurse and receptionist to step forward.

"Who the hell let you know she was in here?" I ask, as my own voice raises.

"Sorry. He's the mayor. I thought he should know his daughter was here," the receptionist chimes in, but at least she looks sheepish about the commotion it's caused.

"Yes, I'm the mayor so remove him," Holden says.

"Sorry but the mayor doesn't trump husband," Niko adds, causing Holden to scoff again.

"He's not her husband yet, and he won't be if I have any say in it."

"That's where you're wrong. They've been married for a few weeks now. Here. I took a photo of the marriage certificate knowing it would come in handy where you are involved," Niko says, as he casually hands his phone over to Holden showing him the marriage certificate. The colour of Holden's face turns to a dark red and I don't say I blame him. This isn't how we wanted them to find out.

"Now as her husband, I'd appreciate it if you stopped threatening me. If you'd like to see Sophia, that's fine but I won't have you upsetting her," I tell him, crossing my arms over my chest. Kennedy steps up beside Holden and grabs his forearm.

"Please Holden. I want to see she's alright," she says softly, as her husband fumes at me.

"Fine," he relents. A huff is all he gives to show he's settled himself down.

"She's right in there but please don't wake her," I tell them.

"Thanks Lorenzo," Kennedy says, and Holden nods at me, finally calm enough to see his daughter. I'm glad he backed down as I didn't want to have the mayor kicked out of the hospital. I let them walk back to Sophia without me, giving them some space.

"Did you have to blurt that all out?" I roll my eyes at Niko, who smiles broadly at me.

"You're welcome," he says, patting me on the back and leading me to a chair down the hall. Ally comes rushing through the doors and towards us as we sit.

"Is she alright?" she chokes out between breaths, as she breathes deeply like she ran all the way here.

"Yeah, she'll be fine. They've got a drip in her now and they're keeping her in here for observation. Her parents are back there with her now," I tell her, as she drops into the seat beside Niko.

"I told them that Lorenzo is her husband now," Niko spills, causing Ally to gasp.

"How did they take it?"

"Not as bad as I thought. Plus, there's nothing he can do about it now," I tell them. My stiff neck calls for some relief, so I move my head from side to side in an effort to stretch it.

"I wouldn't be so sure about that Lorenzo. Don't underestimate the lengths that man will go to when it comes to Sophia," Ally says. I close my eyes, not ready to think of anything that he may throw at me. I drop my head backwards against the wall as I rest and wait. My leg bounces, the only sign I'm awake.

A while later, Kennedy's voice breaks through my thoughts.

"Thank you, Lorenzo. We will let you get back to her," she says, as my eyes flash open to find her in front of me with Holden at her back.

"You're welcome," I say. "Do you wanna go see her Ally?" I ask.

"Yes please. I'll be quick," she informs me. She jumps from her seat and speed walks back to where Sophia is being monitored.

"Don't forget you only have a few more weeks before you need to be out of the premises Mr. Moretti," Holden states.

"Holden not now," Kennedy scolds, but he pays her no mind.

261

"I'm perfectly aware of when I need to be out of there," I tell him.

"Enough Holden, this is not the damn time. Let's go," Kennedy snaps, pulling on his arm to make him leave. He grunts at me before walking away, ahead of his wife. "Thanks again Lorenzo. Can you please let Sophia know we were here," Kennedy asks, and I nod before she hurries away to catch up to her husband.

"Are you doing okay man?" Niko asks, when it's the two of us.

"Yeah. I've never been so scared in my life," I admit, which causes him to reach out and squeeze my shoulder.

"I can only imagine but she's good now. You did good."

"Thanks."

Ally appears about twenty minutes later and informs us they are moving her up to a ward and they'll come tell us once they have her settled.

"Do you want a coffee or anything?" Niko asks, and I nod in response.

The nurse comes and finds me before Niko returns so I flick him a text to let him know which room to find us in and Ally and I follow the nurse. As I enter the room, Sophia's eyes find mine and my heart leaps out of my chest.

"Soph, you okay?" I ask. My feet rush to her as I take her hand in mine.

"Yeah," she croaks. Her voice is still scratchy. I squeeze her hand tightly as I lift it to my lips and deliver kiss after kiss to the back of it.

"Hey girl," Ally says, coming up beside the opposite side of the bed and pulling a chair closer.

"Your parents were here earlier too," I inform her, which she nods to before her eyes close again and before we know it, she's asleep.

Later a doctor arrives and checks out her chart.

"Which one of you gentleman is her husband?" he asks, as his eyes flicker back and forth between me and Niko.

"I am," I tell him.

"Is it alright to speak freely or would you like to talk in private?" he asks.

"Soph, wake up," I tell her, as I shrug her arm gently. Her sleepy eyes open and noticing the doctor she becomes more awake. "The doctor wants to talk to you. Do you want Ally and Niko to leave?" She shakes her head, so the doctor carries on.

"It says here that you, Sophia, are allergic to peanuts. Is that correct?"

"Yes. They said they don't use peanut products at that restaurant though," she croaks.

"No but it has come back that you are also allergic to shrimp. Your husband said you ate a piece of chicken, but we believe it was shrimp you ate and that caused the reaction," he informs us.

"That makes sense as I'm not a big seafood lover, so I haven't tried shrimp before."

"You're probably already meticulous with having the peanut allergy so you'll need to add shrimp to the list in future," he says.

"Thanks doc," I say, holding out my hand for him to shake.

"Before I forget, the baby will be fine with all the allergy and EpiPen stuff going on. It should have no effect on them, so you don't need to worry," he states, and my eyes widen.

"Baby? What baby?" Sophia's shaky voice echoes my thoughts.

"It says here you're pregnant. Is that not correct?"

"No," Sophia says.

"Well, the blood test has come back positive for pregnancy so I'd say that congratulations are in order. I'll have them set up an ultrasound to confirm if you like?" he says, and I nod as I'm speechless. "Very well, someone will be along shortly." He leaves the room and I turn back to my stunned wife along with Niko and Ally, who are sitting there with equally stunned faces.

"A baby?" I whisper.

"I'm pregnant?" Sophia says, and I sit next to her on the bed staring into her eyes as I take her hands.

"Well, we have been having a lot of sex," I admit.

"Okay I think that's our cue to leave. Congrats guys. We will leave you to digest this news," Niko says, before planting a kiss on the top of Sophia's head and dragging Ally out of the room.

"Ring me after the ultrasound Soph," Ally calls out, as she's being pulled away.

"A baby?" Sophia whispers at me.

"A baby."

"Are we ready for a baby? We just got married. People are going to think we have lost our damn minds," Sophia starts rambling.

"Hey, hey, hey, take a breath. All that matters is us and how we feel and think. No one else's opinions matter, okay?"

"Okay," she agrees. We sit in silence for a bit, dwelling in our own thoughts before a lady in purple scrubs wheels in a portable ultrasound machine.

"Hi, I'm Tia, I'm here to do an ultrasound," she states, as she sets everything up. I hold onto Sophia's hand, and she squeezes mine tight. "I'll get you to lift your gown and cover the bottom half of you with the blanket so I can see your stomach," she instructs.

Sophia lifts her gown and Tia squirts a gel onto her stomach.

"Sorry, this might be cold," she says, as she waves the wand around, spreading the gel. Sophia squeezes my hand harder, and I return the gesture as my heart beats wildly in my chest. Tia is quiet for a few minutes while she presses buttons on her machine before she turns the screen to us. "This little blob looking thing right here," she points to the screen, "is your baby. It measures about six weeks. I'm going to turn this up and see if we can hear the heartbeat," she says, before a galloping noise comes from the machine. My eyes widen as Sophia's grip tightens and I turn to her. Her face blurs as I take in her glassy eyes. Her thumb wipes away the tear that has leaked out of my own eye.

"I'll leave you two to it. There's a couple pics as well," Tia says, before she quietly leaves the room with her machine.

"We're having a baby," Sophia gushes, and I reach for her, pressing my head into the crook of her neck.

"We're having a baby," I repeat, as a smile lights up my face. I lean back and cup her face as we stupidly smile at each other.

"People may think we are crazy, but I don't care. I'm crazy about you and that's all that matters," I tell her, as I take her lips in mine and let happiness wash over me.

Chapter Thirty Two

Sophia

Lorenzo treated me so delicately as he took me home this morning. We are still living in our bubble not having told anyone our news. Lorenzo rang Niko while I rang Ally but apart from those two, it's one big secret. We've been resting in bed all day since I got home, and my mum has been ringing but I've been avoiding her calls. It's now late afternoon and there's a knock on the front door.

"I'll grab it," Lorenzo says, kissing my head before he hops off the bed. He leaves the bedroom door open so I can hear him.

"Is Sophia here?" my mum's shaky voice asks.

"Is everything okay?" I hear Lorenzo ask, before my mum's head pops into my doorway.

"Oh Sophia," she says, as she rushes to my side of the bed and pulls me into a hug.

"Mum? Are you alright?" I ask, as this isn't normal behaviour for her.

She leans back and stares at me before she takes my hand in hers.

"I've got some news. It's about your father."

"What's he done now?" Lorenzo scoffs, as he takes his seat back beside me.

"Well, he's dead," she states.

"Dead?" I shriek, caught off guard.

"What?" Lorenzo asks.

"Yes, dead as a doornail. And you know what? Good riddance. I'm sorry Sophia but your father was a horrible man. I should have left him years ago, but he threatened to marry you off to some old buddies of his and I couldn't let him do that. So good riddance I say. I'm sorry I haven't been honest with you about him, but I did hope he would change," she rushes out, and I sit there in shock listening to her talk.

"How did it happen?" Lorenzo asks, probably not sure how to respond to the rest of her rambling. Her loud laughter has me wondering if she's lost her mind and is in shock herself.

"That's the best part. The police rocked up to the house today and were planning to arrest him on embezzlement charges and then while they were talking to me, another pair of police men turned up to deliver the news he was dead. He had a heart attack at that brothel on the outskirts of town apparently. The prostitute fucked the life right out of him, she did," Mum says, which causes Lorenzo to howl with laughter which Mum joins in with. I can't hold my laughter in anymore either. He was my dad and I do feel sad, but he had it coming to him. So, the three of us sit there laughing uncontrollably for a good few minutes.

When the laughter dies down Lorenzo squeezes my hand.

"Mum, we have some news."

"Yes?" She looks between us expectedly.

"I'm pregnant," I squeal, and she covers her mouth with her hand before tears stream down her face.

"Oh, golly that's the icing on the cake of a perfect day. Congratulations both of you," she says, before wrapping me in a hug.

"Do you want a coffee or tea Kennedy?" Lorenzo asks.

"I'll have a black tea if you have some please."

"Coming right up," he says, before he kisses my forehead and turns to leave.

"Oh Lorenzo, I'm pretty sure with the embezzlement charges against Holden, the contract you signed for the sale of your auto shop will be null and void now. It'll take a long time for the police to go through all Holden's accounts and transactions, so I'd say you won't have to move premises if you don't want to," she states, and Lorenzo's mouth pops open.

"Really?" he squeals, and I cover my own mouth with my hand to cover my laughter at his pure joy. He looks like a kid who got his favourite toy back.

"Yeah. I'll have our lawyer look it all over and reach out to you and let you know personally," Mum tells him, and Lorenzo steps towards her and wraps her in a hug himself before releasing her to go and make her tea. She turns to me with a wide smile on her face.

"I am so happy for you honey. Lorenzo is a good man and I'm sorry for anything hurtful I've said in the past few weeks about him. I knew he signed a contract with your father so I worried he was in it to benefit himself through Holden, but I can see that's not the case. I only wanted what's best for you, but I see now he loves you."

"Thanks Mum. It may not have been the most conventional way of everything turning out but I'm happier than I've ever been before," I gush.

"Now don't worry about Dad's funeral or anything, I will have a small service, but I'm tempted to send him to be buried with no service for what he's done. It's up to you if you want to attend or not as well but I totally understand if you don't," she says.

"Let me know the details and I'll let you know."

"Tea's ready," Lorenzo calls out, as he knocks on the door. We all walk down to the kitchen and spend the rest of the afternoon gushing over baby stuff and my mum saying she's too young to be called Nana. It did turn into the perfect day and my heart couldn't feel any lighter.

Chapter Thirty Three

Sophia

"Renzo?" I call out, as I walk down the hallway to the kitchen.

"Morning, how are you feeling?" he asks, as he turns to me from where he stands at the stove shirtless, cooking.

"Like death. Why do they call it morning sickness if I get sick all night," I whine, as he holds up an arm for me to cuddle under. My arms wrap around his waist as he kisses my head.

"I'm cooking eggs. Would you like some?"

"Maybe after some ginger beer," I moan, as I want to eat and drink what I used to but now I must worry about things coming back up if my stomach doesn't agree with it.

He grabs a glass from the cabinet and hands it to me. The fridge door needs an extra tug to release and then I grab the bottle out to pour the amber liquid into my glass.

"Are you and your mum still going shopping?" he asks, as he begins plating our eggs and toast for us as I pull out a chair and bring the glass to my lips for a sip.

"Yeah. Are you sure you don't want to come along? Shouldn't we be doing all the baby shopping together?" I ask, as my head tilts to the side.

"I don't mind. It'll be good for you and your mum to have some time to get your relationship back on track and if baby shopping helps then I'm all for it. Don't make any of the bigger purchases. How about you make a note of what you like and then you and I can make the final decision together. Deal?" he suggests.

"Deal. That sounds perfect. Mum and I can gush over all the baby clothes." I can't help the excitement bubbling out of me. It still doesn't feel real some days that I'm pregnant.

"Well eat up so you've got energy for all the shopping you two are likely to do."

"You know when all of Dad's money affairs are sorted, I was thinking we could pay off the mortgage on this place. Mum reckons I should be getting an inheritance when the lawyers sort it all out."

"You don't have to do that Sophia."

I reach across the table and grasp his hand before I say, "We're a team Renzo. It'll be our money, and this is our home. Plus, if the mortgage is paid off then you could ease up with work and possibly give up the job at the bar so you can have more time at home for when the baby arrives. It's purely selfish reasons," I tease.

"You know that sounds perfect to me. I've been meaning to talk to you about the bar job as I was thinking it's becoming unrealistic to travel back and forth so much."

"See, paying off the mortgage would make it easier. Will Ted be alright if you leave?"

"Yeah, he'd be happy for me as I have a beautiful wife I need to come home to every night now," he says, as he winks at me.

"Is that so?" I smile at his remark.

"It is. Now eat up before I get hungry for my wife and then you have to cancel shopping with your mum," he teases.

"That doesn't sound so bad," I tease back.

"Later trouble." I let out a laugh before I finish my ginger beer and then take small bite sizes of my eggs, seeing how my stomach feels as I eat.

"What about this one?" Mum asks, as she holds up a newborn grey overall set with a cartoon elephant on the front.

"Oooh that's so cute," I gush, as I reach for it and hold it in my hands before dropping it in the trolley which is filling fast with baby clothes and accessories.

"We've gotta make sure we don't get too many newborn sizes in case the baby is bigger and doesn't fit newborn sizing," Mum informs me.

"I hope the baby isn't too big so that I can't push it out." My feet stop in their tracks as the thought of pushing a baby out hits me.

"You'll be fine Sophia. You were nearly nine pounds and I birthed you fine," she tells me, as she links an arm through mine and pushes the trolley with her other hand.

"I'm glad we have been able to reconnect Mum. I know we haven't always had the best relationship, but I feel without Dad in the way we are starting to rebuild it and that makes me happy," I admit, and my mum stops us. Tears shine along her lower lashes before she pulls me in for a tight hug.

"I'm glad too honey. I'm so sorry for everything over the years. I wish I'd been strong enough to stand up to your father when I had the chance," her shaky voice says.

"Let's focus on the future and our fresh start. We don't need him tainting any more of our lives."

"What a fresh start it'll be with the new bundle of joy. I'm so excited to be a nana although I still think I'm way too young," she states, which makes me laugh.

"Well, it's either grandma or nana so take your pick," I tease, which causes her to frown at the thought.

"Would Nanny be better?" she suggests, making me laugh more.

"Come on Mum, we can worry about that later, let's pick out some more clothes." We spend another few hours walking around several shops buying different sized unisex clothes. Mum comes in handy, telling me about all the things I will need that haven't crossed my mind. I gotta admit it's nice to have this mother daughter moment.

I went most of my life thinking my mum was too hard on me and like my father, but I was wrong as she's nothing like him. She was just a scared woman who didn't have the courage to stick up for herself but I'm glad she's free of the burden of my father now. I can only hope she will find her own happiness in the future, whatever that may look like.

Chapter Thirty Four

A FEW MONTHS LATER

Lorenzo

"Lorenzo, you under there?" Niko's voice calls out, above the music. My feet shuffle me out from under the car I'm working on then I stand to greet him.

"You good? What brings you in on your day off?" I ask, as I grab the rag from my back pocket and wipe the grease from my hands.

"Well, your darling wife rang me. I'm on strict orders to drag you out of here and we are to go straight to your house and put the baby furniture together," he explains, which has my eyes darting to where my wife sits at her reception desk, shuffling papers and pretending like she doesn't know what's going on.

It takes ten steps before I'm in front of her and I wait for her to look up. Her usual pink tinge colours her cheeks as she knows exactly why I'm standing there.

"You could have just asked me," I joke, and she lets out a huff.

"You don't understand the anxiety these baby hormones are creating. I need it done now Renzo. Not next week or next month and I don't want to hear we still have time. My brain is telling me I need the baby's room done today." Her chest heaves from her rambling and I can't help the laugh that escapes me.

"Okay little bird, I hear you. Can you get Howie to finish this car when he comes back from lunch?"

"I've already sorted it. You're welcome." This time I laugh louder.

"How did I get so lucky to call you, my wife?" I say, as I round the desk and pull her into my arms.

"You're crazy that's why. But I love your crazy." She kisses me as if she'll never get enough and I don't pull away until the coughing of Niko draws my attention.

"Yeah yeah. I'm coming," I tell him, before kissing Sophia on the cheek in goodbye. "I'll ride home with Niko and leave the car for you to drive home later."

"Sounds good. See you later. Thanks Niko," she calls out to my best friend, who waves goodbye.

"I think she's got us both wrapped around her finger," I joke to Niko, as we hop into his car.

"Don't mess with a pregnant woman my man, that's all I gotta say."

"Yeah, I'm quickly coming to that conclusion," I admit.

"How are things going? Are you missing the bar work?" Niko asks, as he turns on the highway headed to my gramps house which is now the only place I live.

"Nah I needed to give up the second job. Ted was sad to see me go but he's got a new bartender who has taken up the lease for the apartment upstairs too, so it all worked out. I'm happy working at the auto shop and then coming home and relaxing with my wife every night to be honest. No better feeling than that mate."

275

"Yeah, yeah so you keep saying. I don't think I'll be settling down any time soon."

"You should try it. It might suit you," I tease.

"One day I guess."

We pull up to the house and head to the spare room where all the boxes of flat pack furniture sit.

"How about we start on the cot?" Niko suggests.

"Sounds like a good plan." We make quick work of opening the box up and pulling out the pieces.

"Why don't they have written instructions instead of just diagrams?" Niko whines, and I can't help but agree. We've been working on the cot for an hour now and after putting the wrong sides on and having to take them off and change them, we are finally on the right track with Niko screwing in the last piece.

After it sits there finished, we stand back and admire our handy work. With smiles on our faces at our accomplishment, we both hold up a hand for a high five before we let out a chuckle.

"How about I start on the change table, and you can work on the wall decor. Then when you're done, you can help me finish." He nods in reply before grabbing the stack of cute animal wall stickers Sophia picked out.

"You guys still set on not finding out the sex?"

"Nah, we both want it to be a surprise. Doesn't bother us either way." I pull the white wooden pieces out of the box that match the white wood of the cot.

"I bet you're glad you didn't have to move premises in the end. I don't wish ill on the dead but I gotta say, it worked out for you with the mayor's death. Plus, it means he's not here to interfere with the baby now."

"Yeah, I think Sophia is still coming to terms with it because it was a shock. But the way he treated her, she realises she's better off without him. The lawyers finalised everything and the business is securely back in my hands as of yesterday."

"That's awesome man. Seems like it's all working out for you," he says, as he claps me on the shoulder.

"Yeah man it does feel that way. I have the woman I love as my wife, a baby on the way, my business and we are settled here in my grandparents' place. I don't think life could get any better."

"I'm happy for you Renz. Now let's get this sorted then we can relax with a beer," he suggests, making me laugh.

"Sounds good." A warm feeling in my chest spreads as my words circulate. I am one hell of a lucky man it all worked out in the end. I may have started from hard beginnings, but I feel with Sophia at my side, I've finally gotten the happily ever after I always wanted. Like the one my grandparents had.

Epilogue

D DAY

Lorenzo

"Push Soph, push," I encourage her, as I hold one of Sophia's thighs back.

"You can do it honey," her mum encourages from her other side, as her midwife stands between her legs waiting for our bundle of joy to arrive.

"The head is out Sophia. Little breaths that's it, pant for me and I'll tell you when the next push is and then we'll have a baby," the midwife informs us. Sophia looks up at me and I wipe her sweat covered hair back off her face.

"Nearly there, little bird," I whisper, and her face sets with determination.

"Okay push." Sophia gives it all she has before the room falls quiet. One beat, two beats, three beats before I close my eyes with a smile on my face to the sound.

"Waaaaahhhhh," our baby wails through the room.

"It's a girl," the midwife announces, before she deposits her on Sophia's chest and covers her with a blanket so they can have something called skin to skin contact which I've learnt is beneficial to them both.

"A girl?" I ask in shock.

"We have a daughter," Sophia says, as we both look down at the little bundle lying on Sophia. She has a tiny bit of hair you can already see. It's darker than Sophia's but still has her red tinge in it, more of an auburn colour.

"Congratulations," Kennedy gushes, as she peeks at her granddaughter. "Do you have a name?"

I turn to Sophia, and we look at each other smiling before we say in unison, "Sunday. Her name is Sunday."

THE END.

Afterword

I hope you enjoyed the story of Sophia and Lorenzo. With their story I wanted to highlight the importance of building a strong foundation for a relationship to thrive.

Even though their story began in unlikely circumstances at the end of the day if you work and communicate you can still build a healthy life together.

I hope it wasn't too much of a crazy ride for you.

I'm still deciding if I will write a book about Ally and Niko. So that may be a project in the future, who knows.

This story did take longer than I wanted before it was ready for release but sometimes the characters can take their time telling me which path, they want to take.

If you enjoyed this story, please consider leaving a review as they can be hard to come by for an indie author.

Many thanks and I have other books available for you to check out.

Special Thanks

Firstly, I want to thank Bec for working on this book for me. I know it's been hard for you to fit it in, but I appreciate all the help you offer. Even though I don't say it I miss you a lot. And I try not to think of you as it has a horrible habit of making me homesick. Love you.

Tiffany, I hope you know how much I value your friendship and input. I don't think I would be able to get through this journey of writing if I didn't have you to keep me sane every day. Let's hope 2024 is a lot better organised than our 2023. It's funny to think we've only been friends a few years, but I can see you being a friend for a lifetime.

Chelsea, this year you've have been a significant person in my life. I love our conversations and how you try to keep me on track even though I'd rather play solitaire or procrastinate. Even though you are miles away I still consider you one of my closest friends. Don't ever change.

To my darling daughter, who is currently making it hard to write this as you are cuddled up beside me crying as your mismatched shoes have come off for the hundredth time today. My wish for you is that you find a great love. Someone who will cherish you and love you the way you are.

I hope you find someone who listens to you and someone who is kind. Don't ever settle for anything less than you deserve sweetie.

Lastly, thank you to my readers. It makes me happy that people wait for my books to release and enjoy the way I write and the stories I produce. I hope you continue to enjoy them. Fingers crossed I can release more books in the future.

Also by this Author

TNT Trilogy

Who do you turn to when your whole world falls apart?

Tamsyn's world is struck by tragedy. She doesn't know how to cope so she falls deep into a darkness she so desperately wants out of. Everyone around her is unaware of her struggle until the new boy in town arrives and sees a part of her no one else does: pain.

Tate makes it his mission to help Tamsyn while keeping a secret of his own.

Follow Tate and Tamsyn's journey as they fight to overcome their struggles. These two fragile hearts have only two options: shatter or become unbreakable.

This young adult romance features mental health themes and the beauty of true friendship.

Chance and Lacey

A boy, a girl, a boatload of nineties crazes, mayhem ensues, and you end up with an unforgettable tale.

You know those moments in your life, the ones you know are going to change your life in some way? Well the day I met Lacey was one of those moments for me. I knew deep in my bones my life had been changed forever.

Life is a journey not a destination and meeting Lacey was definitely an experience. It was the start of an epic journey full of love, laughter, tears, sadness and all life has to offer.

Inside these pages is our love story. It may not always be pretty and at times the moments may seem inconsequential, but they shaped us and the world around us. A series of defining moments (that don't always follow a traditional timeline) both great and small intertwined to make up the story of our lives.

Come share our journey with us while you reminisce about the good old days or are introduced to some of the crazes we enjoyed in the nineties when we were younger. It may not always be smooth sailing, but I can promise you it will be worth it. Enjoy.

Chance x

This is a young adult standalone romance.

A secret meet cute, enemies to lovers, grumpy hero, second chance romance.

Four magical words to solve almost any relationship problem.

Let me give you some worthwhile advice.

Pissed off a girl?

Reduced a girl to tears?

Made the most colossal mistake of your life?

Make it right with flowers. Sunflowers to be exact. According to the girl of my dreams, they are a surefire way to make sure she knows you're thinking of her, and they scream effort and thought, not like roses. Roses are out boys, sunflowers are in.

Four little words are all you need to know. SAY IT WITH SUNFLOWERS.

You miss a date? Buy her sunflowers.

You forget to buy takeout on your way home? Buy her sunflowers…. the dirtier the better.

Get your minds out of the gutter. I'm talking about the flowers. The dirtier they are the more important she must be to you or something along those lines. You get the gist.

I won't make the same mistake I did the first time around, so I'll make sure I say it with sunflowers. Go big or go home, right? I just hope my big plan isn't too crazy.

Sully x

This is a NA standalone novel containing some domestic violence scenes.